He dared not see
Annabelle Langley again

That was for sure, Ben Jackson thought to himself. Cupid must be laughing his head off, the sadistic little bastard. How could Ben, the conservative, left-brain, goal-oriented young law-and-order district attorney fall head over heels in love at first sight?

He was still thinking of her when the back door burst open, and Annabelle, her face as cheerful as an executioner's, stalked down the back steps and stood staring out at the yard and carriage house.

The effect she had on him hadn't changed.

He leaned back against the trunk of the tree and tried to study her critically in hopes that his rational mind would kick in before it was too late. This could not be happening. His mother must have slipped a love potion into his tea. She'd accused him of being a robot. But robots didn't fall in love.

This *wasn't* love. It was lust. Lust he could handle.... After all, a district attorney with a brilliant career ahead of him wouldn't fall for a woman like Annabelle.

A woman with a scandal in her past from which she'd never escape.

Dear Reader,

Do you believe in love at first sight? I do. I knew the first moment I looked at my husband that he was the one.

Ben Jackson, law-and-order district attorney on the rise, doesn't believe in love at all. He's looking for the right wife—a partner to share his vision, to help build his career.

But he falls passionately for Annabelle Langley the moment he sees her, even though she couldn't be a less suitable choice.

Fortunately, Annabelle would never dream of marrying Ben Jackson. As a matter of fact, she doesn't intend to marry at all. She wants to go back to New York where nobody cares about her past.

Ben wants to uncover the truth so she'll be free to love him. Yet the deeper he delves, the more damning the evidence against her seems. He's not helping her—he's hurting her!

Should he stop? Let her go? Or keep fighting for the love he knows they can have together?

I hope you'll enjoy discovering the answer.

Carolyn McSparren

THE WRONG WIFE
Carolyn
McSparren

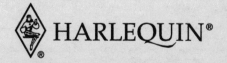

TORONTO • NEW YORK • LONDON
AMSTERDAM • PARIS • SYDNEY • HAMBURG
STOCKHOLM • ATHENS • TOKYO • MILAN • MADRID
PRAGUE • WARSAW • BUDAPEST • AUCKLAND

ISBN 0-373-70921-8

THE WRONG WIFE

Copyright © 2000 by Carolyn McSparren.

Visit us at www.eHarlequin.com

Printed in U.S.A.

For Vonda Milnor, who taught me about heirloom lace.

For Pat Potter, Phyllis Appleby and Beverly Williams,
the greatest brainstormers in the world.

For Emma DeSaussure Jett, who taught me to sew
a fine seam—or as fine as I could manage.

Finally, in memory of Ann Lee, who brought this plot
a good deal too close to home.

CHAPTER ONE

"YOU'VE SUCCESSFULLY avoided falling in love for years," Elizabeth Jackson said to her son. "That's not a good thing."

"For me, it is." Ben Jackson leaned back on the turquoise corduroy Victorian love seat and smiled sardonically at his mother. "Even Cupid couldn't shoot an arrow through all the scar tissue on this particular heart." Ben poked a finger at his chest. "I've had one love, remember. I neither need nor want another. Too painful."

"Ben, you loved Judy, but that was in high school. And her death wasn't your fault."

"It was partly my fault. Although some of the blame must go to dear old Dad."

Elizabeth frowned at her son. "Stop being so sarcastic. All I'm saying is that it's better to feel pain than nothing at all."

"You taught me not to stick my hand on a hot stove, but you want me to hold out my heart and say, 'Hey, somebody come and stomp on this'?"

Elizabeth laid the piece of ecru lace she'd been working with onto the coffee table and gave her son a critical glance. "I'd rather have you bleeding all over my carpet than turning into a robot."

"Whoa! I'm no robot." He leaned forward. "I care a hell of a lot about putting the crooks away."

"That is *what* you do. Is it not *who* you are. Or it shouldn't be."

"If Dad hadn't gotten Elmer Bazemore acquitted of rape and attempted murder he wouldn't have had the opportunity to kill Judy, and you'd probably have those grandchildren you keep talking about."

She leaned across to put her arms around him for a moment. He held himself stiffly away from her. She released him. "Get an emotional life."

"I'm trying, Mom. Within limits."

"Not much chance with the women you date." Elizabeth picked up the lace, adjusted her pince-nez and began to check it for tiny rips. "Everything between you and your girlfriends is so cool and rational. What kind of a marriage would that make?"

"The perfect kind. A partnership that will get me elected to my first full term as district attorney."

"With two point five perfect children to round out the picture?"

"I'm not certain I'll ever have children. I wouldn't want to be an absentee father."

"Your father wasn't exactly an absentee."

"He never attended a PTA meeting or soccer game. He never saw me pitch or Steve catch. He got home in time for maybe two family dinners a month if we were lucky, plus Thanksgiving and Christmas, unless one of his clients popped Santa Claus on Christmas Eve and had to be bailed out Christmas morning."

"His clients needed him."

"So did we. Then he bailed out on us. On you."

"I've long since forgiven him for that. In fact, he did me a favor. If he hadn't left, I'd never have started Elizabeth Lace and become a successful business woman."

Ben slid off the sofa, shoved his hands deep into the pockets of his chinos and strode over to stare out the front window of the big parlor. He knew his mother worried about him, but the still-attractive, slim woman with soft brown hair was busy with her own business, her friends, her suitor—who just happened to be Ben's boss. She was there when Ben needed her, but she seldom intruded as she was doing today.

He watched for Brittany's car. She was invariably early. In his mother's big front yard a dozen different hues of azalea rioted around the aged oak trees while the early April breeze tousled the shaggy heads of Dutch iris.

Ben only felt truly at home in this house where he had spent his childhood. The Garden District, with its aging Georgian houses, was his favorite place in Memphis, particularly now, before summer heat drove everyone inside to air conditioning.

"Sorry, Mom," he said. "I can't forgive Dad for turning the law into a parlor game he played without regard for right or wrong."

"And for Judy's death."

"How many other people died because of Dad and his courtroom antics?"

"He always said if the prosecution did its job properly, they won. His job was to defend his clients as best he could."

Ben leaned back. "Too bad he was so good at it."

"He did get off some people who might have been wrongly convicted, ever think of that?"

"If he did, it was sheer dumb luck that they were innocent. He didn't care about that either. Just the way he didn't care about us."

Elizabeth laid the fragile piece of lace gently on the coffee table again and smoothed it as though it were skin. "We had some wonderful times, Ben. In the early years when we were struggling, your father and I had passion even when we fought. You aren't passionate about anything except getting the felons off the streets."

"I see nothing wrong with that. Besides, I do have passion."

"I'm not only talking about making love." Elizabeth looked him square in the eye. "I'm talking about fighting and demanding and making wild love and driving one another nuts. Your ice princesses don't incite that kind of passion, do they?"

"God, I hope not!" Ben laughed. "If my ice princess and I both know the score going in, we'll never drive each other crazy."

"Boring!"

"I know it's not the life you want for me, Mother, but it's all I'm capable of. Something broke inside me when Judy was killed. So now I intend to marry a woman who fits into my life-style, has the same goals, the same ambitions, the same views of life. Someone who doesn't need the part of me that isn't there any longer. In short, a partner and a friend."

Elizabeth raised her eyebrows. "Job description— one suitable wife. Must be tall, thin, blond, rich, socially adept and completely self-sufficient. Applicants must apply in person.''

''If you like.''

''I don't like, darling, but it's your life.'' She waved an elegantly manicured hand toward the front door at the end of the marble entry hall. ''Are you making a job offer to the one I'm about to meet?''

''Maybe. She fits your description. Plus Brittany is Phi Beta Kappa, has a career she enjoys and is very good at, and would make an excellent public servant's wife.''

''She sounds like a gorgon.''

''She's a wonderful girl.''

''So why haven't I met her before now?''

''Because I didn't want to put pressure on either one of you. That's why she's coming over this afternoon. She really does need a dress for the Steamboat Ball, and she loves your antique lace.''

''Does she know how much one of my dresses costs? Particularly one designed to look like an 1880 riverboat costume. And I assume she wants it to look modern enough for her to wear after the costume ball.''

''Money's no problem. Although I did hope you'd cut her a deal because your poor starving son is only a lowly assistant district attorney.''

''Of course Mommy will be nice to the gorgon, darling. After all, I don't have to live with her. Nor with you, thank God.''

''What's that supposed to mean?''

''I'd hit you over the head with an ice hammer to try to break through to the fallible human being.''

''I will probably be the next D.A. when Phil's

judgeship comes through next month. I have to be above reproach if I'm going to win the election on my own at the end of this term.''

"So your wife must be above reproach too. Have you sicced a private detective on her to see whether there are any skeletons in her closet?''

"Of course not.''

The bell on the front door bonged. Elizabeth stood and smoothed both her skirt and her face and pasted on her professional smile. As Ben followed her to the door, she said quietly, ''You're tempting fate, darling. One of these days, love is going to jump up and bite you. You can't hide away forever.'' She opened the door. ''Brittany, how nice to meet you,'' She held out her hand. ''I'm Elizabeth Jackson. Ben has told me so much about you.''

TWENTY MINUTES LATER, Ben wandered around the big living room that his mother had converted to a showroom for her antique lace dresses. His mother and Brittany sat side by side on the love seat. All he could see was the backs of their heads. They twittered and turned the pages of Elizabeth's display books, while she made quick sketches on the artist's pad in her lap.

He knew both women were making an effort to like one another because of him.

But nothing could alleviate the boredom of listening to the endless snatches of clothes conversation. He drove his hands deeper into the pockets of his chinos and sighed deeply.

"That's enough," Elizabeth said, looking up. "Go away, Ben. You're driving us both nuts.''

Brittany flashed him a radiant smile. "Sweetie, I know this is boring for you. Why don't you go to the club and have a drink. I'll call you from the car when I leave."

"Better yet," Elizabeth said, "go talk to Marian in the workroom." She flicked a hand toward the back of the house. "Everybody else has already gone home, but she hasn't seen you in months, and I've got a new chef d'atelier straight from an upscale Seventh Avenue house in New York. At the moment, she's helping with everything from ordering materials to sewing, but if I could keep her, I'd turn her into a designer. She's very good. Introduce yourself if she's there. Think of it as practice for vote gathering."

"Well…"

"Go. Shoo."

He'd spent many afternoons after school studying upstairs in the workroom, when his mother was just starting to turn a profit with her antique-lace creations and before his life shut down.

Marian Wadsworth was more like an aunt than his mother's employee. She'd even tried unsuccessfully to teach him the fundamentals of sewing. His hands were too big and too clumsy. But she'd been endlessly patient.

And he had been remiss not to keep in closer touch.

He took the back stairs two at a time. The rubber matting deadened his footsteps. He would surprise her.

He tiptoed across the landing to the baize-covered door to the attics, long since converted to work space for his mother's designs. He took a deep breath, grasped the knob, turned it silently, flung open the door, spread his arms and shouted, "Maid Marian, it's Robin Hood returned from the Crusades. Come and kiss me!"

"Are you nuts?"

Ben only had time to glimpse an infuriated female face before the woman dropped to the floor.

"Damn and blast! You've made me spill the paillettes!"

At that point, all he could see was a well-rounded upturned bottom in black leggings.

"Don't just stand there, get down here and help me dig these things out of the cracks in the floor."

"I-I'm sorry," Ben stammered. "I thought Marian was here."

"Well, she's not. I am. She's gone to get some more blue paillettes." The woman at his feet was picking up small flat disks of what looked like blue glass. "Ah, gotcha!" she said, and held up one of the shards. "Are you going to help or not?"

Ben dropped onto his haunches. A completely unruly mass of chocolate curls fell over the woman's face. Her fingers were workmanlike with short, unvarnished nails. He slid one of the fragments of blue from a crack and handed it to her. "Here."

"Lovely. That only leaves about fifty more. We'll never find them all."

She sat back on her heels, pushed her hair off her face and turned to frown at him. She peered over horn-rim half glasses and said, "Ben. Of course it would be you."

Her eyes were the color of dark Barbados rum.

He sucked in his breath and felt suddenly as though he were Butch Cassidy in the last scene of the movie. Everything had turned golden. The world tilted into slow motion.

"Close your mouth, Ben Jackson. You look like a dead carp."

He tried to snap his mouth shut, but only succeeded in gulping. "Uh...wha...who?"

"You don't even recognize me. Par for the course."

He wanted to say, "You look edible, luscious, wild and sexy and dangerous and crazy and I want you."

"Uh, familiar" is what he said. *He* controlled his libido—it didn't control him. Or never had, until now. Then the penny dropped. "Annabelle? Annabelle Langley?"

He heard the door open behind him. "Ben! Belle! Why are you two crawling around on the floor?"

He tore his eyes away, and reached a hand back to Marian as though she were offering him a lifeline.

"Get up, Ben, you'll get filthy," Marian Wadsworth said.

He stood easily and realized he was smiling stupidly at the woman on the floor.

"You going to leave me down here?" The woman held out her hand.

Ben took it automatically and felt the same jolt he'd experienced once when he'd plugged his electric razor into a bad socket. The hair on his arms stood up.

She pulled against him, and a moment later came up against his chest.

The hair on his arms wasn't the only thing that came to attention.

"Sorry, Marian," Annabelle said, and stepped back. She kept looking at him warily. Why not? He must look as fatuous as Bottom after he turned into a jackass in *Midsummer Night's Dream.* How appropriate.

"Ben surprised me. I dropped the paillettes. You think we'll have enough if I don't find them all?"

Marian held out a small cardboard box, perhaps five inches by seven. "Plenty. You have to stop squirreling things away in your apartment, Belle. Or at least develop a decent filing system."

"Sorry. Next time, I'll go do the hunting." She glanced at Ben. "It's safer." She picked up a fragile length of white Belgian lace off the worktable, and took a three-inch glass-headed dressmaker's pin from a large pincushion on her wrist.

"I'm sorry I didn't recognize you at first." Ben said. "You were in my brother, Steve's grade. Right?"

"It's been a long time. High school." Annabelle stuck out her hand. "I was a lowly freshman when you were a senior, but everybody knew the president of the senior class. I'm your mother's new chef d'atelier."

Ben closed his eyes and whispered, "I am going to *kill* my mother."

"Ben!" Marian said.

"Oh, God." Ben opened his eyes. "I didn't mean—I'd never…"

"Get out now, please," Annabelle said. "Before I toss you out."

"It's just an expression."

"Now!" She crunched up the lace in her hand. "Ow!" She held up her hand. The pin had embedded itself in her left index finger. She yanked out the object and raised her finger to her lips to suck the drop of blood, but didn't manage to catch it before it fell on the lace she held in her other hand. "Now look what you've made me do."

"Ben," Marian said quietly. "Go downstairs. I'll handle this."

"But…"

"She knows you didn't mean anything by your remark. Go."

Confused, embarrassed, and feeling like the biggest klutz in this or any other universe, Ben went. He took the stairs fast and turned not toward the living room, where he could still hear Brittany's voice, but toward the kitchen, and then out the back door into the yard.

Without a conscious thought he grabbed the branch of the oak tree, planted his foot in the crotch and swung up and into the leaves. His hands and feet remembered as though he were still a boy of ten who hid out in his tree whenever he wanted to avoid chores or wanted to read a book. Then when he was 18—the summer after Judy died—he'd practically lived up here for a couple of months.

He covered his face with his hands and braced his back against the big limb twenty feet up. Thank God the tree had grown enough to support his weight. He hadn't given that a thought.

He did not dare see Annabelle Langley again, that was for sure.

How could he go back in and charm Brittany when, as of ten minutes earlier, she had ceased to be an important part of his world? It wasn't her fault. It was his mother's.

Cupid must be laughing his head off, the sadistic little bastard. How could Ben Jackson, the rational, left-brain, goal-oriented young law-and-order assistant district attorney on the rise, fall head over heels in love at first sight? And with a woman who had killed her mother?

BEN WAS STILL PROPPED along the branch of the tree fifteen minutes later when the back door burst open and Annabelle Langley, her face as cheerful as an executioner's, stalked down the back steps and stood staring out at the backyard.

The effect she had on him hadn't changed.

He tried to look at her critically, compare her to Brittany in hopes that his rational mind would kick in before it was too late. Hadn't his mother accused him of being a robot? Robots didn't fall in love.

Yet something in Annabelle ripped through his defenses.

He did not like it, didn't want it, didn't approve of it. Passion hurt, feeling hurt. Love meant loss. Hideous, horrible loss that came with pictures that exploded inside his brain without warning, even now.

He couldn't afford empathy. He could not be open to emotion and do his job properly. He owed his entire focus to the people he was sworn to protect. One less criminal on the street meant one less victim—one less Judy.

Annabelle couldn't see him, didn't know he was

there. He might have said something the instant she came out that door, but the opportunity had already passed.

So he studied her dispassionately. What was the big deal?

She was at least three inches shorter than Brittany. Brittany was model slim. Annabelle had curves; she wouldn't fit into chic clothes nearly as well, assuming she ever wore anything more chic than the leggings and baggy shirt she had on at the moment. He didn't care. Naked she'd be gorgeous, and naked was how he wanted her.

Brittany's straight, blond hair fell with flawless precision around her face.

Annabelle's hair looked as though it had escaped from an unclipped standard poodle, taken root on her head, and kept growing until it reached her shoulder blades. He longed to run his fingers into it and feel it curl, bury his face in all that extravagance.

This wasn't love. It was lust. Lust he could handle.

Annabelle didn't seem to care much about her looks. At the moment she'd eaten off her lipstick, her nose was shiny, and she had a smudge of blue pattern pencil along her jaw. But then, she'd been working all day. Hard, physical labor. Ben remembered that much. Sewing might look easy, but it knotted the shoulders and wounded the hands. As he had wounded her hand—and more. God, how could he have been so stupid and clumsy! His remark must have cut her deeply.

Now, Brittany was something else. She was in public relations. She never met a stranger. She smiled easily. She could schmooze anyone.

So how come Brittany suddenly seemed to him as unformed as a lump of Play-Doh? How come her blond good looks now seemed as bland as cornstarch? And this wild woman made him want to leap on her out of his tree and drag her off to his lair to be his mate for life?

He groaned, threw up his hand to hit himself in the forehead, and overbalanced.

"Hey!" he yelped as his feet lost their purchase. He grabbed for the limb over his head just as the one he sat on gave way under his weight.

He fell. He grabbed at a couple of branches to slow his progress, wrenched his shoulder, and managed to catch himself eight feet from the ground, where he hung for a moment before he dropped ingloriously onto the grass.

Annabelle stared at him openmouthed.

"I can explain." He stood up and held his hands in front of him, palms up.

She took a deep breath. "Are you all right? You look a mess."

"I'm fine."

"What on earth were you doing in that tree?"

She took a few steps toward him, and reached out to brush the lapel of his jacket.

"I can explain," he said again.

It took all his willpower not to grab her wrist and drag her into his arms. The touch of her fingertips raised the hair at the nape of his neck, and several other portions of his anatomy that hadn't been this out of control since he'd turned thirteen.

"So?" she said with her eyes on the shoulder of his jacket where she brushed off leaves and twigs.

"So what?" He stared down at her. That blue smudge was adorable.

"You said you could explain."

"Oh."

He closed his eyes as she continued her progress around his body, brushing him off lightly. She grabbed the shoulders of his jacket and wrenched it back into place, then walked around in front of him again with her eyes just above his belt buckle.

"You can take care of the rest of you."

Thank God. If she'd tried to brush off his chinos, she'd have been in for one hell of a surprise.

"And your hair. You're wearing a crown of leaves like Pan."

He swept his hair back from his forehead and brushed down the front of his trousers.

"Well? I'm waiting." She stepped away from him with her hands on his hips. Now, finally, she looked into his eyes.

"I, uh. Look, come sit in the gazebo a minute."

She shook her head. "I've still got an hour's work to do cleaning up the mess upstairs."

"You came outside."

"To keep from screaming in frustration, actually. And then you fall out of the skies practically on top of me."

He shoved his hands into the pockets of his chinos. "Okay. I made such a jackass of myself in there, I came out here and climbed into the tree to calm down and think up some way to apologize. Then, when you came out, I lost my balance."

"You could have announced your presence."

"I know. Sorry."

"Spies do not thrill me."

"I was not spying on you, Annabelle," he lied. "I was thinking that I am not usually a social nitwit. I'm sorry."

"Apology accepted." She turned to go back into the house.

Suddenly the day seemed dark. "Wait!" He reached for her forearm. "How about dinner?"

"What?"

"Dinner. Me, you, tonight."

"Now I know you're crazy." She pointed toward the house. "I think you already have a date, Mr. District Attorney. And I suspect she's wondering where the heck you've gotten to."

He let her go, and leaned back against the trunk of the tree. This could not be happening. Not to Ben Jackson. His mother had slipped a love potion into his tea while they were waiting for Brittany.

He had a brain tumor, or an aneurysm that had burst suddenly. There had to be some rational explanation.

He closed his eyes. Whatever had occurred, he had to fix it, exorcise it, reverse the spell, before it devoured him, his career plans, his goals and the rest of his life in a hapless, fruitless pursuit of a woman who not only was unsuitable in every respect, but who obviously didn't even *like* him.

"WHAT HAVE YOU been up to?" Elizabeth Langley said to her son. "You're a mess."

"I—uh—I tripped on the patio. The bricks were slick."

"Really." His mother accepted the explanation

readily enough, or so it seemed to Ben. "Brittany and I have designed her dress for the ball. Period enough to work for the Steamboat's 1880 theme, but modern enough to wear to the symphony or one of the secret-society parties during carnival."

"Can I see the design?"

Brittany laughed. The sound, which had enchanted him only hours before, now sounded as raucous as a crow's. "No, you cannot, you naughty thing. It's bad luck!" She stretched back on the couch as his mother picked up her sketch pad and notebooks and went to put them back into the armoire in the corner.

"Actually, that only applies to wedding dresses," his mother said.

Brittany giggled. Ben decided he must have been drugged to be able to change his opinion about a woman this beautiful so quickly and so totally.

He blinked, opened his eyes and hoped against hope that the Brittany he had liked would be back.

No such luck. He could still appreciate her beauty, but she no longer moved him any more than if she'd been carved out of marble.

"Now, children, off to dinner you go," Elizabeth said. "I have my own plans."

Ben tried desperately to think of some way to get out of his date, but he'd been raised better than that, and Brittany hadn't done one thing wrong. The responsibility was his alone, his and his witch mother, who had set him up and cast a spell on him.

Maybe it was like the twenty-four-hour flu. He'd wake up tomorrow morning cured of Annabelle Langley.

He heard the two women making leaving sounds

without registering the words. He followed them to the door, and held it while they air kissed.

"Coming, sweetie?" Brittany said.

"I'll send him along in a minute," Elizabeth said. "You did come in two cars, didn't you?"

For a moment Brittany's good nature slipped, but the flash of annoyance that crossed her face came and went so swiftly that Ben wasn't certain he'd seen it.

"Of course. See you at the club," she said, and ran her hand down his cheek. He stood on the step beside his mother and watched Brittany glide to her car and drive away with a wave.

"She is a lovely woman," Elizabeth said.

"Uh-huh."

"And very, very clever."

That didn't sound like a compliment.

"She will look extraordinary in the dress we designed. Daddy, I take it, has money?"

"Pots of it, according to the grapevine."

"Do I need to start designing her wedding dress?"

"Uh—I'd hold off on that."

"Ah." His mother narrowed her eyes at him. "You can't have cooled off so quickly."

He ignored her remark. "If I don't get out of here, I'm going to miss our reservations at the club." He kissed his mother perfunctorily and started down the concrete stairs to the front yard.

"Are you going to bring her to my regular Thursday-night dinner party?" Elizabeth called after him.

Damn! His mother's legendary Thursday nights. "I don't know. I'll call you."

"Fine. It doesn't have to be Brittany, you know. Any girl will do so long as she's not an airhead."

"Right." He climbed into his car and drove away much too fast for the narrow street. He scared a small woman who was walking a large bull mastiff. He knew he should have stopped to apologize. She was probably one of his mother's neighbors, although he didn't recognize her. She would be one of his constituents, if he ever became district attorney. He needed to remember he was a lawyer first, a man second.

The hell he was.

CHAPTER TWO

ANNABELLE SHUT THE DOOR to the backyard and leaned against it with both hands behind her back. There was no point in throwing the bolt against Ben. He'd just walk around to the front. His mother would let him in, assuming he didn't have his own key to her house.

Annabelle's heart raced, the pulse in her temple throbbed, and she knew she had a film of sweat on her upper lip, despite the cool early-April air outside.

The kin of my enemy is my enemy. Her grandmother had drummed that into her head since she could remember. Grandmere was already having triple conniptions because Annabelle was working for Elizabeth, Hal Jackson's ex-wife. The idea that Annabelle might be attracted to Hal Jackson's son would probably give her a stroke.

And she *was* attracted. Heck, she'd always been attracted to Ben, although she hadn't seen him since he went off to college.

She'd known about Judy Bromfield's death, of course; it had happened the summer after Ben graduated from high school. The whole thing had been horrible, especially when it came out that Ben's father had been responsible for getting the man who'd raped and murdered Judy off on another charge only two months earlier.

Annabelle remembered Ben as cheerful, funny, wildly successful at everything he did. The golden boy. Now, although he sounded much the same, there was something cold at the center.

She recognized the wariness in Ben's eyes. She saw it in the mirror every morning.

Back in high school, she'd thought he was the warmest, kindest person she'd ever known because he treated her the same way he treated everybody else.

Now he was asking her to dinner, and she longed to go, but didn't dare. The only way to avoid becoming as big a slut as her mother had been was to avoid temptation like the plague. From the electrical connection she'd felt when she brushed off his clothes, Ben was a combination bubonic and pneumonic, with a big dash of anthrax thrown in.

Besides, he *was* Hal Jackson's son. Grandmere would go crazy. Working for Elizabeth was bad enough.

But how was Annabelle expected to make enough money to support herself, not to mention avoiding the loss of her skills and reputation, when she'd come back to Memphis to look after Grandmere?

Elizabeth's job offer had been a godsend. It would actually enhance Annabelle's reputation. And it gave her a place to live while she was here as well.

Annabelle would not live in the mansion with her grandmother. The day Jonas had driven her to the plane for New York and design school, she'd made a solemn vow that she would never live there again.

Elizabeth had offered Annabelle the apartment over what was now a four-car garage, but what had originally been the carriage house. It was furnished— rather charmingly, as a matter of fact. Elizabeth Langley never did anything halfway. It was almost as large as her loft in SoHo. It even had a fireplace.

Now that she had shoved some of the furniture out of the way, set up a trestle table and brought in a sewing machine and serger, she had plenty of room to keep working until all hours of the night.

Better than sleep. Back where it had all happened, her dreams were even more troubled. She would not resort to pills. Reality was bad enough. Altered reality was a horror not to be contemplated.

She began to climb the steps to the workroom once more. What kind of human being marks the day she will finally be free as "when Grandmere dies?" A monster, obviously. But then, once a monster, always a monster. At least here everybody expected her to behave monstrously.

Ben had remembered her instantly; he'd gotten all embarrassed over his remark about killing his mother. In New York no one would have made the connection. In New York she was not Annabelle Langley, the bad seed.

"You all right?" Marian Wadsworth's callused fingers stopped plying her needle for a moment and let the piece of Venice lace she held lie loose in her lap.

"Fine." Annabelle shoved her hair out of her face for the fiftieth time since morning. "I am going to shave my head like a Buddhist nun."

"It would grow back wilder than before."

Annabelle picked up a foot-long piece of rayon seam binding off the floor and tied her hair into a ponytail at the back of her head. Without a rubber band, the binding would hold for an hour or so before it slid off.

She saw the glint of one of the missing paillettes in the crack between two floorboards and bent to pick it up. Then she saw another and dropped onto her hands and knees. "Funny thing. Ben Jackson nearly fell on me."

"I beg your pardon?"

"He was up in that big old oak. I didn't even know he was there, then suddenly, wham, he drops out of nowhere at my feet."

Marian laughed and picked up the lace. "When he was a child he shinned up that tree whenever he wanted to get away." She turned serious. "After Judy was killed, I think he practically lived up there all summer. It's where he did his grieving. Is he all right?"

"Yes, Marian, your darling is all right, and incidentally, so am I."

"I can see that, Belle, that's why I asked about Ben."

"I brushed him off and sent him back inside looking amazingly little the worse for wear. Ah, gotcha!" she added as she found another paillette.

"He was always one of those Teflon children who came from school looking as neat as he did when he left home." Marian shook her head.

"I, on the other hand, looked as though I'd been through a wrestling match ten seconds after I dressed.

Used to drive Grandmere frantic.'' She sat back on her heels.

''How is she today?''

''Cross your fingers. I haven't had a single call from the sitter, or nurse, or whatever they're calling themselves these days.''

''Caregiver, I think, is the current word.''

''Damn expensive, when all they seem to do is sit around and watch soap operas.''

''Maybe this one will do a bit more.''

''Mrs. Mayhew does seem more conscientious. She keeps Grandmere's room and bathroom clean, and sees to her own bedroom and bath, but I'll probably have to get a cleaning team in for the rest of the house before long or the spiders will take over.''

''Well, don't you try to do it. That place is big as a stadium.'' Marian bent to her needle. ''And all those knickknacks and sitarounds to dust. Why not ask Jonas to help you out?''

''His hands are already full with Grandmere's garden. At least the neighbors can't complain about that. He's not getting any younger either, you know. He does the marketing and takes her back and forth to the doctor's.''

''How long can you keep this up?'' Marian asked.

Annabelle dug her fingers into the aching muscles along the tops of her shoulders. ''As long as I have to. She's always been terrified of nursing homes. I can't do that to her.''

Marian mumbled something as she bit off the thread.

''What?''

''Never mind.''

"Don't bite the thread that way if you expect to have any teeth left when you're seventy, and don't mumble," Annabelle said. "Tell me what you said."

Marian picked up the embroidery scissors that hung from a silk cord around her neck and ostentatiously clipped the end of the thread she'd just bitten. She sighed and looked at Annabelle. "I said it would serve the old witch right."

Annabelle plucked the last paillette from the crack and rose easily to her feet. "I don't want putting her in a nursing home on my conscience as well."

"Pooh! Stop it. Get it through your head that you don't carry any weight or any guilt for what happened to your mother. Your father admitted it and went to jail for it."

"To save me, you mean. Everybody knows that. Grandmere—"

"Mrs. Langley is a poisonous viper who did everything in her power to destroy anyone and everyone who crossed her path. Lord knows why it gave her so much pleasure, but it did."

"She took me in and did the best she could with me. She's a very unhappy woman," Annabelle answered.

"Oh, no doubt. If there were an object lesson in the Golden Rule, she is it. Not one of the nasty things she has ever done to anybody has made her one bit nicer or one bit happier. She's like one of those poison toads—the more venom she uses, the more she has."

"Why, Marian, I knew you didn't like her, but I never realized you loathed her that way. What's she done to you?"

"Watching what she's done to you is bad enough. And laying so much guilt on you that you came home to tend to her after all these years, and your career in New York and all." Marian sniffled and wiped her hand under her eyes. "I'm glad to have you, but the whole thing makes me sick."

Annabelle slipped the paillettes into the pocket of her shirt and walked around the table to drop a hand on Marian's shoulder. "She's my only family. Besides, I screwed myself up before she got the chance."

"No, you did not." Marian covered Annabelle's hand with hers. "You were a little bitty girl. But all those years in that house with that harpy—well, child, you need about ten years of therapy, is all I'm saying."

"Oh, thank you very much." Annabelle laughed. "I've *had* years of therapy. Otherwise I'd probably be dead. This is as good as it gets. I function extremely well in my own milieu, and people leave me alone. And it's nice to have friends who understand."

"Well, you just understand that whatever you have to do to make your life come out all right, you do it. I mean that, you hear?"

"Yes, ma'am." Annabelle saluted. "Now, where did you put that piece of lace I bled all over? I've got to soak it in some ice water before the stain sets."

Marian indicated the side table with a nod of her head. "Over there. Not much blood. Only a drop or two."

"I'll run it across to my place and put it in the kitchen sink. Then I can flatten it out when I go back after work."

"After work is now." Marian set down her needle and embroidery hoop. "I should have this piece mended in an hour or so tomorrow."

Annabelle leaned over her. "You do incredible work, Maid Marian. Nobody would ever know how much damage this piece endured before Elizabeth rescued it."

Marian laughed. "And now it will have a new life in the Countess So-and-So's gown for the opening of the Paris Opera, or Mrs. Texas Oil for her daughter's wedding." She laid the piece down with satisfaction. "I am good, aren't I? You know, nobody ever called me Maid Marian but Ben, when he was a little boy. I used to read him the stories about Robin Hood. Even then he had a drive to right all the wrongs in the world."

"It fits you."

"True, unfortunately." She carefully spread the piece of ecru lace on the worktable in front of her. The table was covered in fine green felt, so the lacework showed clearly. "There. The actual mending is finished—the tatting, I mean. Now I just have to catch the edges so nothing ravels." She pushed herself to her feet, removed her half glasses, stowed them in a navy leather case on the table, reached into her pocket for a red case, and slipped her bifocals on in their place. "Ah, now I can see you." She peered at Annabelle. "And you look like hell. Go home, watch television, read a book. Go to a movie. Call an old school friend. Get out and do something."

"Nope." Annabelle carefully folded the delicate white lace, slipped it into a piece of tissue paper and followed Marian to the door. "Don't fuss. I'm fine.

This is what I enjoy. I'll put on some Mozart or some Stones, fix myself a quick meal, put this lace in water and run over to check on Grandmere. I don't have time for much else.''

She clicked off the lights in the workroom and followed Marian down the back stairs. As she passed the swinging door to the front of the house, she wondered whether Ben and his current tootsie were still there with Mrs. Jackson.

He was still the best-looking, most charismatic man she'd ever met. And if anything, even farther out of her reach and her orbit than he was when he was a senior and she was a freshman. ''A cat can look at a king,'' she whispered, and opened the baize door a tiny crack.

What she saw was not Ben, but Brittany, now relaxed on the sofa with her long, lovely brown arms stretched along its back, her slim ankles crossed, her streaked blond hair falling as precisely to her shoulders as though her hairdresser had cut it with a laser level. Maybe he had.

Annabelle let the door close softly.

Totally out of her league. Like comparing Claudia Schiffer to Ma Kettle.

And that was just looks. Add in social grace, acceptability, education, and it was like comparing Claudia Schiffer to a female Cro-Magnon.

She walked across the backyard and opened the door to the stairs that led to the apartment that Elizabeth Jackson had turned into guest quarters.

The stairs were narrow and precipitous, but were covered with a creamy plush carpet. The walls were painted the palest yellow, and charming old French flower prints stair-stepped up the wall beside them.

Annabelle kicked off the backless clogs she wore while she was working, remembered the paillettes in the pocket of her shirt, pulled them out and carefully dropped them into a cut-crystal ashtray.

Since she didn't smoke and wouldn't dream of allowing smoke anywhere near the fragile fabrics she worked on, the ashtray was clean. She carefully unwrapped the white lace from its tissue and laid it on the drainboard of the sink in the galley kitchen while she filled a bowl with ice cubes.

She filled the sink, dropped in the ice cubes and swished them around before she began to inspect the lace.

The piece was good-sized—several yards. She fingered it to find the spots of smeared blood so that she could immerse only that area and as little of the rest as possible. No sense wetting the whole thing. It would weigh a ton and possibly damage the fragile stitches.

Aha. She found the first spot. Amazing that such a little thing as a pinprick could make such a mess. "Who would have thought the old man had so much blood in him?" she said idly, realizing as she said it that one of her starving-actor friends said quoting from *Macbeth* was bad luck.

She snapped on the light over the sink and glanced down at the lace across her hands.

She froze. A sound she couldn't begin to recognize rose in her throat.

She hadn't bled that much.

The lace in her hands was drenched, dripping with

gore, and her hands were covered in bright fresh blood, so thick she felt as though she could dye the water scarlet.

"No!" She dropped the lace, turned, shoulders hunched, head bowed.

She felt her gorge rise and fought the urge to vomit. "No." She nearly yelled the word. She felt the world spin, her vision blur.

After what seemed a lifetime, but was probably no more than a few seconds, she managed to force herself under control. She took a deep breath and turned back to the drainboard.

She was nearly afraid to look at her hands.

Her hands were dry and clean. She picked up the lace. Maybe eight or nine dots of brownish dried blood stained it. She stared at it, frowning, puzzled.

Then she shook her head. "Trick of the light, obviously. Sunset through the window."

She realized she was speaking aloud. The sound of her own voice in the silent room was momentarily comforting. "Stupid. Ought to get my eyes examined." She rubbed the bridge of her nose where her half glasses sat during the day. "It's Ben's fault. He's the one that fell out of the tree, and here I am with the concussion and hallucinations."

She slipped the bloodstained portion of the lace into the ice water, sluiced it around gently for a minute, then left it immersed. As she dried her hands, she almost expected to see blood on the towel. Ridiculous.

She walked over to the armoire in the corner that held the stereo and television. She didn't want to listen to the news. It was always bad. She'd had enough mayhem for a lifetime.

She flipped through the meager stack of CDs. Vivaldi? Mozart? Too orderly. Too optimistic. She needed angst. She found an old version of the *Kindertotenlieder.* Peachy. Enough angst there for a whole hundred years' worth of the Black Plague.

But triumphant at the end.

That didn't happen in real life. In real life you muddled along and hoped to survive with your brain and your body intact and without causing too much damage.

In her case, it was a little late for that already.

CHAPTER THREE

WHILE HER TV DINNER microwaved, Annabelle curled into a tight little ball in the yellow club chair beside the empty fireplace. She dug the heels of her hands into her eyes, and then ran her fingers down her face. When she touched her cheeks she realized they were wet with perspiration and her fingertips were actually shaking.

What had happened with the lace? She could tell herself it was a trick of the light, but she knew better.

Jonas once told her that Governor Huey Long of Louisiana carried around a mock certificate of release from the Louisiana state mental institution as proof that he was sane. She had often wished she had a certificate like that so she could point to it and say to herself, "See. You are not a nutcase."

In a pinch, she could call on a couple of excellent psychotherapists to certify she wasn't any crazier than so-called healthy people.

Okay, so she hated cocktail parties and meeting new people and speaking in public.

But hallucinations? Never, not in all her years. Not even when the nightmares had still been coming at least once or twice a week.

And she hadn't had the nightmares for years.

Until she'd come back to Memphis to work for the

wife of the man who had failed to defend her father successfully. But they'd been divorced for years. Hal Jackson had disappeared years ago just as her own father had disappeared when he'd been released from prison.

Her New York roommate, Vickie, had begged her not to leave New York. Annabelle managed to keep paying her half of the rent so that Vickie didn't have to sublet. She needed her place to come back to when she left Memphis. Together she and Vickie had done a bunch of work decorating the SoHo loft, and they'd never be able to find another one now at anything like a reasonable rate.

But family was family. That was all that mattered, really. Grandmere needed Annabelle because there was no one else.

When Annabelle had had no one else, her grandmother hadn't hesitated to take her in.

She'd fed and clothed Annabelle, sent her to the best schools, even tried from time to time to act like a regular grandmother. It wasn't her fault that she'd failed so miserably. She was a dragon by nature, and the disastrous circumstances under which she'd acquired Annabelle had destroyed the way of life she cherished, turned the woman into a bitter recluse.

It didn't even matter that she'd made Annabelle pay psychologically over the years. Grandmere had done the best she could. Now it was Annabelle's turn. That was the way families worked.

She couldn't manage to look after Grandmere from eighteen hundred miles away any longer, to turn over her care to unknown women who came and went almost as often as they changed Grandmere's antique linen sheets.

Six months wasn't much to give back for all those years and all those school bills. Dr. Renfro said his best guess was that Grandmere probably had less than six months left.

Annabelle dreaded losing the old woman. They had always had a love-hate relationship, but when Grandmere died, the last tiny root that tethered her to home would be gone. She'd be forever adrift.

Right. The old lady would outlive them all if will was any criterion.

The microwave dinged. Annabelle turned off the CD and flipped on the television. The news was over. Now she at least had the company of human voices and laugh tracks.

She put her dinner on a tray, took it back to the club chair and ate with little attention to the television sitcom.

Her finger, the one that she'd jabbed with the dressmaker's pin, throbbed. She'd doctored it with antibiotic ointment and covered it with a bandage, but it still hurt. Drat Ben anyway! The thought of him set other nerves throbbing.

She glanced over at the lace, now spread carefully on a sheet of white cardboard on her worktable. At least she didn't see the thing dripping with blood any longer.

After dinner she had to drive over to check on Grandmere, to be certain the current caregiver hadn't given up in disgust as so many of the others had, or that Grandmere hadn't lobbed a silver tray at her head and brained the poor woman.

Amazing how strong Grandmere could be when she was angry. Lying in that big old bed she looked no larger than a kitten.

Annabelle picked up her tray and took it into the kitchen. Then she swung her black sweater over her shoulders. The April nights still got chilly. As she started for the stairs the telephone shrilled.

She yipped. Silly to be so jumpy at sudden sounds. She grabbed the phone and said, "Yes, hello," and knew she sounded crabby.

"Uh, Annabelle?" A male voice. "It's Ben, Ben Jackson."

"Yes, Ben, I recognized your voice." Her body had recognized his voice. She wasn't about to tell him that.

"Look, I wanted to say again how sorry I am…"

"No need. I understand perfectly." She started to put the receiver down. His voice stopped her.

"The thing is, I'd like to make it up to you if you'd let me."

"Not necessary. Ben, I'm kind of in a hurry right now."

"Oh. Sorry. I'll make this fast. Let me take you to dinner Thursday night."

"No thank you."

"It's not a real date, only Mother's Thursday-night thing."

"No way."

"It's right across the yard, Annabelle. You've got to eat."

"I work with your mother—no, make that *for* your mother—five days a week. The last thing she wants is to see my shining face at dinner with all those bigwigs she always has.''

"It's a really small group. Probably people who remember you.''

"Wow! Talk about your really *great* enticement.''

"Look. You're the one who came back to town. You can't hide yourself upstairs in the garage forever. You've got to come out sometime. You play hermit in New York as well?''

"In New York I am plain old Annabelle Langley. Here I'm—well, you know what I am.''

"It's ancient history, and you didn't have anything to do with it. Come with me, please. If only to make me feel less of a jerk.''

"Ben…''

"Next step is I blackmail you.''

"What?''

"I mean, I'll make Mom put pressure on you.''

"That is dirty pool.''

"Don't I know it. Save me. Come with me Thursday.''

She dropped her forehead against her hand. "Okay, Ben. I'll come. But I don't have any dress-up clothes.''

"Whatever you wear will be great.'' He suddenly sounded immensely cheerful. "I'll pick you up at seven-thirty.''

"Pick me up?'' She laughed. "Ben, I live in your mother's backyard. Don't be ridiculous.''

"Then shall we say I will call for you, Mademoiselle Langley?''

"Whatever. Now I really do have to go see about Grandmere.''

"Sure. Sorry. Bye." As he hung up, she was certain she heard a shouted "Yes!" down the line.

"YES!" Ben said as he clicked his cell phone shut. He considered doing a victory dance, but suspected that the anteroom of the men's room at the club wasn't the place to do it. As it was, one of the late golfers raised his eyebrows. Ben grinned at him, and went back outside to find Brittany.

What on earth was he going to do about Brittany? She wasn't responsible for his attack of insanity, but he could not, absolutely, positively and totally could not take her home and to bed. Not tonight, not ever again.

But he couldn't actually say to her, "So, Brittany, sorry about this, but I've fallen madly in love with my mother's new chef d'atelier." That ought to go over big. He'd read somewhere that when a woman asked a man into her bed, it was only gentlemanly to accept. Not as if it would be the first time. Or even the twentieth, come to that.

Was that part of the reason he'd gone crazy? Was the first careless rapture with Brittany dying down?

Actually, there had never been much careless rapture with Brittany. Just workmanlike, satisfying, athletic and inventive sex. She had a great body and one hell of a lot of expertise. Going to bed with her wasn't something any red-blooded male would turn down lightly.

So how come he couldn't just accept the implicit offer? Who would he hurt? Not Annabelle, who didn't know the way he felt, didn't know he existed, probably. Not Brittany, who wouldn't be doing anything she hadn't done with him before. Not himself...

Himself. Taking a woman to bed just to be accommodating was the sort of thing his father did. Over and over again. Casually wounding his family, and ultimately the women he seduced. Ben had sworn he'd never be that sort of man. He wasn't about to start now.

"Ready, darling?" Brittany looked up from her cappuccino and reached for his hand. He took it and helped her up. "Ben, sweetie, are you okay?" she asked. "You look kind of green."

"Sorry, I think I had too many crab cakes," he said as he followed her to the front door. "Would you mind if I went home to bed?"

For a moment her eyes grew hostile, then she smiled and touched his cheek. "You want me to come over and tuck you in?"

He managed what he hoped was a suitably wan smile. "No, I'll be fine after a good night's sleep and some antacid. I'll follow you home and make sure you get inside okay."

"Don't be silly, sweetie. I'm five blocks away and you know what a bear my doorman is. Just go on home, snuggle down, and think of what you're missing." She arched an eyebrow.

He opened her car door and handed her in. As she swung her incredible legs behind the steering wheel he thought for a fleeting instant that he probably ought to be institutionalized for sheer idiocy. "Nevertheless, I will follow you. No argument. I know what can happen to a beautiful woman in five blocks."

"You are a dear," she said, and blew him an air kiss. "Call me tomorrow?"

He nodded and turned toward his own car. So much for honor. He'd have to work out some way to let her down gently without wounding her pride. He suspected she wouldn't go quietly.

"SHH!" The deep voice hissed from the top of the stairs. "The old—Mrs. Langley is asleep already."

Annabelle climbed the broad walnut staircase, turned the corner at the half landing and ran lightly up the rest of the stairs to the gallery that overhung the staircase. With each step the Oriental runner threw up a fine cloud of dust. Have to get somebody in here soon, she thought, before the place becomes haunted by brown recluse spiders and mice. She stifled a cough and whispered back, "Any trouble?"

The woman weighed twice as much as Annabelle. Her pale arms were the size of bolsters and looked about as solid. She rolled her eyes and sighed deeply. "Better'n last night. Didn't throw anything at me."

Annabelle fought to remember the woman's name. There had been so many in the past two months since Grandmere's last attack, and although she knew most of them only through communication with the employment agency, she'd met three just since she came to town. That made one a week. "Thanks, Mrs...." she hesitated. "Mrs. Mayhew." That was it. Beulah Mayhew. She'd come three days ago.

"She don't bother me none," Mrs. Mayhew said. "I've had a whole lot worse. At least she don't outweigh me." She laughed silently and the rolls under her arms jiggled. "Want a glass of sweet tea? I got some made in the icebox."

Annabelle smiled. None of the others had ever asked her to join them for so much as a roasted peanut. "No, thanks. But give me a rain check, please. Do you think I can look in on her without waking her?"

"Annabelle!" A querulous and surprisingly strong voice called from the doorway at the end of the hall. "Is that you?"

Annabelle's shoulders sagged. "Yes, Grandmere."

Mrs. Mayhew rolled her eyes and whispered, "Go say hello. I'll come lay down the law in a little while."

Annabelle's feet dragged over the exquisite Kirman runner that Grandmere had cut down for the hall. The dealer who had sold it to her had been horrified, but she'd told him it was her rug and she'd do as she liked with it.

Annabelle pasted a suitable smile on her face, squared her shoulders and walked across the threshold into that room she'd hated for twenty-three years.

The room was the same size as the living room, and beyond it the summer sleeping porch over the solarium downstairs had been glassed in to create a conservatory. The plants had long since died of neglect, but the room still held the faint odor of decaying mulch overlaid with the acrid tinge of medicine.

Here there were Oriental rugs on top of Oriental rugs. They had always been Grandmere's grand passion. At first Annabelle had felt her grandmother's joy in antique Orientals must signal a kinship between them. Her grandmother must truly appreciate the rich colors and beautiful patterns of the rugs. Then she discovered Grandmere saw them only as visible signs of her wealth. She possessed them as she tried to possess everything and everyone around her.

That was why she liked the ornate pre–Civil War furniture. The high-relief walnut eagle still perched on top of the seven-foot-tall headboard, caught in that moment before it stoops to impale its prey on three-inch talons. Annabelle had nightmares about those talons for years. She still shuddered at the sight of them.

Grandmere lay in the center of the bed, propped on soft, linen pillows edged with fine handmade lace.

The same hawk nose and piercing eyes as the eagle. With age and illness the likeness had become really scary. But she'd lost much of her heavy pale hair, and now pink scalp showed through the fine white hairs that were still beautifully cut and dressed once a week when her beautician visited to do her hair, nails and feet.

Her pale blue eyes, so different from Annabelle's dark ones, held the same mad intelligence as the eagle's.

"Come and kiss me, child, if you can bear to touch this wrinkled old skin."

Fishing for a compliment. A good day, then. Annabelle kissed her cheek and tasted the French powder that Grandmere wore even to bed with the expensive perfume she still imported. "Nonsense. You'll never age."

"Liar." She grabbed Annabelle's wrist and pulled her down close to whisper, "That woman is torturing me to death. I have fired her a dozen times, but she refuses to go. You must do it.''

"What kind of torture?''

"She beats me.'' Grandmere frowned at the door. "And she steals. She stole the pearls your grandfather gave me for our tenth wedding anniversary.''

"The pearls are in your safe-deposit box at the bank.''

"She's starving me to death. Look at her, then look at me. She eats her food and my food too. I haven't had a mouthful all day.'' The old voice turned querulous once more.

Annabelle pulled gently away and glanced at the silver tray on the side table. The meal might not be gourmet, but it seemed adequate. She could tell from the European way that her grandmother had laid her knife and fork at angles across the plate when she finished that Mrs. Mayhew had not eaten her grandmother's dinner. "Would you like me to bring you a sandwich?''

Grandmere sniffed. "A sandwich? What wine does one drink with a sandwich?''

"You can't have wine, Grandmere.''

The pale eyes flashed. "You've drunk it all, haven't you, you loathsome child?'' She began to cry. "The Napoleon brandy that your grandfather bought. The champagne. It's all gone, isn't it? You've drunk it or sold it, haven't you? That's what your mother would do—sell what she couldn't swig down.''

"No, Grandmere. The wine is there. You have the only key to the wine cellar, remember?''

"You've had a duplicate made. Wouldn't put it past you. You're in it with *her*.'' Abruptly she turned her face into the pillows. "Leave me alone the way you always do. Everybody always leaves me alone."

"You're not alone, Grandmere. Mrs. Mayhew's here. I'm here now. Jonas is here."

"Jonas?" The old woman cackled. "Jonas? Oh, that is rich. Jonas!" Suddenly she thrust Annabelle away. "Get out and don't come back. You're just like *her*. Evil! The bad seed! I knew it when I took you in. Get out!"

Annabelle stood. She was well aware they were no longer talking about Mrs. Mayhew but about Annabelle's mother. Grandmere had despised Chantal on sight and never ceased reminding Annabelle that she had been the only one to see what a scheming hussy the woman was.

Annabelle might as well leave. Grandmere would call her back later, accuse her of running out, but at the moment staying would only provoke another outburst. That was the way it always went. "Good night, Grandmere. Sleep well." She bent to touch the old lady's cheek with hers and drew back just in time to avoid the sharp red nails that clawed at her. Just like the eagle.

"I said get out. Whore! Slut! Look at you. Just like her!"

Annabelle backed away. As she reached the door, her grandmother sat up. "How many husbands have you seduced this week? The only thing you've ever done right in your miserable life was to kill her!"

Annabelle fled past Mrs. Mayhew, who stood in the doorway with her mouth open. She nearly tripped on the staircase where the brass bar had come loose from under the stair tread on one end. She knelt to push it back into place. She couldn't afford to have Mrs. Mayhew break her neck.

As she fled out the back door she heard her grandmother calling after her querulously, but she did not stop. By the time she slammed the door of her car and turned on the ignition she was crying. Anger? Pain? Loss?

Tonight had been really bad. She'd heard that some elderly, sick people lost their connection to the present, and kept getting today mixed up with yesterday, but Grandmere's mind had always been sharp. Too darned sharp.

She took a deep breath. Grandmere had always been so angry at life, and now she had nothing to look forward to except death. It must be hard to see Annabelle with her life ahead of her. At times like this, she wanted to hate the old woman, but as she'd told Marian, Grandmere was all she had. All she had ever had since her father disappeared.

As she drove by the elaborate four-car garage, she saw the lights were still on upstairs. It was only nine o'clock. Surely she could call on Jonas.

But not without phoning first. She used her cell phone, and, when he picked up, told him that she was downstairs and asked for permission to visit.

"Of course, Miss Langley."

When he opened the door, she hugged him. "What's with the 'Miss Langley' stuff, Jonas?" He stood aside to let her into his cozy living room. A book lay open on the arm of his easy chair under a reading light. The room was furnished in castoffs from the big house and some of the finest rugs. Jonas at least appreciated them.

"You're all grown-up now. I shouldn't be calling you Annabelle."

"Bull. I'll always be Annabelle to you. You got any cold beer?" She collapsed on the brown velour sofa and laid her head back. The nerve along her right temple throbbed. She massaged the pulse gently and hoped it wouldn't keep her awake.

"Lite or regular?"

"Oh, Lite, please, if you have it." The beer should at least help her relax. She patted her hips. "Always Lite. And I'll take it straight out of the bottle, thanks."

Jonas handed her a long-necked bottle covered with ice crystals and took his own to the easy chair. "And then you'll belch loudly?"

Annabelle laughed. "As loudly as possible. Make sure she hears me all the way across the backyard. Times like this I wish I chewed tobacco so I could hawk and spit."

"Well, I don't. She get to you tonight? Was it a bad one?"

"Worse than usual. Now she says that Mrs. Mayhew beats her, steals from her and is starving her."

Jonas snorted. "Nonsense. I watch pretty closely and I'm a fair judge of people. Beulah Mayhew's the best you've had. Let's hope she stays. When you going back to New York?"

"I can't, Jonas, not right this minute."

"You should get out of this town as quick as you can. Put her in a nursing home. I know you don't want to, but I've been checking them out. They're expensive, but there are a few good ones."

Annabelle shook her head. "I can't abandon her.

As much as I hate to admit it, she didn't abandon me, and she could have.''

''No, she saw to it that you paid for her generosity every day of your young life.'' His face clouded. ''There are times I could kill her myself.''

Annabelle finished her beer, went over and set the bottle on the drainboard by the sink. ''Well, don't. You'd get caught and then where would I be? You're my only friend in the world. Thanks, Jonas. By the way, what I could see of the yard looks lovely as always.''

''I try. Hard to get decent help these days.''

''At least money is not a problem. Not for her, at any rate.''

''For you?''

''Not at the moment.'' She brushed her lips across his cheek.

''If you do need money, let me know. I have some put by.''

''I'm fine, Jonas, really. Elizabeth pays me better than I deserve, and I get the apartment rent free.''

''Just remember, I'm here if you need me.''

''I always need you. I'd never have gotten this far without you. And if you ever call me Miss Langley again, I'll deck you.'' She trotted down the steps and waved over her shoulder. She could see Jonas standing in the open door of his apartment in her rearview mirror until she turned out of the driveway.

Before she went to bed, Annabelle carefully rolled the clean, dry lace between sheets of acid-free tissue. The blood had come out completely, thank God. The lace was from an early-twentieth-century wedding dress. With luck it would become another bride's treasured memory. With luck, yards of fine Swiss batiste, some supervision from Mrs. Jackson's chef d'atelier, and the fine mending and sewing talents of Marian and the other seamstresses.

Annabelle stripped and pulled on the oversize silk pajama top that served as night wear. As she looked at herself in the mirror and picked up her toothbrush, she murmured, "Elizabeth needs a chef d'atelier the way I need a third leg." She knew she was only a glorified seamstress and purchasing agent. Marian and the Vietnamese women who sewed for Elizabeth needed precious little supervision.

Still, she was grateful to Elizabeth for making a place for her, giving her a fancy title and even providing living quarters rent free.

"Your being here frees me to go to lace auctions and hunt garage sales for old lace dresses and things, and allows Marian to get on with the sewing and mending," Elizabeth told her. "Of course I need you."

Kind woman. They were all kind. And she was grateful. Only sometimes she got so tired of having to be grateful.

CHAPTER FOUR

"WHY DID I AGREE to this?" Annabelle said to her reflection. Maybe she'd simply tell Ben she'd changed her mind about going to Elizabeth's dinner party. Elizabeth obviously had no idea Ben planned to bring her, otherwise she would have mentioned it. She probably thought he was bringing the tall blonde he'd been looking at dress designs with.

She bundled her masses of hair into a semblance of a French roll and sprayed it long and hard with a hair spray that was guaranteed to hold like superglue, but tendrils still escaped around her face and at the nape of her neck. The heck with them.

She pulled on an ankle-length black skirt and slipped her feet into a pair of chunky black shoes. God, she looked as though she'd been working in the salt mines of Transylvania!

She flipped the shoes off and into a corner of the closet, then ripped off the skirt and threw it onto the floor after them. Once, just once, she wished she were six foot four and weighed ninety-six pounds like the models in New York. Instead, she resembled her roommate Vickie's two rescued alley cats, Dumpy and Frumpy.

She pulled a pair of black slacks off a skirt hanger and climbed into them, then a flame-orange turtleneck sweater, and over that a wildly patterned Tibetan quilted tabard.

Lord, she'd burn up at a dinner party in April!

Off came the tabard and sweater. Off came the slacks. Onto the floor.

Okay. Something simple but elegant. She reached into the back of the closet and pulled out the black Chinese silk cheongsam Vickie had made her for Christmas. She'd never had the nerve to wear it. It fit perfectly, but the style was more suited to the tiny Chinese ladies from the Lower East Side and Mott Street. When she glanced at her watch, she nearly whimpered. Ben would be on time, of course. And that gave her five minutes.

She yanked the silk dress over her head, pulled on a pair of high-heeled black strappy sandals she'd bought in a moment of madness because they were on sale, grabbed her small black purse—the closest thing she had to an evening bag—and did up the fancy gold frogs along the neck of the dress.

She hadn't even looked at the mirror when the bell at the foot of the stairs sounded, and a moment later she heard Ben's voice. "It's open. Okay if I come up?"

"No! I mean yes!" She shoved the closet door closed on the disaster inside. He might take one look at her and offer to take her to McDonald's instead of his mother's house.

She heard his footsteps at the top of the stairs and turned to face him.

"Suffering succotash," he whispered.

She caught her breath. "I'm sorry, Ben. I told you I didn't have anything to wear."

He shook his head. ''Couldn't prove it by me. You look gorgeous.''

''I do? I mean, I don't. I feel like a sausage.''

''You don't look like any kind of sausage I've ever eaten. Come on. You know how Mom is when people are late.''

''Ben, are you sure you want to do this?'' she said, but his hand was already warm on the small of her back as he herded her toward the staircase.

''Yes, ma'am, I do. It'll be all right. You'll see.''

They walked out into the fragile April night, into fairy lights that glimmered in the trees in the Jackson garden, and deputized for the wan sliver of moon that rode above their heads. She could smell the azaleas and the early roses.

She looked up at Ben as he tucked her hand under his arm. ''Watch your step, Princess Turandot, the paving's uneven.''

''Wasn't she that opera bitch who beheaded all her suitors?''

''Ah, but in the end she was vanquished by love.''

As I hope you will be, Ben thought. He heaved a sigh of relief. At least he hadn't been totally daffy when he'd fallen for Annabelle. With her hair up and those little curls around her face, and that incredible Chinese dress, she was the most luscious woman he'd ever seen. Wildly sexy. Next to her all the blond beauties looked as though they'd come out of the oven too soon and been stored in the refrigerator too long. Annabelle radiated heat.

He had heard all the stories about her mother, the hot-blooded Cajun from Lafayette, who'd refused to wear stockings and white cotton gloves in the summertime and went barefoot in the Langley garden.

And had inspired such desperate passion in her husband that he had killed her. At least he'd gone to prison for it. He knew the gossip as well, of course. That he'd lied to protect his child, the real killer.

Looking down at Annabelle, he refused to believe this beautiful girl could do anything that heinous even by accident.

He couldn't change his life's direction. He still wanted to be district attorney, and then maybe governor…senator.

So, if he intended to do all the things he planned with Annabelle by his side, there was only one solution.

He'd have to change Annabelle. At least in public. In private he hoped he read the signs right—that she was every bit as sensual as she looked.

"I can't do this," Annabelle said when they were three steps from the back door.

"Sure you can." His hand on her back grew a little more urgent.

"Who's going to be there?"

"No idea. Probably some politicos, a college professor or two. Nobody special."

She stopped dead. "Who would you consider special? Prince Charles and the Dalai Lama?"

"Come on, Annabelle. I'm right here. I made Mother promise to seat us together…"

"She knows you're bringing me?"

"Of course. Why wouldn't I tell her?"

"She didn't mention it."

Ben shrugged. He removed his hand. "It's just not a big deal to her."

"More likely she hoped one of us would come to our senses. That would be me." Annabelle started back toward her apartment.

"Oh no you don't," Ben said, and reached for her arm. "Just remember the old saw about visualizing everybody naked."

"Are you crazy? Besides, what if they're thinking about me the same way?"

I certainly will be, Ben thought, but he suspected to say so would have been really, really counterproductive. He gulped instead.

"Do you intend to stand out there all night?"

Both of them jumped.

Elizabeth said from the darkness just inside the back door, "You're the last to arrive. You've missed cocktails. We're almost ready to sit down to dinner."

"Elizabeth," Annabelle began.

"And don't even dream of chickening out at this point, Annabelle." Her voice softened. "Come on. It's going to be fun once you plunge in." She opened the screen door and held it back. "It's a tiny group."

Annabelle sighed. So did Ben, but his sigh was of relief.

Annabelle moved toward the door as though it were the route to the gallows. As she reached the lights over the steps, Elizabeth said, "My dear, where did you get that dress? It's marvelous. Perfect for you."

"My roommate. She's a designer for a small house. She made it for me as a Christmas present."

"Well, if she ever needs a job, tell her to look me up."

"I don't think Vickie would leave New York even to become head designer for Chanel."

Elizabeth followed Annabelle down the short hall to the green baize door into the front of the house. "With computers, she could work on the third moon of Jupiter, assuming there is one." Elizabeth pushed open the door and stepped through. "Everyone. Here is my errant son, finally, and for those of you who don't know or don't remember her, this is Annabelle Langley, who's running Elizabeth Lace for me."

Annabelle stood blinking in the light. She was the youngest person in the room. For a moment the faces swam in front of her eyes and she wished she'd brought her glasses. Then a tall, gray-haired and very distinguished man stepped into her field of vision with a broad smile on his face and his hand extended.

"Welcome, Annabelle. I, for one, am delighted that you came back to rescue Elizabeth. She's been working entirely too many hours to suit me."

She took the proffered hand and shook it.

"I'm Ben's boss, Phil Mainwaring."

She gulped. "Nice to meet you, sir."

"God help me, when beautiful women start to call you sir, life is over!" Mainwaring laughed.

Annabelle glanced at Ben. Didn't he know who Mainwaring was? Well, obviously he knew since he worked for the man. Didn't he know who Mainwaring had been? Did it really matter so little to everyone after all these years?

She felt her shoulders begin to relax. Maybe she'd been kidding herself. The murder was over twenty-five years old and had passed into Memphis legend by this time. Maybe people regarded her as just another one of Ben's girlfriends.

"Come along, all, let's sit down or the salmon mousse will ooze," Elizabeth said, taking Phil Mainwaring's arm and leading him toward the big dining room across the hall from the room that served as a showroom during the day and a living room at night.

An hour later Annabelle realized that she was actually enjoying herself. The conversation was intelligent and funny. Not, thank God, about fashion.

Ben didn't seem to be watching her as though she were a time bomb. The group was small—only eight. Annabelle worked very hard to remember names.

Elizabeth Jackson and Phil Mainwaring were apparently an item. Across from Annabelle sat a grizzled and shabby professor of religious studies from the university with his equally grizzled wife who looked as though her skin covered knotted ropes. They were both Ph.Ds, apparently. May and Gene Dressler or Ressler, or something like that.

The other couple, if indeed they were a couple, were charming, suave amateur actors who worked at the local community theater every chance they got and made pots of money doing something financial together during the day. She had no idea whether they lived together or not, but they certainly seemed to act very much like an old married couple. For the moment, she couldn't for the life of her remember their names, and it was a bit late in the evening for her to ask again. She'd have to find out from Ben.

The meal was excellent and served by a caterer, so Elizabeth didn't have to leave the table. The mousse was followed by a lemon sorbet, a salad and then by duck à l'orange and vegetables.

After the salad plates were cleared, the doors to the kitchen opened and the caterer and his assistant rolled in a flaming chocolate bombe covered in meringue and whipped cream. The flames came not from brandy that had been set on fire, but from a little garden of birthday candles on top.

Ben started singing "Happy Birthday" and everyone else joined in except Elizabeth, who sat at the head of the table laughing and clapping her hands.

A birthday party? Ben had landed her at a birthday party without bothering to tell her that's what it was? Annabelle felt her face turn purple with chagrin. What would she do if the dessert was followed by the opening of presents? She hadn't brought a single thing. She gave Ben a look that would curdle milk, but he only grinned back as though he hadn't a clue why she was upset.

"Oh, what fun! It won't explode, will it?" Elizabeth stood, sucked in a deep breath and blew out all the candles while everyone laughed and applauded. "Whew! Thank the Lord you didn't put the whole number of my age on top. We'd have set the house on fire."

Annabelle noticed that when Elizabeth sat down Phil Mainwaring covered her hand with his, and they smiled at each other.

"Speech!" shouted Gene what's-his-name, who had drunk, and was still drinking, quantities of the excellent red wine. Annabelle thought he was more than a little tight. From the dark look his wife threw him, she wasn't the only person who thought so.

"No speeches. I am merely glad to be a year older and surrounded by friends and family." She grinned at Ben. "The only thing that would make things perfect is for Ben to make me a grandmother before I am in my dotage."

"Hear, hear!" Mainwaring raised his glass.

At that moment a clock somewhere chimed a single note for the quarter hour, and Professor Gene knocked over his full wineglass on the white lace tablecloth.

"Gene, you idiot!" his wife snapped.

Annabelle watched the dark red river flow across the table straight toward her.

The room seemed to go dark. The wine became thick, bright blood reaching out to stain her hands.

If it reached her she'd drown.

Vaguely she registered activity—the caterer rushing in from the kitchen, noise, people trying to apologize and act calm and smooth out the awkward social situation. She couldn't take her eyes off the blood that rolled toward her like a sea.

"No!" She stood so fast her chair toppled onto the floor. She backed away with her hands in front of her to stop that terrible tide. She had to get away from it, had to run, had to hide where it couldn't reach her, couldn't drown her.

She had no memory of reaching the backyard or flying across it. Her sandaled feet clattering on the stairway to her apartment brought her to her senses.

Annabelle opened the door and nearly fell into the living room.

She pulled off her sandals with hands that were

still shaking, then kicked the shoes all the way into the corner. Suddenly she felt terribly cold.

That's when she heard the thud of footsteps up the stairs and Ben's voice calling her. "Annabelle!" Then louder, "Damnation, Annabelle, answer me!" He shoved the door open so hard it bounced off the wall with a thwack that made her jump.

She stood, hunched, her back to him.

He took her by her arms and turned her to face him. She couldn't meet his eyes.

"What was that all about? Are you all right?"

"I warned you, Ben, I really did." Her belly began to flutter as she fought to keep from crying. "I'm so sorry." She gazed up into his face. "Don't look at me like that. I really am sorry."

In an instant he looked merely stunned and confused. "It's okay. Come on back."

"No!" She wrenched away from him and hugged her body as though she was shivering.

She glanced up to see Ben's face over her shoulder as he squared his shoulders and set his jaw. She had a terrible desire to giggle. She'd seen him with that kind of look in high school, when the football team was down twenty points and it was up to Ben Jackson to save the day.

"Annabelle," he said in a tone he must use to redress recalcitrant witnesses. "You've seen plenty of drunks before, and everybody spills the occasional glass of wine. It's no big deal. Gene is devastated. He keeps staring around and asking what he said to upset you."

"Oh, poor Gene. It's not his fault."

He held out his hand. "Please come back with me and tell him that. You'd relieve his mind."

"No! I couldn't."

"Listen," he said reasonably, as though he were trying to persuade a frightened puppy out from under a chair, "these people are my friends. They want to be *your* friends. Come back, and I promise you nobody will make an issue of it. Say you got a cramp in your leg, or the salmon mousse disagreed with you. They'll be all over you with sympathy."

"But it wasn't that, Ben."

"Then what was it?"

"You wouldn't understand," she said in a very small voice. "Nobody would."

"Try me."

She shook her head.

"For Pete's sake, Annabelle."

That was too much. "I have just embarrassed the heck out of myself in front of a bunch of people I barely know, plus my employer, and I'm not going to go back and make another fool of myself."

He opened his mouth, but she cut him off and stepped close to him. "And another thing. Didn't it occur to you to mention to me in passing that this was a birthday party for your mother?"

"Huh?"

"Well, didn't it?"

"I didn't think it was a big deal. Not like we were giving presents. It's just another Thursday."

"It is not. It is a birthday party, and there I am singing 'Happy Birthday' with a stupid grin on my face and trying to act as though I knew all along, and then that drunken buffoon spilled all that red wine, and…'' At the memory of the wine on the lace tablecloth, her eyes closed, and she swayed.

''Annabelle?'' She felt Ben's hands pulling her against his chest, his strong arms encircling her, holding her close against him. ''Belle?''

She could feel the dry heaves as she gulped convulsively. No tears. There were never any tears, just this gulping and hiccuping while her throat and eyes burned. Other people cried. What was so wrong with her that she couldn't? Was that another symptom that she was a monster?

He put his fingers under her chin and tilted her face up. She squeezed her eyes shut and tried to quell the shivers in her stomach.

''God, you are so beautiful,'' he whispered.

She felt his lips against hers, gentle, warm, moving back and forth across her lips, his tongue barely touching, teasing, tasting. She wanted to resist, to tell him this wasn't the time or place, but the cascade of warmth within her wouldn't allow her to do that. Instead, her own lips parted and her tongue darted out to meet his, to intermingle, to taste the remains of sorbet, the hint of sweetness on his lips.

His hands slid down her back and below her waist, holding her against him. His whole body felt rock-solid, so wonderfully, comfortingly male. Yet his erection wasn't comforting at all, but disturbing, because she felt the heat in her own loins answering as she moved against him in a slow rhythm that she couldn't seem to control.

No. It was up to her to control it, not to fall over backward at his touch, or to let herself feel all the conflicting emotions he evoked. She sucked in her breath and pulled back from him, her eyes wide. "Go away, Ben, please, right now."

He pulled her into his arms again. "I don't want to," he whispered into her hair.

"You've got to go back to your party." She slapped his hand away. "Stop that. You go tell them I succumbed to the vapors or something."

"Come with me."

"Ben!" This time she used enough force to overbalance him so that he had to step back a couple of paces. "Read my lips. I cannot, I will not go back over to that house tonight. I'll write everybody notes tomorrow, including the caterers if that's what you want…"

He sat on the sofa and took her hands. "It's not what I want. It's what you need. If you don't come back now, the next time it'll be harder to crawl out of that shell. How can you ever hope to feel at ease in social situations…"

"Who said I have to?"

"I do, dammit."

She started to smart off back at him, then stopped, tilted her head and looked at him quizzically. "What do you have to do with it?"

Amazingly, he blushed and stammered, "Because I—I want what's best for you."

"And the reason for that would be…?"

"That wasn't exactly a friendly kiss we just exchanged. My ears are ringing."

"Even in the South you no longer have to marry me because you kissed me, Ben."

"What if I want to?"

This time she laughed. "Right. Like I'd be the

perfect district attorney's wife.'' She walked to the corner and picked up her shoes. ''Look, Ben, I'm tired, and I'm feeling like a nitwit. I'm not up to facing those people tonight. Please just make my apologies to your mother and her guests.''

''You won't change your mind? Or even tell me what went on?''

''Nope.''

His shoulders sagged. ''Fine. I can't pick you up and carry you over there. Well, I could, but you'd probably kick and scream or something equally unattractive.''

''You got that right.''

He straightened. ''However, Miss Annabelle, this is far from over. I intend to find out what's causing this. And when I do, you and I are going to fix it.''

He turned on his heel and made what he probably considered a dignified exit.

As he reached the top step, she applauded slowly.

He paused, then rocketed down and slammed the door at the foot of the stairs behind him.

Annabelle held her pose until she heard him running across the backyard, then she sank into the club chair.

Two hallucinations in one day. Some kind of record. She probably ought to get a CAT scan or an EEG or something. She might have an aneurysm about to pop or a brain tumor.

Maybe Ben was at the bottom of it. She'd been in Memphis for almost a month now without anything worse than bad dreams. Then suddenly Ben Jackson drops out of a tree, and the craziness starts. Was it her hormones?

Was her body finally betraying her for all the years of militant asexuality?

She didn't know what was going on, but *something* was definitely out of whack.

CHAPTER FIVE

THE GUESTS WERE STANDING at the front door air kissing and saying their goodbyes when Ben walked back into his mother's dining room.

She turned a concerned face to him. "Is Annabelle all right?"

He smiled cheerfully. "A touch of migraine. She says she doesn't get them often, but they come on suddenly. She was afraid she was going to throw up."

"Poor kid," the professor said. "I'm sorry about the wine on the tablecloth, Elizabeth. That chime startled me."

"My birthday clock from Phil," Elizabeth said. "It's antique ormolu."

"Too damn noisy," Phil said comfortably. "I can disconnect the chime mechanism if you like."

"Please. It's beautiful, but a bell ringing every fifteen minutes is a bit much. Do you mind?"

"Not a bit. I'll do it tonight if you like."

Elizabeth smiled at Phil. Ben caught the relief in her eyes. His mother would never say anything unpleasant about a gift. But he knew she'd go nuts listening to that thing, and would probably end up hiding it in the broom closet and only bringing it out when Phil was around.

"I'm just glad I didn't cause her migraine," said Gene.

"Lucky, you mean," his wife said.

He seemed to have sobered up quickly.

"Please tell her we're sorry and look forward to seeing her again," May added, and squeezed Ben's arm. "She really is a lovely girl, Ben. So different from the girls you usually squire to these things."

He kept the smile pasted on his face as he stood at his mother's shoulder and waved everyone away except Phil Mainwaring, who stood in the doorway with his arm around Elizabeth's waist.

"Well," Phil said, giving Ben a lift of the eyebrow. "Time for another cup of coffee?"

Ben shook his head. "I'll get out of the way and leave you two kids alone. Don't do anything I wouldn't do."

Elizabeth laughed. "We wouldn't dream of doing half the things you do, would we, Phil?"

"We would if you'd let me."

"And besides," she said, ignoring Phil's comment, "I want to know what really went on tonight with Annabelle." She slipped out of Phil's grasp. "Sit down for a minute. I feel responsible for Annabelle. If she's in any trouble I want to know about it."

"No trouble that I'm aware of," Ben said as he followed his mother and Phil into the living room, where they sat down. He stretched his legs in front of him and slouched on the back of his neck.

"You look awfully grumpy," said his mother. "Surely she didn't dump you quite that soon."

"She didn't dump me because she hadn't taken

me," Ben said. "Frankly, I don't know what went on tonight either, except that she warned me she's not at ease with people. At school she was an outsider—far outside. In high school there's always somebody who's considered weird, who bears the brunt of the jokes and the snickers and the innuendo. She was that somebody."

"I certainly hope you didn't join in," Elizabeth said.

Ben shook his head. "No, but I didn't do much to interfere either. Hell, Mom, she was four years younger. In high school that's practically a generation. I mean, we grew up as neighbors, but we weren't ever close. She's much nearer Steve's age."

"And your brother was off at military school," Elizabeth said with a touch of sadness. "He's never really been home since the eighth grade."

"You did what you had to do. Don't blame yourself."

"Maybe if I'd been a better mother…"

"Since your younger son has turned from a blossoming juvenile delinquent into a model citizen, you apparently did the right thing," Phil added. "Actually, Ben, it's not surprising that Annabelle is a bit dysfunctional, growing up as she did in that mausoleum with Mrs. Langley trying to convince her she was a bad seed. Maybe she should have stayed in New York."

"No, she shouldn't have!" Ben said with such vehemence that both the others stared at him. He stammered, "I—I mean, she's got to face this town if she's going to move from dysfunctional to functional."

"She functions perfectly well when she's working," Elizabeth said.

"She needs to be at ease with people, learn to handle sticky social situations, entertain graciously..."

"Oh my God," Elizabeth said, and sank back against the cushion of the peach sofa as though she'd been slugged. "Not Annabelle? Ben, I know what I said, but I never dreamed it would be Annabelle's name on that arrow."

"I have no idea what you're talking about."

Elizabeth's eyes narrowed. "Right. So you brought Annabelle because Brittany couldn't come tonight?"

"Drop it, Mom."

"If I'd thought for a minute—"

Sitting next to Elizabeth on the couch, Phil cleared his throat. "Excuse me, but what are you two talking about?"

"Mom." Ben's voice was a warning.

After a moment his mother nodded. "Fine. It's nothing, Phil. An old family joke. Nevertheless, Ben, I am right, aren't I? About your getting struck by that arrow?"

"What if you are?"

"It's worse than unfortunate. Under the circumstances, it's downright catastrophic. But for you or for her?"

"Look, if you people are going to talk in riddles, I'm going home," Phil said, getting to his feet.

"No, stay," Ben said. "I'm going. I've got to go over depositions at the crack of dawn if I'm going to be ready for the preliminary motions in the Mac-Cauley thing."

"Indeed you do, and I, as your boss, demand it." Phil dropped back onto the couch and slipped his arm around Elizabeth's shoulders. "So go away, grasshopper, and return when you have all the knowledge of assault with a deadly weapon at your fingertips."

"Or at least the knowledge of the *State versus Cadwallader*."

"Indeed. Good case law."

Ben bent to kiss his mother's cheek. "Do me a favor, and just leave this alone. Promise me."

Elizabeth sighed. "Okay. I don't know whether to be happy or sad for you."

"Let me in on the joke," Phil asked a little plaintively.

She touched his cheek. "The mother's curse. You wouldn't understand since you don't have children."

"Not your fault, Mom." Ben straightened his shoulders. "It will work out. You'll see. I can handle this."

"I hope so, I really do."

"Not another word, you get me?"

"My lips are sealed."

"Thanks, Mom. Good night, you two."

It *would* be all right, dammit, Ben thought as he walked slowly down the concrete stairs to the sidewalk where his little yellow car waited for him.

He would learn to control the feelings Annabelle engendered in him. There was nothing wrong with what his mother considered passion. But he couldn't allow passion—love—to interfere with his focus. And maybe he could help Annabelle to feel more comfortable in social situations. A win-win situation, as Phil Mainwaring would say.

He drove around the block and headed toward his apartment. Suddenly the car veered as though it had a mind of its own, and he found himself parked in his mother's back parking area beside Annabelle's car.

Her lights were still on. He dialed her number on his cell phone. When she answered, he asked, "May I come up?"

"It's late."

"I know. I won't stay. I want to report what happened back at my mother's."

"Do I care?"

"Don't you?"

"Yes," she sighed. "All right, come up, but just for a minute."

Annabelle met him at the head of the stairs. He caught his breath. Her wild mane of hair tumbled over her shoulders like an image in a painting by Burne-Jones or Dante Gabriel Rossetti.

The room was lit by a fluorescent work light suspended over her worktable. The rest of the space lay in shadow.

"You've been working at this hour?" he asked.

"Helps me calm down. You want a beer or a glass of wine?"

"Beer, please." He leaned against the worktable and watched her. She had changed into a corduroy robe of dark maroon that swirled around her naked ankles when she walked.

She handed him the beer. "Why are you looking at me that way?" Her hand went to the shoulder of her robe and pulled it higher.

"I'm seeing you in a garden."

"I beg your pardon?"

His finger traced her cheek, touched her earlobe. He could see her shiver beneath his touch. "It's as though I've never seen the world bloom before."

She stepped back. "Drink your beer, please. Tell me what happened at the house, then go."

He came out of his reverie. "Gene was happy he hadn't caused your migraine, and everyone agreed that you were a delightful dinner companion. They would like to see more of you."

"Really?"

"I'm not making it up. Now it's your turn. Tell me what really happened."

"It's too crazy." She turned away.

"I won't laugh or have you committed." He put his hands on her shoulders and pulled her gently back against his chest. For a moment she resisted, then with a tiny sigh she let her head rest against him. He began to knead her shoulders. "Your shoulders are one big knot."

"Sewing does that to you," she whispered.

"This isn't sewing, it's tension. Is it your grandmother? Some memory of the past?"

"Partly." She made an "Mmm" sound. "That feels wonderful."

Felt pretty good to Ben too. He bent his head and ran his lips down the side of her throat.

She sprang away instantly. "Don't, Ben."

"Why not? We both liked it." He caught her hands, drew her to him and slipped her hands around his waist. "You did like it."

"That's not the point. I shouldn't like it."

"Yes, you should." He slipped a finger under her chin, tilted her head up and kissed her softly.

She kissed him back. His arms went around her, brought her closer, while his lips deepened the kiss, teasing her with his tongue until she opened to him and responded.

"Ben," she whispered against his mouth.

"Hush," he said softly.

One moment he could feel her body stiffen, held awkwardly away from his, the next she seemed to capitulate, become almost boneless in his arms. He felt as though he were drowning in the richness of her mouth, her tongue, her hands that swept up his back and then down again.

He broke the kiss and slipped her robe down from her shoulders, trailing his lips down the soft swelling of her breast.

He found the zipper on the front of the robe and slowly eased it down, parting the corduroy so that it lay like an open vee revealing her breasts, cream white with soft honey-colored nipples already erect and waiting for his tongue.

When he began to massage her nipple, she gave a tiny sob and kissed his throat, finding the throbbing pulse. Her tongue was like a burning wick of a candle.

"I want you so much," he whispered against her breast.

Her hands came up and cradled his head. Her back arched and those soft sounds came again and again.

He ripped off the polo shirt he'd worn to dinner. "Annabelle?" He held her eyes. Hers were enormous, pupils dilated, her mouth soft and bruised.

Without taking her eyes off his, her fingers found the slide of the zipper.

He held his breath as her fingers slid the zipper open all the way.

He reached for the open neck and slid the robe off her shoulders. It slithered to the floor in a puddle around her feet.

She stood before him naked, her eyes almost frightened.

"I'm…" she began. "I mean, I'm not very…"

"It's all right, love," he whispered as he gathered her into his arms. "I am."

He took her hand, brought it to his lips. "We'll be fine." He led her to the bedroom. He could hear her breathing, shallow, quivery. She probably hadn't been with many men before. He'd have to go slowly, gently, let her see how much she meant to him, how much this beautiful gift of her body meant.

She lay on the bed and watched him as he undressed. Only when he stripped fully and she saw him exposed and erect did she utter a sound. He lay down beside her and began to caress her softly.

When he reached the spot between her thighs she opened to him instantly, and her own fingers found him and slid along him as though she were exploring an unknown land.

She was an unknown land to him too, but a paradise of riches. He pressed his fingers into her.

Suddenly she arched her back and cried out.

He sat up, leaned over her. "My God, Annabelle, I didn't know!"

She caught his hand in both of hers. He could see

the glint of unshed tears in her eyes. "I can't even do this right," she said.

"Shall I stop? Do you want me to?"

"No! Please, please, no."

"I don't want to hurt you."

"Somebody has to, don't they? Sometime, I mean? Ben, I'm so sorry."

He wrapped his arms around her, pulled her up against his chest. "Sorry? To offer me such a gift?" He held her, kissed her hair, her face, her eyes. She clung to him.

"Ben, please, do whatever you have to. I'll be all right."

"You're certain?"

"Yes."

"We'll take all night if we have to."

She'd made him feel clumsy and stupid again when he wanted to be her knight in shining armor. He'd had no idea she was still a virgin. He didn't know how to make love to her, how to keep from hurting her. He wanted her, but what mattered now was what she wanted, needed.

Then he saw her lying white and still beneath him, her eyes closed tight, her hand clasping his. Was he wrong to long for her so? To want this from her?

He began kissing her at her throat and trailed slowly down her body. She arched against him. He spread her gently and bent to kiss her where he'd probed her, and was rewarded with a cry that wasn't pain this time, but pleasure. She dug her fingers into his hair and her hips began to move against him.

Then she arched one final time. He could feel her spasm, hear the inchoate sounds she made.

As she began to slide back down the far side of her orgasm, he knelt above her, taking all his weight on his forearms. His body knew what to do if his mind was still confused.

She gave one cry when he slid into her. He could feel her tear, feel the wetness that he feared was her blood. He held himself still, afraid to move, afraid to invade her farther.

Her hands encircled his hips. "Yes, Ben," she whispered. "Yes."

He kissed her and felt her lips part, but whether in pain or pleasure, he couldn't later be certain.

But after a moment she began to move with him, against him, matching his rhythm, and finally wrapped her legs around his waist. He could feel the world begin to slip away from him into that tiny space where they were joined. He groaned as he tried to hold himself away a little longer from the top of the mountain.

She dug her fingers into his shoulders and suddenly the mountaintop was upon him. He soared into free flight.

Afterward, he held her cradled against him, kissed the tears on her cheeks, stroked her back.

"Will I get pregnant?" she whispered.

"No, love, I took care of that."

"Did I bleed much?"

"I have no idea."

"Will you stay a little while? Hold me a little?"

"Yes, love." He ran his fingers through her hair, then reached down and pulled the duvet off the floor to cover them. "Sleep now."

She cuddled against him. A moment later he heard her breathing become soft and even.

He wished he could sleep so guiltlessly.

THAT NIGHT Annabelle had the nightmare for the first time in a dozen years. She heard the crackle of the flames that reached out to draw her in, the bells that tinkled as though they danced away from the heat.

Monstrous shapes formed and reformed in the shadows. She tried to hide, but they eddied about her, choking her with the odor of something sharp and metallic.

She kept wiping her hands down the front of her dress, but when she looked at her palms, they were still wet and red.

She ran and ran until she tripped and fell into blackness.

She always woke before she hit bottom. She'd heard that if you ever actually hit bottom you died. Assuming there was a bottom.

"Annabelle!" The voice was familiar, male. It called her from a million miles away. She came awake thrashing frantically against strong arms that held her.

"It's all right."

She froze. She stared up into the concerned gray eyes of Ben Jackson.

Everything flooded back in an instant. What had she done? She'd been so careful, so guarded for so long, and then, bang! She barely knew Ben Jackson, really.

"You were having a nightmare."

She slipped away from him and sat up, crossing

her arms over her naked breasts. "Sorry. Happens sometimes."

His fingertips stroked her back. She shivered with the remembered pleasure of his touch.

"Are you all right?" he asked gently.

"Fine. Why wouldn't I be?" Keep it light. A meaningless encounter. He'd definitely consider it only another conquest. A night off from bedding Brittany or Ashley or Heather. She mustn't let him know how horrified she felt at her actions.

"Lie down. Let me hold you."

"I'm thirsty. And I have to go to the bathroom." She glanced at the clock. "You'd better go home, hadn't you? We both have to get up early in the morning, and we definitely wouldn't want anyone to see your car outside."

"Annabelle!" He grasped her shoulders, sat up behind her and wrapped his arms around her. "I don't give a damn if the whole world sees my car. What I couldn't bear is if you're sorry."

She twisted in his arms and buried her face against his naked shoulder. The dark hair on his chest tickled her nose. Lord, she loved the smell of him, the taste of salt on his skin. "I'm not sorry." But she was, desperately. She'd started on the road her grandmother had predicted. Staying a virgin had given her a way to prove to herself and to Grandmere that she wasn't a slut like her mother.

"Thank God," Ben whispered against her hair. "Let me stay."

She shook her head. "No, Ben."

"I won't touch you if you don't want me to." He stroked her hair. "Did I hurt you?"

"I told you, I'm fine." The ache she felt between her legs was a combination of pleasure and pain. At the moment pain predominated.

"I promise you, the next time won't hurt."

The next time? There would not be a next time. She nodded. Anything to get him away so that she couldn't see him, feel his touch, long to have him back inside her, long to touch him, to caress him. She felt her groin tighten. "For now, go home, please."

He sighed. "If you're certain you're all right."

He reached across her to flick the switch on the bedside lamp.

"Don't!" She grabbed his hand. She'd die if he looked at the sheets. Maybe she was acting like an eighteenth-century heroine, but Grandmere had drummed it into her head for so long—slut, slut, slut.

Without a word, he slid off the bed and began to dress. The thin moon sent just enough light through the narrow windows to silver his body. He was so beautiful, and so completely at ease with his nakedness.

When he was dressed, he knelt on one knee on the bed to kiss her. "Sleep well. I'll call you in the morning."

She listened until she heard his car start and drive away before she slid out of bed and turned on the overhead light.

The stain on the sheet was barely visible. Surely she must have bled more than that! She changed the sheet quickly, then took a shower to wash the scent of sex off her skin and out of her hair.

She'd known Ben was dangerous to her peace of mind.

Her guard was down, she was vulnerable, that was it. From now on, she'd be armed against his attraction.

She would not be another in his long line of mistresses.

And to a man like Ben, she would be nothing more.

The instant she climbed back into bed, she fell into a deep, dreamless sleep.

She awoke to the song of the dratted mockingbird that had taken up residence outside her window. She glanced at the clock. Five-thirty in the morning. She started to roll over for another hour and realized her throat felt dry and itchy. She laid the inside of her wrist against her forehead. Fever!

Her eyes burned and her tongue felt as though somebody had covered it with dirty shag carpeting.

Retribution couldn't come this swiftly. She must have been coming down with whatever it was for two or three days.

That explained the hallucinations.

Not a brain tumor. Just a plain old head cold.

She popped a couple of cold capsules, drank a large glass of water straight out of the tap and climbed back into bed.

She'd have to call Marian to say she was sick.

She groaned. If Elizabeth had spotted Ben's car outside until all hours, she'd never believe the cold story. She'd think Annabelle was too worn out making love to get out of bed.

Ben had probably been infected too.

Undoubtedly. She'd helpfully shared every germ in her body with him.

She'd wondered what she could possibly offer Ben that he didn't already have.

A ripsnorting cold was not exactly what she'd had in mind.

"I APOLOGIZE," Elizabeth said.

"Huh?" Ben slipped the phone between his ear and shoulder so that he could continue to sign the papers his secretary, Dixie Guest, stuck in front of him.

"Last night. I was certain you were lying about Annabelle's migraine."

He dropped his pen and put his hand to the phone. "What are you talking about, Mom?"

"She really was coming down with some kind of bug."

"She's sick?" He heard the panic in his voice. "What with? Who's looking after her?"

"Hey, calm down, lover boy. It's just a virus. I'm sure she'll be fine tomorrow or the next day."

"How do you know?" Visions of hemorrhage flooded his mind. God, he must have been crazy to make love to her last night and even crazier to leave her before he was certain she'd be all right.

"She called Marian this morning and said she wouldn't be in to work, so of course I went over to check on her. She was swigging down orange juice and looking miserable—runny nose and all."

"Did you call Dr. Vickery?"

"No, Ben, I did not call Dr. Vickery. She popped

a couple of Tylenol and told me not to come too close in case it's the flu.''

"So you just left her there alone?'' His voice rose dangerously.

"Ben, you didn't act this concerned when I had an emergency appendectomy. You have got it bad.''

"I don't have anything except a sick friend and a coldhearted mother.'' He started to hang up the phone, then said, "Thanks for calling.''

He shoved the remaining papers on his desk back into the "to be signed'' folder and grabbed his jacket off the back of his seat.

"Whoa, hoss!'' Dixie said. "You sit your rear end back down and sign those papers.''

"I've got an emergency, Dixie. I'll sign them tonight and have them on your desk first thing Monday morning.''

"Monday? Ben…''

"All the judges are halfway to the eighteenth hole by now. If it'll make you happy, I'll bring the papers back tonight.''

Dixie sniffed. "You are the boss, although sometimes I cannot understand why.''

He bent to kiss her cheek. "Say hello to Gus for me, and have a good weekend. Take off early yourself. You deserve it.''

"Damn right I do.'' Dixie patted her graying hair into place as Ben closed the door of his office on her.

He stopped by the health-food store and spent eighty-five dollars on holistic flu remedies, heavy-duty vitamins, herbal concoctions guaranteed to clear a fever and a quart of homemade chicken soup. Then he stopped by the ice-cream store and picked up

rocky road and raspberry sorbet. He considered diamonds, but she'd never accept them. Roses? Not if
she was already sneezing.

The spare key to her apartment was still under the
potted geranium outside the back door. He shifted the
plastic bags he'd looped over his arm, unlocked the
door and called up the stairs, "Annabelle, it's Ben.
I'm coming up."

A moan. "Oh, God, no."

Annabelle lay on the sofa in a nest of comforters,
quilts and half a dozen down pillows. On the muted
television, four extremely large ladies attempted to
pull one another's hair out.

Annabelle pointed the clicker at the set and shut it
off. "Go 'way, Ben," she croaked. "And don't look
at me. If you do you'll turn to stone."

"Your hair does kind of look like snakes. They're
not wriggling much. I'll be okay." He bent to kiss
her.

She put up her hands in front of her face. "Don't.
I mean it."

"Sure." He set his bags on the kitchen counter,
pulled the two quarts of ice cream out of one of the
sacks and opened the freezer. Six TV dinners and a
bag of shrimp. He set the ice cream on the top shelf.

"I've brought chicken soup and herbal medicine."

"That was sweet, but I really need sleep. With
luck, this stupid fever will break in a couple of hours
and I'll be fine tomorrow."

"Tomorrow's Saturday. You can stay in bed all
day if you want."

"I've got Grandmere, remember."

"She doesn't need what you've got."

"Neither do you, Mr. Assistant District Attorney, and I'm not just talking about this bug."

He dropped the bottles of medicine onto her lap. "I need everything you've got, bugs and all. Here. Take a bunch of these while I heat the soup."

"Ben, please." She sounded plaintive. "Just watching you is making me tired. Besides, it's four o'clock in the afternoon. I never have dinner before seven."

"Did you have lunch?"

"No, but—"

"Then how about a nice cold dish of raspberry sorbet while I fix you some iced tea?"

Her eyes widened. "Raspberry sorbet? Really? How on earth did you ever find that?"

"We have our ways." He sat on the coffee table and reached for her hand, which she immediately shoved deeper under the covers. "Seriously, are you all right? I've spent the day alternately worrying about you and cussing myself. I tried to call, but the answering machine was on."

"Ben, I am fine. Really. Except for this stupid cold I am physically perfectly all right." She ran her hand across her forehead. "Besides, I suspect in a few hours you're going to know precisely how I feel."

"What?"

"After last night, my germs are your germs."

"I don't just want your germs."

"Oh, please." She was suddenly serious. "Thank you for coming over and for caring about me and for the sorbet, but that's as far as it goes. You and I— well, there just can't ever be a you and I, and the sooner we both admit it the better off we'll be."

He felt as though he'd been kicked in the stomach. For the first time since high school he'd opened his heart a crack, thought there might possibly be a chance to make himself into a human being again. He'd forgotten what the pain of loss felt like. He'd have been better off if he'd remembered ahead of time. Last night he'd been certain she wanted him as much as he wanted her.

Apparently she'd had second thoughts.

All day he'd had visions of the way she would look with their children in her belly. He'd thought about kissing every laugh line that showed up around her eyes; about doddering beside her into old age. He'd made up a whole lifetime for the two of them between motions before Judge Hawkinrood and opening arguments.

The thought of being without her gave him such a wrench that he twisted suddenly in his chair with actual physical pain.

"Ben? Are you okay?"

"No, I am not okay." He brought her a dish of sorbet, thrust it at her and began to prowl the room.

"Um, this is wonderful," Annabelle said.

"Why?" he asked.

"Why what?"

"Why can't there ever be a you and I?"

She set down the empty dish. "Sit down, Ben. Listen to me. I've been thinking about this all day."

"If it's all that old nonsense about your mother's death—"

"It's not nonsense, Ben. It's the truth. I shot and killed my mother."

"First of all, you didn't. Your father went to jail for it."

"Grandmere says he was covering up for me."

"Even if you did, it was an accident. You weren't quite four years old, for God's sake. You didn't even know what a gun was, much less what would happen if you picked it up."

"Doesn't matter. It happened. Maybe if you were a businessman or a banker it wouldn't matter. Maybe if we moved to Fargo, North Dakota, to raise hogs it wouldn't matter. But you are an up-and-coming assistant district attorney known for his tough stance on crime and criminals. The law-and-order D.A. The first newspaper reporter that sees us out together in Memphis is going to write up some cute little article for the *Commercial Appeal* or the *Memphis Flyer* about practicing what you preach."

"Who cares?"

"You do, or you should."

"Do you actually remember shooting her?"

"What little I remember has been so colored by what everybody has told me through the years that I have no way of knowing what really happened."

"So maybe your father actually was guilty."

"Okay. Say he was. So I'm a murderer's kid instead of a killer. And not only a murderer's kid, but a slut's kid. Everybody knew my mother slept around. That's why my father is supposed to have killed her. Any way you cut it, Ben, I am off limits to you, and as soon as the situation with Grandmere is resolved, I'm going back to New York and my anonymous life so that you can marry yourself a Brittany or a Tiffany or a Heather."

"I don't want Brittany or Tiffany or Heather. I want you."

"You can't have me. Not ever again."

He started to speak, then thought better of it. A moment later, he said, "Tell me you didn't want me last night."

She turned away from him. "Last night was last night. Today I may be sick, but I'm in my right mind. I refuse to screw up your life."

"I don't accept any of that. Most of all, I don't accept that you are a bad seed or that you have bad genes." He stood up. "I'll put the soup in the refrigerator. Heat it in the microwave when you want it."

"You're going?" She sounded surprised.

"You said yourself I'm probably going to come down with what you've got. Besides, I've got some work to do." He leaned over to kiss her, but she waved him off. He put the soup into the refrigerator none too gently and noticed that there was nothing inside it but a gallon of orange juice and some lemons. "I forgot your iced tea."

"I'll fix some later."

"Fine." He walked to the head of the stairs before he turned to say to her, "I am also the can-do district attorney. You may have missed that one. I don't give up, I don't give in, and if things aren't right the way they are, then I damn well find some way to fix them."

CHAPTER SIX

THE FIRST THING Ben noticed when he opened the door of his apartment was the blinking light on his answering machine. He threw his suit jacket at the back of the sofa, yanked his tie loose and tossed it after the jacket, kicked off his shoes and began to unbutton his shirt as he walked to the side table. Seven messages. He sighed, stripped to his undershorts and punched the button.

"Ben, darling, it's Brittany. Are you all right? I know we've been playing telephone tag. Call me."

He pulled a beer from the refrigerator and sank onto the couch to listen to the rest of the messages. He'd called Brittany twice, both times when he'd been pretty sure she wouldn't be available.

The next three messages were all from Brittany. Same song, different refrain.

The fourth was from his secretary, Dixie. "You were wrong about the judges. Henderson was in long enough to rule on your pretrial motion. You lucky devil. The evidence from the search goes in. See you Monday."

He'd fought hard to get the evidence of the search of Thomas MacCauley's premises admitted into evidence despite the defense lawyer's finagling. He should be feeling elated. Instead, he felt miserable.

The fifth call was from his mother saying she'd check on Annabelle and hoped that he wasn't getting the same thing she had.

The sixth was from Phil Mainwaring. "Great job, young grasshopper. I'm still not Judge Mainwaring, but the powers that be say I'm a shoo-in for the appointment. And guess what that means about my successor as D.A. See you Monday."

The final message came in a high, elderly, but surprisingly firm voice. "This is Victoria Langley. I do not normally speak to recordings. I am making an exception in this case because I wish to see you this evening at eight o'clock. Be on time."

Ben stared at the machine. Victoria Langley? Annabelle's grandmother? The dragon lady herself? There was no possible way she could know about him and Annabelle. She'd never spoken to any member of his family since his father had allowed her son to accept a plea bargain in his wife's murder.

So far as Victoria was concerned, Hal Jackson was solely responsible for her son's term in prison and subsequent disappearance. The scandal had caused Victoria to withdraw from her place in society. In her eyes, Hal was also to blame for that. What could the old lady possibly want with him?

He reached for the telephone to tell her he wouldn't be available, then let his hand fall. It might have something to do with Annabelle. If so, then he wanted to know.

He might be able to pump her about the night Annabelle's mother died. He wouldn't put it past the old lady to have shot the woman herself and let her son take the blame. From what his mother said, she'd hated—what was the woman's name again? Something Cajun. Auvern, no, Aucoin. That was it. First name something fancy. Chantal.

Chantal Aucoin from Lafayette, in deepest, darkest Louisiana. No wonder old Mrs. Langley hated her on sight. He'd heard his mother talk about how Raymond Langley came home with her after a few months of working in one of the banks the Langleys were associated with. And how Mrs. Langley took to her bed for a month, wouldn't speak to either of them.

Back then, people still counted the months between marriage and the birth of the first child. He suspected, in Annabelle's case, it might have been a tad shy of nine months. That was something he could check.

He didn't even know Annabelle's birthday. Didn't know what her favorite color was, or what movies she liked, or whether she enjoyed long walks in the country.

He was in love with a complete stranger, a stranger he'd known all his life. He must really be bewitched.

Had Annabelle's mother produced the same effect in her lovers?

AT FIVE MINUTES TO EIGHT Ben rang the front doorbell of the Langley mansion. He'd parked under the elaborate Georgian porte cochere and walked around to the front. He had no intention of using the tradesman's entrance.

He stood under the anemic light on the porch and straightened his tie by the reflection in the glass of the front door. He'd taken another shower, shaved again and dressed in his soberest lawyer suit. He carried an equally sober briefcase, which held his laptop.

A weak light came on inside and the sheer curtain on the door was pulled back. A moment later the door opened to a large woman in tight stretch pants and a flowered Hawaiian shirt.

"Hey, you must be Ben Jackson. Come on in. Lord, am I glad you're not late. She has been a caution ever since she called you this afternoon."

He had been told by his mother that the house had once been full of laughter and that Mrs. Langley had given wonderful parties with masses of food. But that was before her son went to jail.

Now the place looked as though it were peopled by ghosts.

"I'm Beulah Mayhew," the woman said as she led him up the angled staircase. "I look after her. Frankly, if it weren't for that precious Annabelle, I'd have left already. Mrs. Langley is a terror most of the time, although she can turn sweet as sugar."

"How is she tonight?"

Mrs. Mayhew leaned over to whisper, "I think most of her moods are put on when she doesn't want to do something or wants to drive me and Annabelle nuts. She keeps saying she's losing it, but I think she's sharp as a tack."

"Do you know what she wants me for?"

"Something sneaky, you can bet on that." She stopped at the top of the stairs to catch her breath, then laid a hand on Ben's arm. "You wait here. She made me practice how to announce you, just like she's the Queen of Sheba." Mrs. Mayhew walked to the double doors at the end of the hall, opened them,

stepped inside, said, "Mr. Jackson is here, Mrs. Mayhew," and moved aside to let him enter.

When he saw the fragile person propped up in the
huge bed, he wondered why Annabelle should be so
in awe of her. Until she lifted a languid hand heavy
with diamond rings. He didn't know whether he was
expected to shake it or kiss it.

He came forward, took the bird's hand with its
long and probably fake talons in his, and was surprised at the strength of her grip.

"Pull up that chair, young man. Under the light. I
want to look at you."

He did as he was told.

Her face remained in shadow. "Just like your father. Handsome as the devil and probably just as
wild. Are you a drunk and a womanizer too?"

"Not so far," he said. "But after tonight, who
knows?"

She narrowed her eyes at him, then she laughed.
High, thin and pretty scary.

"I have driven a number of men to drink. Not,
however, to womanizing. I was impossible to re-
place."

The woman was flirting!

"Go, look at that picture over the fireplace."

He obeyed.

"Turn on the light. I don't usually keep it lit. It's
too depressing."

The portrait was exquisite, the subject breathtak-
ingly beautiful, a pale, ethereal Celtic princess in a
chiffon afternoon dress surrounded by irises and
roses.

The artist had captured the set of that delicate little

jaw, the steel in those soft blue eyes. Mrs. Langley
had been ravishing in her youth, but in her portrait
there was evidence of the formidable woman she
would become.

"It's beautiful."

"No, *I* was beautiful. Old age, Mr. Jackson, is a
bitch, and don't let anyone tell you differently."

If she had let loose a string of four-letter Anglo-
Saxon cusswords he couldn't have been more startled. He went back to his chair and sat down.

"I want to give you something. As my lawyer, that
is."

"But I'm sure you have plenty of lawyers…"

"Be quiet." She reached under the covers and
withdrew an envelope. "There is a thousand dollars
in this envelope. I assume it is enough to retain your
services."

"Ma'am, I'm a prosecuting attorney employed by
the county."

"Does that prohibit you from doing other work as
an attorney?"

"Not legally, but if there was a conflict of interest—"

"There will be none, I assure you." She sat up.
"Mayhew, Mayhew, come in here."

"Yes, Mrs. Langley?" Beulah stuck her head in
the door, then came all the way in.

"You look like a small tropical island," Mrs.
Langley said. "An island that has endured a particularly nasty typhoon."

Beulah grinned and winked at Ben. "Uh-huh."

"That box, the one I asked you to get out of the
attic this afternoon. Do you have it?"

"Yes, ma'am. It's by the attic door. Y'all want me to go get it?"

"No indeed. I have no desire to see it again in this lifetime or the next. Is it sealed?"

Beulah nodded.

"Very well. When you leave, Mr. Jackson, please take the box with you. Put it somewhere safe."

"Ma'am, if there's something valuable inside, it ought to be in a bank."

"Nothing of monetary value whatsoever, of that I assure you. It had better not show signs of tampering, Mrs. Mayhew."

"No'om. I don't tamper."

"Then I want Mr. Jackson to take possession of the box this evening." She pointed to the letter. "Inside this envelope are sealed instructions in my own writing as to what to do with the box after I am dead. Until then, no one is to open it for any reason. Can I trust you to follow my wishes?"

Ben longed to say no. He wanted to open the thing now. It probably contained something to do with Chantal Langley's murder. It might hold the proof to clear Annabelle's name. It might even contain Victoria's confession that she, not her son, had murdered her daughter-in-law.

"I'm waiting. If you won't do it, there are a great many lawyers who will. There'll be another thousand dollars in my will for you if you do as you're told in this matter."

"Before I answer, Mrs. Langley, I have a question. Why me?"

"You are Hal Jackson's son. It is appropriate that you should receive this box and no other lawyer.

From what I have read and heard about you, you have a certain steel in your backbone that your father lacked.''

''My father was a good defense lawyer by his definition.''

She waved him away. ''If he had been a good lawyer with the best interests of his clients at heart, my son would not have gone to jail and my life would not have been ruined. Nor, as a matter of fact, would your mother's.''

Ben drew back. ''My mother's life is not ruined.''

''Your father left Elizabeth with two sons to support and without the social cachet of a prosperous professional man as her husband. That she has succeeded as well as she has despite those odds is to her credit. It is not to your father's credit that she has been forced to become a seamstress.''

Ben gulped. Was she serious? His mother would howl with laughter when he told her Mrs. Langley had called her a seamstress.

In any case, that box, whatever it contained, was better off in his hands than anyone else's.

''Very well, Mrs. Langley. I accept your retainer.''

''Say the words, Mr. Jackson. Give me your solemn promise where Mrs. Mayhew and I can both hear and witness it. Your father was inept, but he was not totally dishonest. I can only hope you are like him in that respect and in no other.''

''Very well, Mrs. Jackson, but a thousand dollars is too much money.''

''That is my concern, not yours.''

''Then I, Benjamin Jackson, attorney-at-law, do hereby swear and promise that I will take possession of the box that Mrs. Mayhew gives me tonight and keep it safe and unopened until such time as you shall be dead, at which point I can open your letter of instructions and follow them." He hoped Mrs. Langley did not notice his substitution of "can" for "will."

The old woman nodded. "Even if I say burn the box without opening it?"

"Yes." Would he break his promise once the old lady had gone to Glory? He hoped that would not be necessary, but if he could save his relationship with Annabelle by breaking his word, then he might do just that.

"Good. I could tell you a great deal about Chantal's death that no one else knows, but if there is a heaven, and if I manage to attain it, I prefer to sit on my cloud while you set the cat among the pigeons. Now take your money, take that box, and go. I'm tired. Mayhew, show Mr. Jackson his box and let him out. Then come back here and get me ready for bed."

Not a single please or thank-you. At the bedroom door, Ben turned to look at the tiny woman. She lay back against the pillows with her eyes closed, her breath shallow.

"Mrs. Langley," he said gently.

Her eyes flew open.

"You really were a beautiful woman." Then he shut the door behind him.

THE BLASTED BOX squatted beside him on the seat of his car. He half expected the thing to start ticking. It was not a cardboard box, but a very fancy round hatbox covered in some kind of flowered silk, long since faded and fraying at the creases. Several layers of duct tape sealed the closure. He considered X-raying the damn thing.

The letter and money in his pocket might have been coated in acid the way they burned his skin. What had he gotten himself into? As an officer of the court, he was duty bound to present any evidence of the crime to the courts, but he had no way of knowing whether this box contained any. It might be an old hat, for all he knew. Or a dozen feather boas. Or old love letters from Mr. Langley. Hell.

He looked up as an angry driver gave him the finger for straying out of the lane.

He felt light-headed and a little sick at his stomach by the time he'd carried the box up to his apartment. Before he set it down on the kitchen counter, he shook it gently. Not a sound.

He shoved it onto the top shelf in the very back of his walk-in closet, and stacked blankets and towels that he didn't use in front of the thing.

His throat was so parched he downed two glasses of water as he pulled off his clothes and dropped onto his bed. Annabelle had been right. He was coming down with whatever she had. The perfect ending to a perfect day. Despite the heat he could feel when he laid his hand against his forehead, suddenly he was freezing.

As he crawled under the covers and turned out the light, all he could think of was that blasted, bloody box and his damn stupid promise.

ANNABELLE'S FEVER BROKE at three o'clock on Saturday morning. She had fallen into an uneasy sleep on the sofa, and woke to find herself and her comforters drenched in sweat. Her temperature was normal, but she felt as though she'd been beaten with sticks. She rolled over and went back to sleep—mercifully without dreaming—until nine o'clock in the morning.

She took her time straightening the apartment and soaking in a shower, then she telephoned to check on her grandmother.

Beulah told her about Ben's visit the night before. "I'm afraid it took some out of your grandmomma," Beulah said. "She's pretty weak this morning. Keeps drifting in and out of sleep. Didn't want to eat her breakfast."

"You're off this afternoon, aren't you?"

"Supposed to be, but I can stay if you're still not feeling good."

"No, I'm fine. Just a little tired, but I don't think I'm contagious. I'll be over in an hour or so."

"Well, if you're sure. I have some shopping to do, and I need to run by and see my grandbabies. I declare, they are the most adorable children. Hurts my heart not to see them every day."

Annabelle felt a sudden hurt in her own heart. Had her grandmother ever called her adorable? Even before Chantal's death? If so, Annabelle didn't remember. As she was leaving the house, Elizabeth shouted from the back door, "Annabelle, feeling better?"

Annabelle nodded and walked over to her. "I'm sorry about yesterday, and even sorrier about your dinner party."

"Don't give it a thought. Time for a cup of coffee? I assume you're on your way to Mrs. Langley's."

"I'd love one. Extra heavy on the caffeine."

"How about some orange juice and some food to go along with it?"

Annabelle followed her inside. "No thanks. I had homemade chicken soup and rocky-road ice cream for breakfast. Ben's contribution."

"I see." Elizabeth poured the coffee and handed it across the breakfast counter, then poured herself another cup. "He's apparently down with the same thing you had. When I called him this morning he just growled at me. Thank God it's only a twenty-four-hour bug."

"I'm sorry. I should probably return the favor and take him some sorbet this afternoon on my way home, but I have no idea where he lives."

Elizabeth wrote the address down for her. "I'm very proud of Ben, you know." Then she twirled her cup nervously in her fingers for a moment before continuing. "He's going to be appointed our new district attorney as soon as Phil Mainwaring's judgeship comes through."

"No wonder you're proud of him."

"He'll be appointed to Phil's unexpired term, of course, but by the time the next election rolls around, he should have proved his ability. He should have no difficulty being elected on his own merit. He's already the choice of the high muckety-mucks who still run things around here. He's very much his own man. It just so happens that he believes in being tough on crime."

Annabelle nodded. "I appreciate your telling me," she said. "Ben's safe. I won't endanger his career."

Elizabeth blushed and stared down at the cup she

was still spinning. "It's hateful to have to worry about public opinion and gossip." She looked up, and Annabelle swore she could see a mist of tears in the other woman's eyes. "At least until he has this appointment safe and sound, he needs to be squeaky clean. Nothing the newspapers can use against him. After that—you know I'm fond of you. You're good for Ben."

"I'm not good for anybody."

Elizabeth caught Annabelle's hand. "Yes you are! Ben is showing signs of actually turning into a human being instead of this perfect android who runs on circuits instead of blood."

"That's not my doing."

"Can't be anything else." Elizabeth studied her coffee as though it fascinated her. "Did you know Judy Bromfield?"

"Not really. She was older."

"Ben and Judy were truly in love, I think. They'd have survived the separation of college."

"I remember that she was a nice girl. And pretty."

"Bright, charming—all the good things a mother hopes for in a daughter-in-law." Elizabeth closed her eyes and leaned back. "Ben managed to get through his father's abandoning us the way he did, but when that monster killed Judy, and Ben knew his father was responsible for getting the creep off on another case just a couple of months earlier—frankly, I was afraid he'd hunt his father down and kill him."

"Ben's father didn't kill Judy."

Elizabeth's eyes turned flint hard. "Ben said that you can't blame a tiger for dismembering a goat, but you can damn well blame the keeper who leaves the tiger's cage unlocked. Hal never tried to apologize or even explain." She shrugged. "But then, he always ran from unpleasantness."

"Ben went on to college that fall, didn't he?"

"That's the thing I'm trying to explain to you, Annabelle. Ben went off to school, joined the right fraternity, made straight As. On the surface he was the same old charming Ben. But when he came home for Thanksgiving, he was a different person. Hard, driven, empty."

"He's never seemed hard to me."

"He's learned to cover it up better. But there's this core of ice inside. And I'm starting to see signs that you're melting it."

"I'm sorry, Elizabeth." Annabelle got up and backed away. "Ben is not my responsibility. The minute Grandmere dies, I'm off to New York."

"But—"

"I promise you I won't abuse your hospitality while I'm here. I won't do anything to hurt Ben's career."

"The heck with his career. I'm not being fair, but I'm a mother. Don't hurt *Ben*."

"He won't get close enough to get hurt. Thanks for the coffee, Elizabeth. I really have to get to Grandmere's. Monday morning I'll be back at work." She practically bolted to her car.

Her hands were shaking when she turned the key. Ben had already gotten too close. She couldn't avoid him. There must be some way to return the relationship to friendship. Elizabeth didn't want her son hurt? Understandable. But did anybody give a damn if Annabelle got hurt?

When she relieved Mrs. Mayhew, she found that Grandmere was still asleep. Annabelle used the telephone in the hall to call Ben's number, half-afraid to wake him up. She told herself she should check on him since she'd given him the bug. It *wasn't* that she wanted to hear his voice.

"Hello," he croaked on the fourth ring.

"Sorry you're sick, Ben. I feel responsible."

"Annabelle?" He seemed to perk up for a moment, but only a moment. "If you felt like this the other day when I came by with the food, why didn't you shoot me when I bothered you?"

She flinched. Ben didn't mean anything by his remark. She had to learn that people said things like that casually. "The good thing is it doesn't last long. Look, I'll bring you some raspberry sorbet on my way home this evening if you'll tell me where you got it. You won't have to get up, just ask the doorman to let me in."

"How about lemon instead of raspberry?"

"Fine. Go back to sleep."

As she set the phone back into its cradle, she realized she was breathing hard, and she had that wriggly feeling in the pit of her stomach. She loved his deep voice, even when it sounded all scratchy.

"I need some water!"

She sighed. "Right away, Grandmere."

BEN'S APARTMENT was austere, modern, impersonal, but with a spectacular wall of windows looking over the river. Annabelle put the sorbet in the freezer, empty except for a bottle of vodka, and walked over to the door of what must be his bedroom. "Ben?"

A half groan, half mumble answered her. She opened the door softly.

The California king-size bed stood against the far wall. Lumpy with dark comforters and piled with pillows, it didn't seem to have anyone actually in it. Then Ben raised his head. "Even this doesn't change my feelings for you."

"That's a pity."

"Tell me I'm not dying."

She walked over and put her hand against his forehead. "Not dying, just feverish. Lie back and close your eyes." She reached for the topmost comforter. "And get some of this weight off you before you elevate your temperature into the stratosphere. Want some sorbet?"

"With some ice water?"

"Coming right up."

When she came back, he had propped himself up, but left the sheet at his waist. She glanced at him and quickly averted her eyes. Remembering what it felt like to sleep against that chest made her stomach heat up again.

He drank the water greedily, handed her the glass and started on the sorbet.

"Where's your bathroom?" she asked.

He pointed.

The bathroom was palatial. It held a walk-in shower, a whirlpool tub, and miles of black-and-white marble. She ran cold water in one of the two sinks, wrung out a washcloth and was back in time to take the empty bowl from him.

"Here, lean back, put this across your forehead.

And don't ever talk to me about my unruly hair again. Yours looks like straw that's gone moldy.''

He groaned, but closed his eyes and let her lay the cloth over his eyes.

"The fever will probably break tonight, and you'll be fine by morning."

He grabbed her wrist. "Don't go. Stay and talk to me."

"You need sleep."

"I need tender loving care and somebody to wring this thing out in some more cold water."

"Fine. I'll bring you another one. Then you can alternate."

She let the water run for several minutes, needing the time to let her own pulse return to normal. Finally, she wrung out another washcloth and started back to the bedroom.

"Poor baby!" The voice was deep and anguished. "I had the doorman let me in, darling, the minute your mother told me you weren't feeling well."

It was that blonde. The one Ben had brought with him to look at dress designs. Annabelle shrank against the wall beside the bathroom door.

"Brittany," Ben said.

"Sweetums, you don't sound happy to see me."

Through the crack in the door, Annabelle saw Brittany start toward the bed.

"I'm highly contagious," Ben croaked. "You shouldn't be here." He pulled the sheet up under his chin.

Annabelle walked out of the bathroom with the washcloth in her hands. "Hi," she said. "Come to visit the sick?"

Brittany gaped. Her eyes flashed from Annabelle to Ben and back again. She recovered quickly.

"Hello, I'm Brittany. I don't believe we've met," she said, and extended her hand. "Are you contagious too?"

"I'm Annabelle Langley, and I gave it to him." Annabelle held the washcloth in both hers. "Sorry, I'm wet."

"Of course you are. Well, Ben darling, since you're so obviously in capable hands, I'll be on my way." Brittany turned on her heel and gave a tiny wave over her shoulder. "Call me when you're feeling up to doing something interesting."

At the last minute, she flubbed her exit by closing the bedroom door a bit too hard. A moment later the front door slammed.

"Sorry."

"Oh, God," Ben said, slid down and pulled the sheet over his head.

"Should I go after her and explain?"

"Explain what?"

"That I'm just a concerned friend."

"The hell you are." He reached for the other washcloth.

"The sooner I'm out of here the better. I'll let your mother know you're ticked off enough to be on the mend."

"Kiss me. Think of it as my last kiss."

"That's what got us into this in the first place. Bye, Ben."

He called after her, but she kept walking. She hoped that Brittany was egocentric enough not to tell a living soul she'd run into Annabelle tending Ben.

If she mentioned it to anybody, Ben could find himself in deep political doo-doo.

Deep down, Annabelle suspected that given the proper incentive, Brittany could be a real vindictive bitch.

BEN'S FEVER BROKE before morning, as Annabelle had predicted. He soaked in his shower until the hot water ran out, stripped his bed and changed the sheets. Normally he left all that to his housecleaning service, but he couldn't bear to slide his clean body back into that sweaty bed.

He expected to fall asleep immediately. Instead, he lay with his eyes open until he gave up and fixed himself a salami and cheese sandwich and a glass of milk.

He sat in his leather club chair, propped his feet on the coffee table and flicked on the television. He clicked through channels of evangelists and infomercials touting the latest exercise equipment until he landed on an old black-and-white movie.

He watched for five minutes before he realized what he was seeing. He'd been an A.D.A. for long enough to know that age was no barrier to the commission of appalling crimes, but the killer in this movie was a child—an evil child. He grabbed the remote, changed the channel and saw that his hands were shaking.

Annabelle was not evil. He refused to believe that she could have shot her mother even accidentally.

The problem was that Annabelle had been convinced of it. Maybe her grandmother had started filling her head with tales simply as a means of exculpating her son. Maybe she truly believed Annabelle was guilty. Then the gossip had started, grown, taken on a life of its own.

Raymond Langley could have come home when he was released from prison, admitted his crime to the world as he had admitted it in his plea bargain. He had served his time. No one could punish him further. An honorable man would have forced the world to listen, forced his daughter to understand her father was a murderer but that *she* wasn't guilty of anything. Then if he wanted to disappear, let him. Good riddance.

Langley was a coward as well as a killer.

Somebody had to prove to Annabelle that she was innocent.

She needed a champion, an Ivanhoe. A Ben Jackson.

But Ben had sixty or seventy hours of work every week just to keep up with his caseload. Then there were the political lunches and dinners, the schmoozing, the handshaking and backslapping. He'd probably been susceptible to Annabelle's germs only because he was run-down. Not nearly enough time at the gym. Forget golf and tennis, unless he was stuck in some political foursome he couldn't get out of.

He didn't have time to breathe, much less open up a twenty-five-year old closed case.

Annabelle would be horrified if she found out he'd even considered looking at those files. She might never forgive him.

And, a tiny voice in his head kept asking, what would he do if he discovered Grandmere had been telling the truth?

CHAPTER SEVEN

"I'M FINE, Mom," Ben said when he phoned his
mother on Sunday morning. "A twenty-four-hour
bug. Look, I need to ask you something, and you're
not going to like it."

Elizabeth sighed down the phone lines. "What
now?"

"I need to get in touch with my father."

This time Ben heard no sigh, no gasp, nothing. He
waited. "Mother?"

"Unfortunately, I can't help you." She sounded
remarkably normal. "I don't know where he is or
what he's doing. Frankly, I don't want to know."

"Have you any idea if he's kept in touch with any
of his old friends?"

This time he heard the sigh. "Call your brother,
Ben. You do have Steven's number, don't you?"

"The last number I had for Steve was care of some
company called Executive Specialties. I'm not certain
what they do."

"Steven is very closemouthed, but I gather it's
some kind of organization that protects business-
men."

"Right up Steve's alley. Okay, Mom, I'll get in
touch with him." He hesitated, then said, "Aren't
you going to ask me why?"

"I can guess. You want to talk to your father about Chantal Langley's death and her husband's conviction."

"Right."

"Don't do it. Annabelle won't thank you."

"Even if I find out she's innocent?"

"Even then. I know how you go about solving problems. You define it in your own terms, then you define the steps you think you need to take to resolve it, then you go at it like a junkyard dog in a three-piece suit."

"I take it that's not a compliment?"

"In some ways your approach is admirable. But you can't simply manipulate other people's lives to achieve the solution you want."

"That's unfair. Annabelle is suffering..."

"Yes, she is. But will she suffer more or less because of the old wounds you plan to open? Will she benefit or lose? Are your motives altruistic, or do you want to clear her name so that you can go on to transforming her into the perfect public servant's wife? The woman you think you want?"

Ben felt stung. He started to protest, then closed his eyes. "Maybe I'm fooling myself, but I truly believe that the truth does set us free, no matter how unpalatable it is. That's why I became a lawyer. If I can free her from doubt and innuendo, from stupid gossip, then if she walks away from me afterward, at least I'll have done her that much good."

"Are you being entirely honest with yourself? With her?"

"God in heaven, Mom, a week ago I didn't believe I would ever care again about a woman the way I care for her. If this is love, then it's a blasted train wreck. I'm trying not to get crushed."

"Then let me get you Steven's number. He's on some job in Philadelphia at the moment. He does keep in touch, even if he never comes home."

Five minutes later Ben dialed the number his mother had given him. After four rings, a gruff voice picked up and said, "What?"

"Not hello?"

"Ben? What the hell are you doing calling this number? Is it Mom?"

"She's fine. Everybody's fine. Look, I need a favor. How do I get in touch with Dad?"

For a moment he thought his brother would refuse to give him the information. Then Steve reeled off a telephone number. "He's living on a boat in some marina on Lake Michigan. That's all I know."

"When was the last time you talked to him?"

"Couple of months ago. My birthday."

"Jesus, Steve, I totally forgot."

"So did I. Anyway, he sounded sober. He asked about you and Mom. I think he misses you both."

"He should have thought of that before he walked out."

"Yeah. We all make mistakes."

"What are you up to? Who are these people you work for?"

"Just a bunch of guys who solve problems." His voice left no room for questions. "Tell me about you."

When Ben hung up ten minutes later, he realized he knew no more about his brother's life than he had before he called. But that was Steve. They hadn't been close since Steve got shipped off to military school, and then went into the army. He'd always felt Steve resented him for staying home and doing well. Yet Steve was the one who'd kept up with his father. Strange guy, his brother.

A boat in a marina? Would the telephone number ring in the boat itself, or in some harbormaster's shack where no one would answer it on a Sunday?

Was his mother right? Should he leave the situation alone? The last thing he wanted to do was hurt Annabelle.

He glanced at his closed closet door. Should he break his promise to Mrs. Langley and open that blasted box she'd given him? He'd never gone back on his word as a lawyer before.

If his feelings for Annabelle turned him into a self-ish, dishonest man, what good were they? If he lost her through his own stupidity, he'd never dare to be anything but a robot again.

He picked up the telephone and invited Annabelle to breakfast.

THE ONLY COLOR she wore came from the wildly patterned scarf that she'd used to pull her hair into a ponytail. As he pulled out of his mother's driveway, he asked, "Why do you always wear black?"

"I don't always."

"Usually." He waved a hand at the April morning. "It's spring. Most women dig out the pink and blue."

"Are you telling me you hate the way I look?"

"No! God, no. I'm asking a question because I want information. No hidden agenda."

He felt her eyes on the side of his face and knew his ear had turned red. He kept his hands on the wheel and his face resolutely facing traffic.

"Okay. First, black is a uniform in New York. Especially in the fashion industry, and particularly among the little backstage people like me who weigh well over ninety pounds and stand less than six feet tall. Not that models look all that gorgeous off duty."

He glanced at her. "I thought they looked gorgeous all the time."

"Let's face it, most of them would look spectacular in a toe sack. But when they're not working, a lot of them go around with no makeup, limp hair, ratty old jeans, oversize sweatshirts and broken-down running shoes. And carrying enormous bags full of all their stuff. It's a business, Ben."

"How did you get into it?"

"Grandmere actually had a dressmaker who came to the house when I was little. She took pity on me and started teaching me to sew my own doll clothes, and then Grandmere decided I should be able to do the fine hand sewing that girls had learned back in the Dark Ages when she was a girl, so I had to endure hours of pulling threads out of white batiste and doing embroidery and laying in entredos lace and all that stuff."

"Didn't you hate it?"

"Hey, what else did I have to do? Actually, I liked it, all except the part where Grandmere criticized every stitch. I asked for a sewing machine for my birthday, and got it—although it was actually Jonas who gave it to me."

"Jonas?"

"Jonas. He's head gardener and driver and jack-of-all-trades. He's been there since I was twelve or so, and he practically raised me, although I never really took to gardening, much to his dismay. He's made the Langley gardens famous among garden people. They're on all the tours every spring."

"I don't have much time for garden tours."

"Anyway, since I didn't have a man around, I went to Jonas whenever my bike sprung a sprocket or whatever they do. He's one of the few people who don't take any guff from Grandmere."

"And he gave you a sewing machine?"

"Sure did. He drove me to my lessons at the art academy, and I think he bugged my grandmother about sending me to New York to design school. He's sort of a surrogate father."

Ben decided he'd have to look up this paragon. If anyone knew about Annabelle, it would be Jonas. Impulsively, he reached over and squeezed her knee.

"What was that for?"

"I'm glad you had somebody, that's all."

"I had Grandmere."

"Yeah, and I had chicken pox."

Annabelle laughed. Ben didn't think he'd ever heard her laugh before. It was just a short bark, cut off as though it embarrassed her, but his spirit leaped. One of his college buddies always said that if a guy could make a girl laugh, he could win her.

"You said 'first.'"

"What?"

"The first reason you wear black."

"Oh. It got to be a thing in high school. Grandmere loathed it, but didn't know how to stop it. I was already a weirdo, so I might as well look the part. Then, like I said, I worried because I wasn't a size two. And black does make you look skinnier. Finally, you can mix and match black with great accessories and get by with a whole lot fewer clothes that fit every occasion. And I could make my own. Satisfied?''

''All except the skinnier part and the weirdo part.''

''If you'd ever looked at me in high school, you'd have seen I was a lump. Then I went to New York and all that walking and late nights, and the weight just came off. I still can't pig out, but I can eat like normal people.''

''Good, because I intend to feed you champagne and truffles for breakfast.''

''Where?''

''The Peabody Brunch. On the Skyway.''

''No! I thought you were taking me to a pancake house or a greasy spoon.''

''You deserve the Peabody.''

''I deserve to have you listen to me. Please, Ben. Otherwise, you can take me home.''

''Why? What's wrong with it?''

''All those people, all that noise, possibly people I knew, definitely people you know. Shaking hands, being introduced, stared at, assessed.''

He pulled over to the curb, cut the engine and turned to her with his left arm on the steering wheel. ''I want to show you off, is that so bad?''

''As in, hey, look at the New York weirdo my mother hired? Or as in, hey, look who's come back to town so you can all gawk?''

''Neither. I realize coming back to town has

brought things back to you, but believe me, around here you're very old news.''

She stared at him, eyes wide, mouth set. He laid his right hand on her knee again.

"Trust me. I have the inside track to most of the scandals in this particular neighborhood. You're real small potatoes.'' He gave her a reassuring smile.

"You swear? And if I get uncomfortable we can leave?''

"Absolutely, cross my heart et cetera, et cetera, and so forth.''

She nodded.

Twenty minutes later they stepped out of the elevators onto the Skyway floor of the Peabody Hotel and claimed their reservations. As they followed the waiter to a table on the dance-floor level closest to the dessert tables, Annabelle whispered, "Ben, isn't there someplace in a corner?''

The waiter turned with a smile as he held her chair. "Sorry, madam, we're even more crowded than usual today.''

She nodded and sat. There was no menu to hide behind. Around them tables groaned with everything from traditional breakfast food to chefs dispensing crepes and blinis, to cracked crab and mounds of fat, pink shrimp. A hovering waiter filled their champagne flutes.

"A toast,'' Ben said, raising his glass, "to new beginnings.''

"How about to good sense?''

"Ben, my boy!'' a voice boomed from over her shoulder. "Good to see you. I'm surprised our next district attorney isn't slaving away in his office, Sunday or no Sunday.''

Ben stood and held out his hand. "Councilman." He indicated Annabelle. "Annabelle Langley, may I introduce Councilman Mark Adler?"

The councilman shook her hand. "Hello, young lady." An instant later he dropped her hand as though it were red-hot. "Langley. I thought you looked…" Then in a too-hearty voice. "Never forget a face. Probably hit me at 3:00 a.m. where I know you from. Hah-hah." He swept on.

Ben sat down again.

"Ben." Annabelle leaned across and laid her hand on the table. "See, I knew this was a mistake."

Before Ben could answer, a handsome young couple stopped by to be introduced, and as soon as they left, a tall young man took their place. Annabelle found herself drowning in a swirl of unfamiliar smiling faces she wouldn't remember because she couldn't meet their eyes. Their names vanished from her memory before they turned their backs.

It became a parade. Annabelle sat with a fixed smile on her face, her hands twisted under the table in her napkin, her heart pounding, while Ben bobbed up and down, shook hands, slapped backs, kissed cheeks.

Ben seemed to know everyone, and what was worse, everyone knew him.

Finally, the parade slackened off. "Sorry," Ben said. "People I know through work."

She tried to smile, then froze. "Ben," she whispered.

"Ben, sweetie." Brittany leaned over Ben's shoul-

der and kissed his ear. "How nice to see you well."
She smiled at Annabelle. "Taking your little nurse-
maid out for a treat?"

Ben smiled back and pushed himself away from
the table once more.

"No, don't get up. Oh, I don't think you know
Trent Wellfleet, do you?"

The man at her side was not as tall as Ben, nor as
good-looking, but Annabelle recognized that the shirt
and slacks that slipped so casually over his slim
frame hadn't come from this part of the country.
Probably not from the United States.

"Trent's thinking of opening a branch of his in-
vestment firm in town," Ashley said as she slipped
her arm through his. "Usually he lives in London.
Nice to see you." She dragged the unprotesting and
obviously smitten Trent off toward the dessert table.

"Please, Ben," Annabelle whispered. "Take me
home."

"I'm sorry about all this, but you can see nobody
cared who you were."

"Except that Adler person."

"Possibly. Doesn't matter if he did."

"I'm suddenly not very hungry." She stood. "You
stay. I'll catch a cab." She started for the exit at what
she hoped didn't look like a run.

"Annabelle," Ben called. "Wait. I'll take you
home." He tossed a couple of bills onto the table and
went after her.

She punched the button for the elevator in the
foyer and prayed it would arrive before Ben caught
up with her. When the doors opened, she found her-

self face-to-face with Elizabeth Jackson and Philip Mainwaring.

"Annabelle," Elizabeth said. "How nice to see you."

"I'm just leaving."

"Hello, Mom, Phil," Ben said. "Please come back, Annabelle. We can join these two. Phil's going to generate more interest than I ever would."

"Perfect," Annabelle said, and brushed past them into the elevator. Before she could hit the button for the lobby, Ben grabbed the closing doors, forced them apart and came with her.

"Go back. Join your mother. No reason your morning should be screwed up. Aren't those people your constituents or something?"

"You're the only constituent I care about."

She leaned against the back of the elevator. "I'm sorry, Ben. It's not so much that they would know me or blurt out anything about me if they did—they're all probably too polite to do that. It's waiting for that widening of the eyes that signals recognition. You have no idea how exhausting it is to be on guard all the time, defenses at full alert, seeing innuendo where none was intended. I don't have to be that way in New York. I knew I shouldn't have come back, but I didn't see any way out of it."

That settled it, Ben thought as he watched her try to slow her breathing. Her fists were still clenched. He intended to find out exactly what had happened to Chantal Langley. If by some terrible chance Annabelle did fire the gun, she was better off knowing than always wondering.

If she had pulled the trigger, she had to come to

terms with the fact that it was an accident and let go of her guilt. "Come on," he said as the elevator doors opened. "We still need to get breakfast. One greasy spoon coming up."

"Sorry, Ben," she said, "I've got work to do."

"But it's Sunday," he called after her. He'd had visions of a long, lazy afternoon making love to her, teaching her, pleasing her.

"I know. Thanks, anyway."

"How about dinner tomorrow night?"

She stopped six steps from the bottom. "I don't think so. I've got Grandmere to see to."

"You have to eat."

"Not a good idea. Thanks, Ben." She fled.

That was the only word for it. She fled from him like some damn nymph being pursued by a satyr.

He'd never felt this hunger for any woman. Not even for Judy. But then he'd been a boy. Now he was a man.

Which meant the pain of loss would be greater.

The moment he slammed the door to his apartment behind him and ripped off his jacket, he threw himself onto the leather couch and began to dig around on the side table for the telephone number Steve, his brother, had given him. He dialed before he lost his nerve, not really expecting anyone to answer.

After seven rings, a man answered.

"Fair winds, matey, and what can I do for you?"

Ben caught his breath. He could never mistake his father's rich, lustrous baritone—the voice that his father could play like a Stradivarius when he faced a jury.

The voice that could still cause him to cringe when it was ripened by alcohol.

The old man must be drunk, otherwise, why the ridiculous greeting?

"Uh, hello. Is this Hal Jackson?"

"And who would it be otherwise, me bucko, except Hal Jackson, answering the phone on me own boat?"

The phony brogue wouldn't have been acceptable in a 1930s B movie.

"And who might ye be, me bucko?" Hal Jackson laughed as though he'd made a joke.

Ben dropped his head into his hands.

"This is Ben, Dad."

An instant's silence, then Hal answered in a different accent and a tone that was almost tentative. "Ben? What's wrong?"

Both Steve and his father assumed he would not call except in case of disaster. Not something Ben felt proud of. "Nothing, Dad."

"Your mother?"

"She's fine. I'm fine. Steve sends his love."

"Ah, yes, you had to get my number from someone." Another hesitation. "Since you wouldn't give me a purely social call, I assume you have a business reason."

At one point Ben had admired this man. In fact, Hal Jackson had been Ben's hero. At least he sounded sober now. "As a matter of fact, I'm calling you for both business and personal reasons. I need your help."

"My help? How on earth could an old liberal shyster help the next law-and-order president of the United States?''

''Hardly the next. I'm not old enough to run.'' Ben tried to keep his tone light, polite.

''Oh, well, early days yet. Still time to reinstitute public hangings and firing squads.''

''I didn't call to argue about my political convictions, Dad.''

His father's laugh boomed down the line. ''Probably a good thing. So what do you need? This is costing money. Not the taxpayers', surely?''

''No. I need to ask you about one of your old cases. You may remember it. A shooting. Domestic violence. Chantal Langley.''

After a dead silence, his father asked in a subdued voice, ''Why? Why that case, Ben? Why now, after all these years?''

''Old Mrs. Langley is dying, Dad.'' He considered telling his father about the box, then decided against it. He'd tell Ben to open it and the hell with the client's instructions. Hal had spent a lifetime playing blindman's bluff with Lady Justice. She already wore the blindfold, which made slipping out of her grasp a darned sight easier. His father was a genius at keeping his guilty clients just out of her reach.

''And?''

''And Annabelle Langley has come back to town to look after her. All the old rumors are surfacing. I want to find out the truth about what happened.''

''I can't tell you what my client said to me, Ben, even after all these years. You know that I'm still bound by attorney-client privilege.''

''You plea-bargained him, Dad. He must have been guilty, right?''

''I plea-bargained him because he demanded that I do so. He had no intention of dragging either his mother or his daughter through a trial. I think I could have gotten him off if I'd had an opportunity. I've always regretted that I didn't fight him harder.''

''Wasn't he the only person who could have done it?''

''That's not the point. The prosecution had precious little forensic evidence, and I think I could have gotten that thrown out before a jury ever had a chance to review it.''

''But what about justice? Chantal Langley died. Where's the justice for her?''

''We have had this argument before. If the prosecution does its job properly, then it will make a solid case. If not, then it's their fault, not mine.''

''And a guilty man goes free to kill again.''

''You're thinking about Judy.''

''Of course I am. I never cease to think about Judy. Remembering that if it weren't for you, her killer would have been behind bars, that she'd still be alive—that's what drives my life.''

''To the best of my knowledge, Raymond Langley has not killed again.''

''Not under that name. He disappeared years ago. You wouldn't know, and I doubt like hell you'd care, but he could have committed murders all over the world.''

''Well, he didn't commit this one! Oh, hell, I shouldn't have said that.''

''Who did?''

"Look up the old files yourself. Read the autopsy reports, the police reports. Look at the forensic evidence. Make up your own damn mind, boy, if you're such a hotshot!"

For a moment Ben thought his father had hung up, but then he asked in a studiously conversational tone, "How's your mother, Ben?"

"Beautiful, successful, serene, happy and fulfilled."

"Glad to hear it. And you?"

"Probably going to be the next district attorney if all goes well."

"Married?"

"Not yet. Nobody's made you a grandfather. What about you? Do I have any half brothers and sisters?"

"None that I'm aware of. And no stepmother either."

"Why are you living on a yacht?"

"It's not a yacht, it's a sailboat. It requires all my money and most of my time."

Ben longed to ask his father about his own career, whether or not he was still a practicing lawyer, but didn't know how to phrase the question.

"In answer to that pause," his father continued, "I still practice law in a small way, a very small way. Not criminal law. I'd rather sail."

"And drink?"

"At the moment, no. But tomorrow, you never know."

"Why not criminal law?"

"Maybe I got religion in my old age."

"I doubt that."

"You're my son, Ben. Whatever you may think of me, I will always love you."

"Sure."

Ben dropped the phone into its cradle with more force than he intended. The hell of it was, he still loved his father. Life would be much simpler if he could hate him.

He leaned back against the sofa. The older he got, the more his life looked like Swiss cheese. Holes for both sets of grandparents, long dead. For his brother, whom he never saw and never talked to, for his father who had disappeared, for friends from law school he'd lost track of, most of all, for Judy.

There remained only his mother, Marian, Phil Mainwaring, and now Annabelle.

He had plenty of acquaintances, political allies and foes. Had he been right to cut himself off from his emotions?

How in hell could he be a good prosecutor if he didn't understand people, both good and bad? If he didn't understand himself? Didn't empathize with the victims, their families?

He smoothed his unruly hair. Maybe something had guided him to Annabelle's case. Suddenly he wanted to know for certain not merely who had pulled the trigger, but how and why it had been pulled.

LATER THAT AFTERNOON, he found a very young officer at the other side of the grill of the police storage facility. He presented his credentials and filled out a slip requesting the criminal-case file boxes on the Langley shooting.

"Man, I wish I could help you, but I don't know a darned thing about that stuff back there," the officer said. "I'm pulling desk duty because I sprained my shoulder last week."

"Hot pursuit?"

The officer grinned. "My kid's soccer game. When they were warming up, I tried to show off and dived for an out-of-bounds ball. I guess it's okay these days for a kid to see his old man cry."

"For a sprained shoulder, you bet. Look, how about I come back there and find the box myself?"

The officer looked dubious.

"I won't run off with anything. And I'll check with you before I leave."

"Yeah, okay. Sure. But you got to *promise* you'll sign the paperwork if you want to take anything."

"Fine."

Ben knew the general setup of the storage facility. Shelves to the shadowy ceiling, every one full of cardboard banker boxes labeled with case file, date and disposition. The place smelled of slightly damp concrete and spiders. There'd been a recent furor about the department's destroying old files, but Ben knew that homicide files, even those considered solved, would never be destroyed.

After twenty minutes his hands were dirty, his jacket was dusty and his nose was starting to run, but he'd narrowed down his search to the right area. Glad that he'd brought a pocket flashlight, he searched the top rows first, and finally found the case number well out of reach of even his long arms. He found the metal stairs that slid along the row, climbed up and lifted the box down.

Only one cardboard box. Some cases filled dozens, but this one had been basically open and shut. He took it to a battered wooden table under a single ceiling light and unwound the strings that held the top closed.

Everything, including the yellow lined pads the detectives had used for their notes, had been tossed into the box. For the next half hour he organized the contents in some sort of chronological order, then he began to read the autopsy report, and to check the crime-scene photos. On the surface it seemed a pretty straightforward domestic shooting. One shot, fired from Raymond Langley's .38 pistol. No prints on the weapon except his.

Not Annabelle's. Ben heaved a sigh of relief.

The shot had hit Chantal Langley square in the heart. A practically perfect shot. Raymond Langley had gunpowder residue on his hands.

Ben read further. Annabelle, aged four, had been spending the night across the garden at her grandmother's house.

She wasn't even in the house when Chantal was shot! Did she remember that? Had her doting grandmother ever bothered to tell her? Or was she so set on protecting her only son—and her own social status—that she was willing to toss Annabelle psychologically to the wolves?

He wouldn't put it past the old woman to frame a four-year-old child on the assumption that Annabelle would not be charged. An accident was not a murder.

The first detectives on the scene had taken color Polaroids. During the years, the pictures had faded and turned the color of decaying oranges, but they gave a better feeling for the victim and her surroundings than the official black-and-white ones.

His first impression was of blood. Lots of it. The single shot had apparently not stopped the heart instantly, so that it had continued pumping its contents onto the front of Chantal Langley's white cocktail dress.

She sprawled on her back at the edge of the hearth in the living room in an ungainly tangle of brown arms and legs. She wore high-heeled strap sandals on bare feet. No stockings or panty hose? In October? Her toenails were painted hot-pink. He checked the autopsy report. No underpants, although there had been no sign of recent sexual intercourse. Maybe she didn't believe in underwear.

Chantal had been beautiful, even in death. His heart spasmed at the close-up of her face. Her chocolate eyes were robbed of the light that Annabelle's had, but they were essentially the same shape, as was her heart-shaped face. Her café au lait hair was every bit as wild as Annabelle's and lay fanned around her face as though it were trying to crawl away.

He forced himself to concentrate on the surroundings. The pistol lay on a fat round hassock between a pair of sofas. Apparently the hassock had served as a coffee table, because several magazines had toppled off it onto the floor, while several others remained. The next shot was a close-up of the oil stain found on the hassock. The murder weapon had been cleaned and oiled shortly before the shot, but not cleaned afterward.

His head had begun to throb, probably from the

dust. He rubbed the bridge of his nose and his temples and went back to the report.

Something had struck him as odd, but he couldn't put his finger on it. He spent ten minutes switching between the crime-scene photos and the autopsy report. Then he got it.

Chantal had been taller than Annabelle—nearly five feet eight inches. Her heeled sandals added another couple of inches.

A four-year-old child would be pretty short. Assuming that the gun lay cocked and ready on the hassock for some reason he couldn't fathom, and assuming that Annabelle actually was in the house instead of at her grandmother's, if Annabelle had wandered downstairs, saw the gun, picked it up, aimed it at her mother and either pulled the trigger or let the hammer fall, Chantal Langley's wound should have angled up from below.

Instead, the wound went straight from the front of her sternum through her heart and lodged against a rib. No way could a small child be tall enough for the shot to have gone straight.

He had his proof. Raymond Langley shot and killed his wife while his daughter slept thirty yards away at her grandmother's house.

He wanted to call Annabelle immediately to tell her she couldn't have shot her mother.

No, not yet. Juries had a tough time with ballistic evidence, so might Annabelle. She had over twenty-five years of guilt ingrained in her. What if she didn't believe him? Didn't see that was all the proof he needed?

No, he'd started down this path, and he was darned

well going to follow it. When he did tell her, he'd be able to back it up with evidence of who the real killer was—Raymond Langley, the man who had gone to jail for the crime.

At the moment, what mattered most was that he, Ben Jackson, was certain the woman he loved had never killed anyone.

CHAPTER EIGHT

BEN CALLED ANNABELLE from his car and got no answer. When he called directory assistance he found that old Mrs. Langley's number was unlisted. He pulled over into a parking lot, pictured the number she'd given him in his mind and let his fingers remember the sequence his mind couldn't.

"Langley residence."

"Annabelle? It's Ben. I'll be there in five minutes."

"Ben? Why?"

"No questions. I'll tell you when I get there. Tell Mrs. Langley I need to speak to her."

"She's asleep."

"Then I'll wait until she wakes up."

When Annabelle let him in the back door from the swimming pool, she said, "She's awake now, and wavering between delight that an attractive man is coming to see her and fury that you called at all. What is this about?"

He reached for her, but she ducked away from him.

"How sick is she really?" he asked, letting his hands fall. Apparently he was still in the doghouse about the Peabody. As he probably deserved to be.

"She has good days and bad days."

"And today?"

"A pretty good day, actually. Her whole system is slowly shutting down, Ben. Congestive heart failure, kidneys—she's on a ton of medication, but in the long run it can't help, just make her more comfortable. The doctor says four to six months."

"But she's in no immediate danger?"

"No. Ben, you're scaring me."

"Maybe you'd better alert her doctor. I don't think this is going to be pleasant." He took the stairs two at a time. Annabelle trotted behind him.

At the bedroom door he stopped. "Any sympathy I had for her has evaporated." He walked in. "Good afternoon, Mrs. Langley."

"I hired you, young man, for a specific assignment. That does not give you the right to invade my privacy." She narrowed her eyes. "And in a condition I can only call unkempt."

She sounded strong enough. Looked it, too, sitting up in that big bed. Ben wished he could check the color of her lips beneath their crimson lipstick, or her nails under their fire-engine-red polish. He didn't want to hasten her death, but he had to take what might be his only opportunity to speak to her.

"I think you and I had better speak privately," he said.

Her eyebrows went up. "I think not. Annabelle, you will remain in the room."

"Yes, Grandmere."

"Fine." Ben sat beside the bed and took a deep breath. If he'd learned one thing from the guys in the homicide division about interrogation, it was that counterfeit sympathy worked, confrontation didn't. He tried to tamp down his feelings, and said quietly,

"Who started the rumors that Annabelle had shot her mother?"

"What?" Her eyes shifted and then refocused. "How on earth should I know?"

"Because we both know she couldn't have done it. She wasn't even in the house when her mother was shot. She was here, asleep."

He heard Annabelle's gasp but did not turn around.

"Who told you that?" Mrs. Langley snapped.

"The police."

"You've read the report?" Mrs. Langley's voice rose alarmingly. "You dared to rake up things best forgotten?"

"I warned you, Mrs. Langley, I'm a prosecutor first. I check what I choose to check. Who started the rumors?"

Mrs. Langley lay back on her bed and smiled the same lazy-cat smile in her portrait. "Harold Jackson, your father."

For a moment, Ben felt as though she'd kicked him in the chest. Of course, Hal would have said Jack the Ripper had been reborn if it could have saved his client. He swallowed and said in what he hoped was the same controlled tone, "But Annabelle couldn't have shot her mother, could she?"

"Because she was staying here?" Mrs. Langley glanced at her granddaughter. Ben yearned to turn around to see Annabelle's response, but he didn't dare take his eyes off the woman in front of him. "Oh, yes, when the police came to inform me of Chantal's death, they found Annabelle asleep upstairs in her bunny pajamas."

"Grandmere?" Annabelle came toward the bed.

Mrs. Langley held up a hand to stop her, without taking her eyes off Ben. "Did your police report happen to mention how often Annabelle stayed here overnight before her father was arrested for murder?"

Ben saw where this was leading. He'd asked a question he thought he knew the answer to, only to find he'd asked the wrong question. "I assume frequently. The house is only a few yards away from the cottage the Langleys lived in."

"Chantal and I were not close."

"The understatement of the year," Annabelle whispered.

"I believed in disciplined feeding schedules even for small children. Chantal let the child run wild. I believed in morality in women, appropriate dress, good manners. Chantal believed in none of these things.

"Check your police report, Mr. Assistant District Attorney. The police found Annabelle asleep in a double bed in a guest room with chairs pushed up against the sides of it so she wouldn't fall out. She slept in the bed from that time on, but that was the first time she had ever spent a night in this house."

"Langley brought her to you to give himself a clear field to shoot his wife."

"My son brought her to me, Mr. Jackson, asleep in her blanket, just before he called the police. He was hysterical. I did not know until hours later that Chantal had been dead for some time."

"He didn't want Annabelle woken by the police when they came to investigate the murder."

"Annabelle was immaculately clean when my son brought her to me at midnight. The hair at the nape of her neck was still wet. She was an unusually grubby child who was always bathed just before her regular bedtime, some five hours earlier.''

Mrs. Langley sniffed. ''My son is a fool. He thought he could convince the police he'd heard a burglar, fired a shot without realizing Chantal was downstairs.'' She made a sound in her throat. ''Ridiculous. He'd already handed the police that story by the time Jackson arrived because *I* called him. You didn't know that, did you, boy?''

''So my father started the rumors.''

''Not until later, when Raymond finally told him the truth. The police, of course, not only did not buy that story either, but they felt it was a killer's pathetic attempt to blame his crime on his four-year-old daughter.''

''A four-year-old child cannot commit murder in the eyes of the law.''

''No one ever said she killed her mother deliberately. But Hal feared that if he were to try to convince a jury that Raymond was telling the truth, he'd be laughed out of court, and Raymond would die in the electric chair.''

''In the end he didn't get the chance.''

''No, Raymond, gallant fool to the last, refused to have a trial. The prosecutor agreed to accept a plea of second degree, assuming that Chantal was killed in a crime of passion.''

''And what did Raymond say to you?'' Ben asked. ''Did he ever admit the truth?''

''The only time I went to visit him in prison he swore to me that he had actually seen Annabelle pull the trigger.'' Mrs. Langley began to laugh.

The hackles rose on the back of Ben's neck. He turned to see Annabelle, her hands white-knuckled and wrapped around the bedpost of her grandmother's bed, her eyes wide and horrified. A moment later she ran.

As Ben chased her, Mrs. Langley's triumphant laughter rang down the hall behind him.

CHAPTER NINE

"DON'T SHUT ME OUT." Ben stood outside the door to what he supposed used to be Annabelle's bedroom. "Please." He leaned one hand against the door frame.

Annabelle flung the door open so fast that he nearly fell into the room. By the time he recovered his balance, she was staring out the windows toward the gardens and swimming pool.

"Am I supposed to thank you?" She didn't turn to look at him.

He took her by the shoulders and made her face him. "It's not true. What she said in there. I promise you, it's not true."

"Not true that I did it or that my father swore he saw me do it?" Her dark eyes smoldered, her jaw was set so hard he could see the muscles along her cheekbones tighten.

"It's not true that you did it, whatever your father said, if he said anything at all. I wouldn't put it past that old harpy to lie about that too."

"Too? What else has she lied about? Let me go."

"I owe you an apology. I made a first-year law school mistake in there. I didn't have all the facts before I asked my question. But what she said does not change the fact that you did not, you could not, have shot your mother accidentally.''

''Oh, really?'' She sat on the edge of the high tester bed.

''Yes. Your father was probably scared to death of what he had done. I wouldn't put it past my father to work out the details of that story and convince your father to tell it to the police. Dad would have realized the original burglary thing wouldn't fly.''

''How could he do that?''

''Listen, Annabelle, neither your father nor your grandmother said you killed your mother with malice. At the worst it was an accident.''

''Was it?''

''Four-year-old children do not shoot people except by accident.''

''Oh, really?''

''Can't you remember what happened?''

''I remember waking up in a strange bed and crying because I didn't know where I was. I told you, Grandmere has said so many things over the years I think I remember, but I really don't.''

''How about hypnosis?''

She stared at her hands twisting in her lap. ''Contrary to what they say on television, hypnosis is not always a key to the long-lost portions of your memory. I tried hypnosis my freshman year in college. Nada. Wipeout. And that in itself tends to make me believe I'm guilty.''

He dropped to his knees and took her hands, held them still in his. ''You are not guilty of anything. Even if you had fired that shot accidentally, you wouldn't be the first child to shoot a relative or a friend. It's a terrible tragedy, but with counseling and love and support, those children usually learn to accept that they were too little to be responsible in an adult sense, and definitely not responsible in law. There's a big difference between accident and murder, Annabelle.''

She jerked her hands away. ''So I'm supposed to just accept it? Okay, how's this, Counselor? That gun got downstairs some way. It was normally kept in my father's bedside table. I wasn't supposed to know that, but I did. How about if I took it out of my daddy's bedside table, walked downstairs with it in my hand and blew my mother away because she hadn't given me any ice cream for dessert?''

''No.''

''Hey. Children see this stuff on television all the time. I watched Saturday cartoons. The boulder doesn't actually hurt the coyote when it falls on his head. The kids in my play group played cops and robbers all the time, or humans and aliens. It's possible I thought I could go *bang bang* to punish my mother and then she'd get up and give me my ice cream.''

''No,'' he repeated.

''Why not?'' Her voice had risen.

''Because the entry wound is too high up and the angle too straight to have been caused by a four-year-old child, unless you were born six feet tall and have shrunk every year since.''

''Huh?''

''I went over the autopsy report this afternoon.''

She shuddered.

''I wanted to be able to lay out the whole thing

for you, tell you everything that happened before I told you that part of it. But you need to know *now*. Your mother was shot straight through the heart— one bullet. And it did not angle up. She was too tall for you to have shot her.''

''Maybe she was sitting down.''

''No. The body was lying in front of the fireplace, and forensics would have known if it had been moved.''

For a moment she looked confused. ''Really? Are you absolutely sure?''

''Forensics don't lie. Your mother was shot by someone of adult height. How tall was your father?''

''I have no idea. Tall, I think.'' She seemed bewildered, confused.

''Pictures?''

''None. Grandmere threw away all the photographs of him and my mother. I could meet him on the street and never recognize him.''

''Are you certain she doesn't have any?'' He jerked a thumb at the hall door.

''If she has, they're very well hidden.''

''Well, his arrest record will have his vital statistics and a photo. I didn't spend enough time with those files this afternoon. I'll go back before work tomorrow morning.''

''Ben, don't.''

''What do you mean, don't?''

''Please drop this. If anyone finds out you're doing it, everything will bubble back up like a cesspool. Let it be.''

''I can't. Don't you want to know?''

"You've said I couldn't have shot my mother, therefore my father did it and blamed me."

"Maybe your grandmother did it and blamed you. Did you ever think of that?"

"No!"

"I think your father would be more likely to lie to protect her than he'd lie to protect himself. She hated your mother, didn't she?"

"Oh, yes, she's never made any secret of that."

"And your father?"

"I've always thought he loved my mother. At least when he married her."

"I rest my case. What better way to torment Chantal's child than to convince her she's a murderess?"

Annabelle began to shake her head. Her shoulders hunched and her eyes began to tear. "I won't believe it, Ben. She's not the easiest person to live with, but I think in her own way she cares about me. She'd never spend all these years trying to destroy me. I can't be that wrong about her." She looked into his eyes. "Can I?"

He pulled her into his arms. "I don't know. All I know is that I am going to find the truth, and I am going to lay it at your feet, and then I am going to marry you."

She stiffened. "What did you say?"

"I said, I—"

"You said you were going to marry me."

"Give the lady the prize. That's what I said."

Shaking her head, she pulled away from him. "No, Ben. Never." She held her hands in front of her, fists clenched. "How can I make you hear what I'm saying?" Her voice had risen. "I will not marry you. I loathe meeting new people. I can't pretend to be interested when I'm not, and I don't welcome their interest in me. I do not kiss other people's babies, and since I don't plan to have any of my own, that pretty much leaves the whole baby question moot.''

"That's your choice, although I think my mother would like some grandbabies.''

She jerked away from him. "If you have some antiquated idea that since you took my virginity you have to make an honest woman of me, don't even think it.''

He went to her and took her by the shoulders. "Yes, your virginity was a gift, but I wouldn't care who came before me so long as nobody comes after. Not for me, not for you. Do you think I can ever look at another woman, want another woman? I knew you were the only woman in the world for me five seconds after I saw you in the studio.'' He sighed. "I admit I wasn't too thrilled about it, but I knew. And if you'd admit it, you feel the same.''

She ducked under his arm and got away from him again. "No!'' She rounded on him. "You spring this stupid proposal on me as calmly as if you were asking me to go for a five-minute walk. I will never get married, Ben, not to you, not to anybody. Get it?''

He dropped his hands, but not in defeat. "You're right. I shouldn't have sprung it on you that way.''

She sank onto the bed with her hands between her knees. "You do believe me? You give up?''

"Not at all. But I won't push you, either. At least, not today.'' He sat on the bed beside her, leaned back on the pillows and locked his hands behind his head. His heart was pounding, but he had no intention of allowing Annabelle to see how close he was to losing control.

"We have to clear all this old murder business out of the way first anyway." He sat up and reached for her, but she avoided him and clambered across the bed.

"You don't hear a thing I say, do you? You just go bulling your way straight through to what you think is best. Why do you feel this obligation to me? Is it because of your father?"

That stung. "No."

"Leave this alone, Ben Jackson. Now and forever. If you don't, I'll never speak to you again."

"We can discuss that later as well."

She threw up her hands. "I give up. It's like talking to a wall."

"Good." He looked around. "If you're going to be my wife, I ought to know more about you. My cop buddies say you can tell a lot about people from their bedrooms." He shook his head. "This looks as impersonal as a room from an upscale bed-and-breakfast. Is this the room you've always had?"

She nodded.

"Fireplace, but no knickknacks on the mantelpiece. Lovely old furniture, but no bookshelves. Beautiful rug, but no pictures on the walls except the ones that your grandmother obviously selected." He stood and walked to a door at the side of the room. "Bathroom. Man, look at that tub. You could bathe an elephant in there."

"What are you doing, Ben?"

"Just trying to find out more about you. This

doesn't seem to be the place to do it." He wandered over to another door.

"Ben, don't—"

But she was too late. The door opened on a walk-in closet large enough to be a small room. It even had a round window high up in the far wall. "Ah-ha," Ben said. He flipped the light switch and walked in. "So this is where you did your living."

Floor-to-ceiling shelves on the left were crammed with palettes, paint boxes, blocks of paper, mugs of long dry brushes. In the center stood a built-in table holding a covered sewing machine that had probably been state-of-the-art twenty-five years earlier. Under the table were several wicker baskets holding brightly covered fabric.

Along the far wall under the window stood more shelves crowded with books. He checked the titles. Children's books, art books, design books, old schoolbooks, paperback classics, romances and mysteries.

And dolls. Fashion dolls elegantly costumed and neatly covered in plastic.

The other wall had obviously once held Annabelle's clothes, but was now bare, except that on the floor in the corner sat an enormous brown bear with a goofy expression on his face. Ben turned to Annabelle and pointed at the bear. "Your first prom date, I assume?"

"All right, dammit. That's Montague. Go ahead, laugh. That's why I didn't want you to open the closet door. Santa Claus gave him to me for my second or third Christmas. I know it's silly, but I couldn't ever part with Montague. I've spent too much time crying on his hairy bosom.''

He shut the door gently. ''My bosom's hairy, too. I offer it freely anytime you want to cry.''

''You are incorrigible.''

''From that closet I'd say you are overorganized. Driven, even. Goal-oriented. A control freak. Like me.''

''About my career. My life, on the other hand, flies further out of my control every day I know you.''

''Then think of this as your newest goal. No more murk, no more secrets, no more half truths. Whatever we find, we'll find together and face together.'' He held out his hand. ''Deal?''

''Ben, I don't know—''

''Deal?''

''I will walk away from you afterward.''

''No you won't.''

''I will not make you any promises.''

''I'll accept that for the moment.'' He held out his hand. ''Deal?''

She stood up and took his hand. ''Deal,'' she whispered.

He pulled her into his arms, turned her chin up and kissed her gently. After a moment she wrapped her arms around his waist and leaned against him, her own lips parting, her tongue seeking his. He felt the warmth flood his body. His hands slid down her back, cupped her against him, felt her fit against his loins.

''Annabelle?'' The querulous voice eddied down the hall toward them. ''Where are you? What are you doing? I need some water.''

She broke the kiss. ''Yes, Grandmere. I'm coming.'' As she started down the hall, she whispered over her shoulder, ''I shouldn't have let you kiss me. Go home, Ben. She's probably forgotten you were here already.''

He slipped down the staircase and out the back door. Despite his annoyance with the interruption, he felt elated. She had responded to his kiss, there was no denying that. So she hadn't made any promises. He'd spent his life breaking his long-term goals into shorter and more easily attainable ones. First, find the truth.

ANNABELLE HELD the crystal tumbler to her grandmother's lips. The afternoon seemed to have taken a good deal out of the old woman. ''Do you want me to call Dr. Renfro?''

''Certainly not.'' Mrs. Langley shoved the glass away. ''I'm dying, but not yet awhile. Your luck's not that good.''

''I don't want you to die, Grandmere.''

''Of course you do. Then you can go back to that hell's kitchen you live in and make a million dollars draping outrageously priced apparel on mutant models.''

Annabelle smiled. ''I'll never make a million dollars, and I have a decent job here.''

''As well you should. Elizabeth owes me that much.''

''Owes you?'' Annabelle sat on the edge of the bed. ''What on earth does Elizabeth Jackson owe you for?''

''For not marrying Raymond the way she was supposed to.''

Annabelle blinked. "I beg your pardon."

Grandmere waved her hand. "Raymond pinned Elizabeth in the tenth grade. They were perfect for each other. Everyone knew they'd marry, take their place in society. Then she went off to college and met that Hal Jackson, a devious and ruthless man, and married him. Raymond married Chantal on the rebound."

"Grandmere, Ben is four years older than I am, so the Jacksons must have been married at least four years before my father married my mother. That's one hell of a long rebound."

"Watch your tongue, young lady."

"I've always assumed I was a seven-month baby, that he married my mother because it was the right thing to do."

"You were no seven-month baby. You were born eleven months after your father married that—that woman. I don't say that she didn't have...relations...with him before marriage, only that she did not become pregnant then. She may, however, have told him she was. He was fool enough to marry her on her word alone."

"Ever think he might have fallen in love?"

Grandmere laughed shortly. "No doubt he believed so. Perhaps she used voodoo on him. I wouldn't have put it past her. But you are not a bastard. You are a Langley."

"Hey, what's a spot of bastardy when you're a killer?"

"You are not a killer either. Not in the sense you mean." Suddenly the old woman grasped Annabelle's wrist so hard Annabelle winced and tried to draw away.

"I know you think I am a monster."

Annabelle shook her head.

"Hush. I have the strength to speak now. I may not later. I have always said the best thing you did was to shoot that woman. I never said you intended to do it."

"Then why did you dump so much guilt on me all through the years? Watch me as though I were a land mine somebody might step on?"

Grandmere released her and lay back with her eyes on some far scene that Annabelle could not see. "Raymond was gentle, but he could be stubborn. Not weak, like his father. Raymond had a wild streak that he managed to keep well hidden from me until he brought Chantal Aucoin home. He'd never been away from home except to go to college, and suddenly he was running the family bank in Louisiana. She was a teller, did you know that?" Grandmere spat out the word as though she'd said "whore."

"From the moment you were born with her eyes and her hair and your father's determination to go your own way whatever the consequences, I've been battling for your soul, child."

Annabelle drew back. She couldn't take her eyes off her grandmother's bright blue eyes.

"Yes, your soul. I watched you for every sign that you were like her. Her wildness, her sexual appetites. That woman lived for pleasure—food, wine, jewels, clothes, money, most of all, men. An alley cat is a model of sexual probity compared to Chantal Aucoin."

''I don't want to hear this.'''

''You must. You look just like her. You hunger for sensation and pleasure the way she did. But you are a Langley. You are not trash. I disciplined you to instill the honor and position of the Langleys into you, to dilute her nature with my nurture. You fought me every step of the way. But you didn't win. I'm in your blood deeper than she ever was. When you feel the wildness pulling at you, it's my voice you hear pulling you back—not hers urging you on. No matter how hard you try to flout convention and my rules, you're a Langley, not some bare-legged Cajun trollop with the morals of a muskrat. And someday, because of what I instilled in you, you will do the Langleys proud.''

Suddenly the light went out of her eyes and she sank gasping against the pillows. ''I'm tired. Go sit over there and read a book. I want to sleep.''

Annabelle did as she was told. Grandmere had never in all their years together used words like ''You'll do us proud.'' Annabelle wanted to cry, but as usual, she couldn't. The tears would well up, then subside. How on earth could she do anyone's family proud?

ON MONDAY Ben was caught on the broad marble stairway to his office before he had a chance to drop his briefcase.

''He wants you,'' Dixie said. ''Now.''

''Now?''

''Immediately. Go. Probably something about the MacCauley case.''

Ben sighed, handed Dixie his briefcase and took

the second set of steps two at a time. When he opened the door to Phil Mainwaring's anteroom, he saw that Phil's secretary had not yet arrived, but the door to Phil's office was open. As Ben walked across the room, the antique grandfather clock against the far wall bonged seven-thirty. He knocked on the doorjamb.

Phil looked up from a file open on his desk and smiled. "Good morning, Counselor. Did you catch your errant nymph yesterday? Sit down."

Ben slumped into one of the burgundy leather chairs across from Phil and slid down so that the nape of his neck rested against the back of the chair. He folded his hands across his stomach. "I should have had better sense than to choose the Peabody, Phil. There was a steady stream of people dropping by the table. She's really paranoid about people remembering the Langley case."

"After all this time? Not many do." Phil leaned back in his chair and templed his fingers in front of him. The broad grin disappeared. "That people might rake up the Langley case is only one of the issues, Ben."

"What issues?" He sat up, leaned forward and dropped his forearms onto his knees. He was suddenly alert.

"Okay. If Elizabeth knew I was talking to you, she'd kill me. I like Annabelle, Ben. She's a lovely woman, and unlike most of the other post-debutantes you squire around town, I don't think she's aware of it."

"She's not, although I've tried to tell her."

"She's also smart, and judging from that dinner

party—the part she attended—she's thoughtful and considerate.''

"Go on."

"I had a call last night from Councilman Adler."

"Yeah, he stopped by the table yesterday."

"The good councilman asked me if the girl you were with was Ray Langley's daughter. I had to tell him she was."

"Had to tell him? Why had to?"

"He didn't actually say so, but I was left with the impression that he wasn't pleased that our prospective district attorney was having brunch at the Peabody with the daughter of a notorious society murderer.''

Ben leaned back in his chair, "Oh, for God's sake, Phil! That's ancient history. Did he think I was plotting to go bad on him?"

"I'm merely passing on my impression. Who knows, he may have had an affair with Chantal Langley. Plenty of powerful men did. That could make him uncomfortable around Annabelle. We do not want him uncomfortable at any cost. I told him it was a casual date, that you were old friends, and that you were being nice to her before she went back to New York.''

Ben stood. "You don't have to apologize for Annabelle, Phil, nor for my dating choices. It's none of his damn business whom I date.''

"He wields a lot of power behind the scenes, Ben. When he whispers, we had better hear a shout. This is your career we're talking about.''

"So I'm supposed to drop her?"

"Not at all. I would, however, suggest you use a

little discretion in the places you take her until you have that appointment sewn up."

"Hey, how about I sneak her into my apartment after midnight, screw her brains out and sneak her out into a taxi before dawn? Would that suit the councilman?"

"Don't lose your temper, Ben."

"I'm going to work now, Phil. If I don't, I'm going to say something we'll both regret." He left with as much dignity as he could maintain with his flushed face, his fists and jaw clenched, and the unholy desire to search out Councilman Adler and beat him to a pulp.

ANNABELLE SPENT the morning in the small administrative office beside Elizabeth's kitchen, organizing invoices, paying bills, checking orders, printing out a list of auctions in Europe that might have antique lace for Elizabeth, the kind of detailed work at which she was usually very good.

Today, however, she called the same firm in Toulouse twice to check on the same order of buttons, and made an input error into the tax file that, if she hadn't caught it, would have held the firm liable for over ten thousand dollars in excess taxes and penalties.

When she knocked over her cup of coffee onto the printout and had to run it again, she finally gave up, cleaned up the mess while the second copy came out of the printer, set it on Elizabeth's desk, put her glasses into their case and went upstairs to find Marian in the workroom.

"I need to talk," she said to Marian. The four

other seamstresses didn't even look up from their machines.

Marian, who was meticulously mending a piece of eighteenth-century bobbin lace that was pinned to a velvet pillow, nodded. "Sure."

"Not here. In the kitchen. Coffee?"

"Never turn down coffee." Marian laid out the bobbins carefully so that she could pick up precisely where she had left off, rubbed her hands down the front of her plaid skirt, dropped her glasses onto the velvet cord around her neck and followed Annabelle.

"Is it Ben?" Marian asked as she sat down.

"Of course it's Ben. He's driving me nuts."

"I haven't seen him this emotionally involved for years. He's actually feeling something for a change. He cares about you."

"Care? This is more like a frontal assault from a tank corps. He doesn't listen!"

"Did you ever know a man who did? They think they do, but they don't."

"He looks at me and sees what he wants to see—not the me that's there at all."

"I doubt that. I suspect the woman he sees is a pretty accurate picture. Maybe more accurate than the picture you have of yourself."

"Don't you start."

"Ben is the ultimate fixer. That's why he does the job he does. He wants to fix the entire world so that good people will be free to live happy, contented lives unharried by bad people."

"And he gets to pick who is who? Everything is either black or white?"

"He's not much into moral ambiguity."

"What am I supposed to be?"

Marian laughed. "Good, obviously. If you weren't good, he wouldn't be in love with you."

"Don't call it love. He's infatuated, maybe, or he's got the hots for me, but it can't possibly be love."

Marian laid her hand over Annabelle's. "He wants to tilt at the Black Knight and rescue the fair damsel."

"Marian, I am not fair and I'm not a problem he can solve."

"Did you ever meet Hal, his father?"

"I'm sure I did, but I must have been too young to remember."

"Hal was the ultimate pragmatist. Situational ethics might well have been his middle name. He'd use every trick in the book to get a client off, even one he knew was guilty as sin. Ben grew up listening to his father crow about his latest success in putting one over on this jury or that judge or that prosecuting attorney. Like all small boys, Ben adored his father at the same time he deplored his view of life. And then, of course, Hal walked out."

"I don't know much about that."

"While Elizabeth and the boys were at Destin for the summer, Hal carefully removed every one of his possessions from this house, hid every red cent he could in offshore accounts and had a process server hand Elizabeth divorce papers on her front doorstep when she came home."

"My Lord!"

"Elizabeth was devastated. She'd always known there were other women, of course, but she still thought that deep down he loved her and his family. She certainly never expected anything like that.''

"Poor Ben and Steven."

"They handled it very differently. Ben decided he had to be perfect to make up for his father's failings.

"Steven, on the other hand, acted out. Elizabeth eventually sent him to a military school as an alternative to reform school. He took to the life, joined the army. I think he works for one of those hotshot bodyguard-for-hire places now. Hasn't been home in years.

"Then, just when Ben had finally stopped grieving for his father, Judy was killed, and Ben had to deal with the fact that his own father had gotten Judy's killer off on a prior charge. Worse still, Elmer Bazemore fixated on Judy because he knew she was attached to Hal's family.''

"But why harm someone connected to the lawyer who got him off? That makes no sense. He should have been grateful.''

"He didn't care that Hal got him off. Maybe that added to the thrill. Who knows how that sort of twisted mind works. Ben was working the summer after he graduated from high school as gofer for one of the trial judges and had also been in court during the Bazemore trial several times. Apparently, Bazemore saw Judy one day when she picked up Ben. After he got off, he stalked her and killed her.''

"That's dreadful, but I don't see how I factor in.''

"Whatever he says, I think Ben feels it's his fault Bazemore got a look at Judy in the first place. He feels somehow responsible, though he certainly shouldn't. I do know he's avoided emotional entanglements ever since. He dates, he sends flowers and probably sleeps with them all, but no one has mattered. Until you.''

''You're saying I'm some kind of expiation?''

''He felt helpless when Judy died. If he can help you, that could go a long way to even that score with his father he's always talking about.''

''He's got some crazy idea about reopening my mother's case and proving I didn't have anything to do with her death. That when I know for certain I didn't pull the trigger, I'll be fixed. I'm not broken, dammit.''

''But you're hurting, Annabelle.''

''It's not his fault.''

''Everything wrong with the world is Ben's fault so far as he's concerned.''

''He practically accused Grandmere yesterday.''

Marian looked down at her hands around her coffee cup, then said softly, ''He could be right.''

''Oh, come on! She's a fragile old lady.''

''She wasn't a fragile old lady twenty-five years ago. She could have pulled the trigger as easily as you could.''

''She swears my father told her he saw me do it.''

''If he did not kill your mother, than he went to prison to protect someone else. Much more likely that he'd protect his mother than that he'd protect you. All he had to do was to tell the police there'd been a tragic accident if he'd really seen you shoot your mother.''

Annabelle set down her cup. ''She's not evil, Marian. She's hardheaded and opinionated and the world's worst snob, but surely she wouldn't have raised me to think I was a killer simply to protect herself.''

Marian merely raised an eyebrow.

Annabelle grabbed both cups, took them to the sink and began to wash them viciously. "Ben may be right. Maybe it is time I found out the truth instead of accepting everybody else's word for what happened.''

CHAPTER TEN

BEN COULDN'T FIND the slightest resemblance between the Raymond Langley whose mug shots stared up at him and Annabelle. Chantal Aucoin Langley's genes had overridden her pallid husband's. But maybe he hadn't been quite such a lackluster person when he wasn't being booked for murder.

He looked limp. Bloodless. Empty. A weak man with a weak chin and a sharply beaked nose. His eyes were a watery gray, his shoulders thin. He was six feet two inches tall, but had the look of a man who habitually stooped to make himself seem shorter. The prototypical henpecked male, hag-ridden first by his mother, then by the tempestuous wife he'd chosen.

Why had he married Chantal? Was she his one and only rebellion? Or had he needed to fill his mother's place in his life with someone equally domineering the moment he was out of mama's clutches?

Ben called Annabelle at her apartment as he wound through evening traffic on Union Avenue. No answer. He'd have to ask his mother whether it was polite for a suitor to give his intended a new answering machine.

He called the Langley house expecting to hear Beulah Mayhew's voice. Instead, a deep baritone answered, "Langley residence."

Ben hesitated. "Uh, this is Ben Jackson. I'm trying to get in touch with Annabelle. Is she by any chance with Mrs. Langley?"

"Sorry, sir, Miss Langley has already left."

"If you should hear from her, would you ask her to call me?"

"Certainly, sir." The line went dead before Ben could even say thank-you and goodbye.

It could only have been Jonas, unless Mrs. Langley had suddenly hired a butler, and that didn't seem likely. He remembered he'd wanted to meet the man. This might be a good time to do it, if he could think of an excuse.

The first drops of spring rain hit his windshield, then the heavens opened. He turned on his lights and wipers and saw a dozen flashes light up the sky in his rearview mirror. The thunder that followed six seconds later sounded like cannon fire.

He checked the weather station on his radio and found that there were already warnings in Crittenden County, across the river in Arkansas, and that the entire west Tennessee area was under alert for thunderstorms and possible tornadoes.

Annabelle shouldn't be driving in this. Her apartment had no basement, but his mother's house did. He wanted Annabelle close enough to take shelter should the sirens go off in the Garden District.

He pulled up in his mother's parking area, saw that Annabelle's little sedan was not in its accustomed place and drove out again without stopping.

The wind had picked up so that twigs and newly formed spring leaves whipped across his windshield. The big old trees nodded and twisted above the road.

They'd withstood ice storms, snow, floods and many thunderstorms before this. Only a direct hit from a tornado would be likely to topple these giant survivors, but large branches could snap off and land on top of automobiles.

He cruised past Mrs. Langley's mansion, saw lights on in only two upstairs rooms and turned the corner into the side street. He had no idea where to look for Annabelle, and in this weather he doubted Jonas would be in any mood for company. He cruised by the turn-in at the back of the house, checking to be certain that Annabelle hadn't come back when she heard the weather reports. The area was empty. He drove on.

He nearly missed seeing her little car. It was parked on the street down beside the alleyway that ran behind the Langley property.

He slammed on his brakes, grateful that the streets were practically empty at the moment, and backed up.

Why hadn't she pulled into the Langley parking area if she'd gone back to the Langley house?

And if he knew she was there, why had Jonas lied?

DRAT AND DOUBLE DRAT! The thunder seemed to roll just outside the door of the cottage. Lightning flashed down the small vestibule and claps of thunder followed.

Over the years, Annabelle had disobeyed many of Grandmere's rules, but until tonight she'd never tried to sneak into the cottage in her grandmother's back garden where she'd lived the first four years of her life with her mother and father.

She had schooled herself to forget she'd ever lived there. Why tonight she had taken the key that hung on the key rack beside the back door of the Langley mansion to sneak into the cottage, she had no idea.

She would certainly never have gone in if the weather report had been accurate. This storm front was not supposed to come through until after midnight.

She hated thunder. Her therapist had suggested her fear might be an echo of the shot that killed her mother.

She flicked the light switch and wasn't surprised when nothing happened. Grandmere wouldn't have paid utilities on an empty cottage.

Even though the cottage sat so far back in the garden behind the magnolias that it was invisible from the main house, Grandmere would never have tolerated strangers living here—assuming she could have found someone willing to move into a cottage after a woman had been murdered there. The cottage had lain empty ever since, probably only protected from vandals by Jonas's vigilance.

It must have seemed perfect when Raymond brought Chantal home. Now with the dust sheets covering even the pictures on the wall, the little house was creepy and completely unfamiliar.

Playing her flashlight around to keep from bumping into anything, Annabelle crept tentatively into the living room. Surely here she'd remember what happened the night her mother died.

She stared down at the ashes in the fireplace that spilled out onto the hearth.

Nothing. No visions, no memory, no feelings.

Panic struck with the next clap of thunder.

She raced to the front door and pulled it open.

On the front porch a man stood silhouetted against the storm. She screamed.

"Annabelle?"

"Ben?"

His hair was plastered over his forehead, his clothes were drenched.

"Are you following me? You scared me to death!"

"I saw your car in the street and the open garden gate. If you stay out in this, you'll be sick again. What were you doing in there?"

"Trying to remember, of course."

"And?"

She shook her head.

"Lock up and follow me home. The storm's almost over, and I have something to show you."

"I'll bet you do."

"Don't be so cynical. It's business. Purely business."

She glared at him, then shrugged. "Business it had better be."

WHILE ANNABELLE parked her car, Ben checked his supply of cold white wine and pulled out wineglasses before he changed out of his suit and into sweats.

Annabelle was right to be cynical. He hoped once he got her here, he could convince her to stay with him. He wanted her so badly he ached. And he wanted to prove to her that they could be good together, that he could give her pleasure without pain.

The bell rang. He drove his hands through his wet hair and opened the door.

Annabelle stood outside with her arms across her midriff. "So what's to see?"

"Come in. You want a brandy? Some wine?"

"Lite beer if you have it. The bottle's fine."

After they were settled, she said, "You wanted to show me something. How about we cut to the chase."

"I'm chasing as hard as I can, lady." He picked up a slightly damp manila envelope and handed it to her. "Here."

For a moment she didn't touch it. "What is this?"

"It won't bite. Open it and see."

She pulled out the slick pages and glanced up at him.

"That's your father," he said.

She dropped the envelope on the couch beside her as though it were on fire.

Ben took her hand and began to rub his thumb over the back of it. "Seems like I'm always upsetting you. I can't seem to help it."

She disengaged her hand gently and picked up the envelope again. "Can I take this home with me? Look at it on my own?"

"Sorry. I'm signed out for it. We don't have a color copier at the office or I'd have made you a decent copy and returned the originals. Look, if you don't want to open it..."

"No. I want to see. I'd simply prefer to do it alone." She slid the sheets out and stared. "I ought to feel some kind of recognition. This is a complete stranger, and yet for almost four years of my life he was the most important person in my world. What's wrong with me?''

"I have trouble remembering my father's face, and I was thirteen when he left.'' He took the photos and slid them back into the envelope. "I'll make you some copies on my way to work tomorrow. At least you'll have them.''

"Thank you, Ben,'' she whispered. Suddenly she clenched her fists and shut her eyes tight. She began to tremble.

Ben was beside her on the sofa in an instant, his arms wrapped around her. "You're freezing. I should have given you some dry clothes.''

"I'm not wet, I'm scared.''

She clung to him, buried her face against his shoulder, but after a minute, she pulled away. "In the cottage, when you opened the door, I had that déjà vu thing, as though I'd seen someone looming up in the doorway before.'' She looked up at him. "But how could that have happened? Unless I was already downstairs when my father came home. And if I was already downstairs, then my mother must have already been dead.''

"Not necessarily.'' He took her shoulders. "You've blanked it all out for years. Maybe you couldn't handle that you were there, there when your father came home, when they argued, when he shot her. Maybe you can't remember his face because you don't want to remember what it looked like that night.''

"Is that it? Did I see it? Not shoot her myself, but watch him shoot her?''

Ben nodded. "Possibly. And like every kid in the

world whose parents aren't getting along, like me and Steve when Dad walked out, you turned it into your fault. You couldn't bear to think your daddy, the man you loved, could do a thing like that. Better that you did it.''

She pressed her fingers to her temples. ''Why can't I remember?''

''You don't want to. I've been bullheaded to force you. Say the word, and I'll drop the whole thing.''

She rose from the sofa, strode to the window and looked out over the city. ''I *want* to remember. That's why I went to the house.'' She looked over her shoulder at him. ''But now I'm scared to do it alone.''

''You won't be alone,'' he said as he walked over to her and put his arms around her. ''I'll be with you every step of the way.''

She stepped out of his embrace. ''Don't. Business, remember? Besides, you don't have time, Ben, even if you knew what to do or where to look. And what about your promotion? There's going to be fallout if you pursue this.''

''There already is.'' He bit his tongue.

''That man—Adler—I saw the look in his eyes when he was introduced to me. He remembered who I am. And what I am. How many of the others you introduced me to recognized me?''

''Only Adler. He's the right age. He called my boss, who said I needed to be discreet.''

She pulled away, picked up her purse. ''I won't be responsible for getting your career smashed. It isn't worth it.''

He caught her arm. ''It is. You are. The hell with the councilman. The hell with Phil, for that matter.''

"No."

He pulled her back to the couch. "At first I just wanted to absolve you from this mess. But it's more than that now. If there was a miscarriage of justice all those years ago, then I have to correct it. Much as I hate to admit it, I'm beginning to think my father really might have gotten your dad off if there had been a trial. That doesn't mean he wasn't guilty. But was there enough evidence to convince a jury? And if he could have gotten off, why did he demand the plea bargain?"

"Maybe he felt the honorable thing to do was to accept his punishment."

Ben laughed shortly. "My father would have hated that. If I let the powers that be dictate what I do about a twenty-five-year-old case, how soon before I let them dictate what I do about one that happens tomorrow or the next day?"

She smiled and touched his face. "Pretty good speech, Counselor, but the jury is still out on whether you'd cave under pressure. Or when your career is on the line."

CHAPTER ELEVEN

BEN FOLLOWED Annabelle home and parked beside her car in his mother's backyard. She refused to let him come upstairs to her apartment, so he rang his mother's back-door bell, then used his key. She met him in the hall in a flamboyant brocade dressing gown.

"What are you doing here?" she said.

"Do I need an excuse to come see you?"

His mother touched his cheek. "You never come by without calling first."

"Tonight isn't convenient?"

"Not particularly. I'm dressing. Phil's taking me to dinner. Come on upstairs. You can watch me emerge from my chrysalis. You want a drink?"

"Beer. I'll get it."

Beer in hand, he slouched on the French chaise longue in his mother's bedroom. He could hear her in her bathroom through the open door. "Phil's really pursuing you, isn't he?" he asked.

"Mmmph."

"I said…"

His mother stuck her head out the door. "I heard you, but I was half in and half out of this dress. Come zip me up. It's one of the few things I hate about not having a man around. My arms are never long enough.''

He did as he was told. "Nice dress. No lace.''

"Lace is what I sell, darling, not what I wear.'' She shoved him back in the direction of the chaise. "So, to what do I owe this pleasure?''

"Mother, were you engaged to Raymond Langley?''

Elizabeth stopped in the act of putting on her left pump and stood for a moment like a crane. "That old devil,'' she snapped. "She never forgave me for falling in love with your father.''

"So it's true.''

She sank onto the bench of her dressing table. "Perfectly true. He was my high-school sweetheart, and a kinder, gentler soul you'd never want to meet. He simply killed the wrong woman. He should have bumped off his mother. No jury in the world would have convicted him. Justifiable homicide all the way.''

"But you married my father?''

She swung around and began to dig in her jewelry box. "If I hadn't met Hal, I'd have fallen for somebody else like him. At that age, most woman don't appreciate good men. We want to tame the wild, crazy, charismatic guys.'' She thrust the spike of her pierced earring through her ear hard enough so she winced. "We don't realize until later that it's an illusion. Self-absorbed once, always self-absorbed.''

"How badly was Raymond Langley hurt when you broke it off?''

She shrugged. "Not as much as Mrs. Langley

would have everyone believe. He did marry Chantal after all.''

''Years later.''

''First time he'd been away from momma. It's not so much that Chantal was beautiful, you know, but there was something about her that turned men into taffy. Actually, she wasn't unlike Mrs. Langley, senior. Not on the surface, of course, but demanding, extravagant, hard as nails and single-minded. She wanted money and social position. She intended to have it.''

''Did she have an affair with Dad?''

The pearls in Elizabeth's hand clattered to the floor. She bent to pick them up. ''I am torn between telling you to mind your own damn business, and telling you the truth, what I know of it.''

''I wouldn't ask, Mom, if it weren't important.''

''Because of Annabelle.'' She sighed. ''I cannot see your father spending as much time with Raymond and Chantal as he and I did in those days, without taking her to bed. He took everybody else.''

Ben went to his mother and laid a hand on her shoulder. She covered it with hers.

''I did a fine job of hiding it from you and Steve,'' Elizabeth said with jutting chin.

''Neither of us had a clue until—''

''Until the divorce papers arrived on the doorstep. Hal tried to be discreet about his affairs, but it's a bit like a bull moose trying to be discreet in somebody's kitchen.''

''You stayed for our sakes?''

''Partly. I did love him, you know, and he *was* extraordinary. He had me convinced the rules didn't apply to men like him, and that at bottom, he truly loved me best. Maybe he did, as much as he was capable of loving anyone outside himself.'' She ran her hand up under her hair at the nape of her neck, bent her head and said, ''Fasten these blasted pearls, Ben, will you? My hands aren't too steady at the moment.''

He complied and began to knead her shoulders gently.

He held his mother's eye in the mirror. ''Okay, here's the biggie. Could Dad have shot Chantal?''

His mother wrenched her shoulders. ''No!'' She slid away from him and went to her closet. ''I'm certain whatever they had was long over when she was shot.''

''Humor me, Mom. Where was he that night?''

Elizabeth waved a hand. ''I have no idea. It's been forever.''

Ben said softly, ''Where were you?''

''Ben, if you don't stop attacking me like a prosecutor, I'll demand my own lawyer, and Phil Mainwaring will be here any minute to protect me.''

''Sorry, Mom. It's become a habit. So where were you?''

She began to laugh, walked over and smacked his cheek lightly. ''Damn you, Ben. I had two children, remember? I was at home getting the pair of you to bed, then watching a little television, then I fell into bed myself.''

''Were you asleep when Mrs. Langley called?''

''Hal must have come home by then, because he answered the phone downstairs. I picked it up, heard enough to know who was calling and hung up. I don't eavesdrop. He came upstairs to tell me he was on his way over to Ray's."

"So he *had* been out until late?"

"Ben, your father is many things, some of them unpleasant. A killer he is not. I'd stake my life on it."

"Raymond Langley already did that. Look where it got him."

"HAVE YOU LOST your mind?" Dixie pointed to the four dusty cardboard file boxes stacked in the corner of Ben's office. "You've dragged in every case file from the prosecutor's office and the police and the courts. All on that Langley thing that's been over forever. If you don't have enough to do, I'm sure Mr. Mainwaring will be happy to increase your caseload."

"I'm not working on any of it on company time," Ben said from his desk. "Strictly extracurricular activity."

"Yes, and I know what kind," Dixie said with a sniff. She turned on her heel and strode out.

Ben grinned after her and rubbed the back of his neck. He must have been crazy to request all the Langley files. He had little enough space in his office as it was. The place was starting to look like a warehouse. He bent to the law book in front of him as the door opened and Phil stuck his head in.

"Got a minute?"

"Sure." Ben leaned back.

"What the hell is all that?"

"Okay, okay. I'm taking it home, getting it out of here. I'm just checking a few things, is all."

Mainwaring dropped into the chair opposite Ben. He looked more tired than usual. "The Langley thing. Elizabeth warned me, but I had no idea it had gone this far. In the final analysis, Ben, none of this matters. The case is closed, Langley served his time."

"Justly?"

"He thought so."

"My father doesn't."

Phil snorted. "Hal Jackson wouldn't admit a man was guilty if we found him standing over a dozen newly dismembered corpses with a bloody chainsaw in his hand."

"Of course he would. He just wouldn't let a jury know he did."

Mainwaring chortled. "You're right."

"But he doesn't think Langley was guilty."

"You've spoken to him?" Mainwaring sat up. His eyes were suddenly alert.

"Don't worry. He doesn't plan to drop in on the family manse."

"Good. Where Elizabeth is concerned, I'd prefer to be the only bull in the pasture."

"I must tell Mother how romantic you are when she's not around."

Mainwaring stood. "You do and you can kiss your new job goodbye." He grinned. "Can you come to a meeting tonight at the Hunt Club? Couple of the good ol' boys want to check you out."

"God, Phil, if they don't know me by now…"

"Just do it, okay? You're young, you're brash, and you have a mind of your own."

"And I intend to keep it."

"We all want the same thing here. Less crime, more prevention, and the sociopaths put away where they don't screw up life for the good guys. Come tell them that."

"Fine."

"I'll have Maxine call Dixie with the details." Phil stopped with his hand on the doorknob. "Don't get consumed by the Langley thing, Ben. We have too many hot buttons to worry about the cold cases."

"Mrs. Langley doesn't think Ray was guilty either."

"What?" Phil stopped. "Does that surprise you? She's his mother."

"She keeps hinting that she knows things about that night. Of course, she also keeps trying to convince Annabelle she did it, which I know isn't true."

"How?"

Ben nearly told him about the angle of the shot, then kept his mouth shut. He'd keep his own counsel until he was certain of his facts. "Just a feeling."

"In this office we work on evidence, not feelings. Annabelle's a nice girl, but don't risk your career over her. See you tonight."

"OUR MISS BRITTANY is coming over for a first fitting in twenty minutes," Marian said as she hung up the telephone. "We've barely had time to stitch up her toile. She plans to wear the dress to the Steamboat Ball. I do wish Elizabeth would stop doing favors for Ben's girlfriends."

Annabelle flushed. Ben hadn't actually said he wasn't seeing Brittany any longer. Why should his seeing another woman make her stomach go queasy and her skin heat up? "It's close enough to finished for her to try it on." She machine-basted a final seam and hung the toile on a hanger. Hard to believe this beige muslin thing was the basis for a ball gown. "You fit it, all right? I might accidentally jab her with a pin or two."

Marian laughed. "And I won't? Do you know, Annabelle, I believe you are the first girl Ben's ever shown any interest in who wasn't a size four with blond hair and blue eyes?"

"I don't think I was a size four when I was four." But then, she didn't actually remember being four, except in a fog of moving house and changing from a nuclear family to a Grandmere-centered existence.

"If you're staying, you can get me that bolt of red Brussels lace for her bodice and sleeves. If Miss Brittany approves, of course. Then, why don't you go on home? It's after five."

"I'll stay as long as you do."

"Everyone else has left. I stay because I don't have any life. You do."

"Right. TV dinners and driving over to check on Grandmere. Big whoop." Annabelle opened the storeroom door and turned on the light.

Along three walls were dowels from which hung rolls of Brussels, Valenciennes, Battenberg, Guipure, Spanish—all the different kinds of lace Elizabeth used—as well as bolts of silk, brocade, peau de soie and batiste.

The fourth wall held a rack on which antique afternoon and ball gowns, petticoats, pantaloons, peignoirs and shawls were carefully hung on padded hangers. These were the clothes that Elizabeth bought at auction, garage sales, or found in attics, and from which she took the lace she used in her designs.

Annabelle spotted the roll of scarlet Brussels lace in the shadows at the far corner under the eaves.

As she ducked her head and reached for it, the door behind her swung closed with a crack. She jumped, half turned, then reached once more for the bolt.

As her hands touched it, it seemed to shimmer with moisture. Her hands felt wet, her fingers gluey on the fabric. A leaking roof? She stared down at her hands and saw her palms coated with deep crimson. She began to shake. "Marian!" she shouted. "Marian!"

An instant later the door opened and light from the workroom flooded it. "Honestly, these old houses. Nothing's balanced. Can't get a window up or keep a door open," Marian said. "Couldn't you find it?" She walked in and kicked the edge of an empty bolt into the doorway to keep the door from shutting behind her.

Annabelle turned to her with her palms outstretched. She tried to speak, but nothing came out but a croak.

"Annabelle?" Marian's eyes widened. She shoved Annabelle out the door, grabbed the bolt and followed.

Annabelle sank into the nearest sewing chair.

"Oh, for pity's sake! The dye's run in this corner. We'll have to work around it." Marian set the bolt onto the nearest cutting table. "Now, how on earth did that happen? You'd better wash your hands before that dye sets or you'll really be caught red-handed." She giggled. "Annabelle?"

Annabelle stared at her palms, then wiped them

frantically down the front of her shirt again and
again. She didn't recognize the sound that came from
her throat.

"Oh, Lord, Annabelle!" Marian dropped in front
of her and grabbed her wrists. "I'm sorry. Such a
dumb thing to say. It's dye! Just red dye!"

"Yoo-hoo! Can I come up? I'm dying to see my
lace."

BEN TIPPED his doorman outrageously and kicked the
door shut behind him before he set down the last file
box. He often brought work home but he tried to keep
it organized in the second bedroom he used as his
office.

The Langley case seemed to be breeding.

He glanced at his watch. Hardly time to shower
and shave again before he had to dress for the Hunt
Club thing. The worst thing about politics was the
games one had to play. His father had taught him
that—one of the few things his father had ever said
that Ben agreed with. The men and women who
would be at that meeting seemed to believe that
money and power gave them privileges Joe Public
couldn't aspire to.

Now he was faced with the age-old dilemma. In
order to help Joe Public, he had to get appointed, then
elected for a full term. And in order to get elected, he
had to satisfy the power brokers—without com-
promising his own integrity.

Despite the time pressure, he called Annabelle.
"Hi. I've got those color prints for you?"

"What?"

She sounded confused.

"You know. Your father's picture."

"Yes."

"Annabelle, is everything all right?"

He could hear her bristle over the phone line. "Of course. Why wouldn't it be?"

"Look, I've got a dinner meeting tonight, then I'll drop by your place with the prints. Say, about nine. Is that too late?"

"No, Ben. Don't come over here. Mrs. Mayhew has some kind of family emergency. I'm filling in for her."

"You'll be home by nine, won't you? Or I could come over to Mrs. Langley's."

"I just want to go to bed. Tomorrow night, maybe." She hung up without waiting for his answer.

Every time she rebuffed him he grew more and more uptight. Last night she'd been anxious to see the pictures of her father on her own. Now she didn't seem interested in the copies he'd made.

Maybe she'd suffered a relapse of her cold. She'd been wet and miserable for long enough. He'd drop by on his way home to make certain she was all right. If her light was still on, he'd call her from his car.

If she hadn't changed her mind about seeing him, he'd leave the photos on the front seat of her car. He'd offer to take her to dinner the following night.

AT SIX FORTY-FIVE Annabelle discovered her right rear tire was flat. She called Grandmere's house to try to speak with Mrs. Mayhew before she left.

Her grandmother picked up the phone instead.

"Grandmere, catch Mrs. Mayhew. I've got a flat tire. I'll be a few minutes late."

"That woman left fifteen minutes ago. I was wondering whether you intended to abandon me completely for the entire evening."

"Jonas is there."

"He has gone to some landscape-design meeting tonight. It will take you hours to get someone to come change that tire."

"I can change a tire, Grandmere. I'll be there in thirty minutes, tops. Stay in bed and don't do anything silly until I get there."

"I do not like being here alone. You know that."

"You'll be fine. Now, the sooner I'm off the phone, the sooner I'll have that tire changed."

Thirty minutes later Annabelle rolled into her grandmother's parking area on three normal tires and one small spare. She'd pulled the roofing nail out of her tread and dropped it into her purse. At least the tire could be easily repaired. She didn't want to spend money on a new tire.

She unlocked the back door and called, "Grandmere, I'm here." All quiet. The old lady was probably sulking and wouldn't speak all evening. Sighing, she climbed the stairs.

She tapped at Grandmere's door. No answer. Great. Big-time sulks. "I came as quickly as I could," she said as she opened the door.

Her grandmother lay in her usual position in the big bed, her hands neatly folded across her middle and her fine hair spread on the pillow. Her eyes were closed. Sleeping.

Annabelle tiptoed across the room until she stood beside the bed. The old lady seemed to have shrunk in only twenty-four hours. Her skin was waxen, with a tinge of blue-gray around the mouth.

"Grandmere?" Annabelle said softly. She felt rather than saw the absence of movement in the old lady's chest.

"Grandmere!" she screamed. Without conscious thought she tipped the woman's head back, pinched her nose and began CPR. "I must not crush her chest," she said between breaths.

Nothing. After a full minute—that seemed like an hour—she grabbed the telephone and dialed 911. As soon as she'd given the dispatcher the address, she called Dr. Renfro.

The phone rang for what seemed like minutes before she heard an answer, "Renfro residence."

She was surprised at how calm she sounded. "This is Annabelle Langley. My grandmother has had another spell. She doesn't seem to be breathing. I've called the rescue squad, but I'd appreciate it if the doctor could come to the house right now."

She hung up the phone and went back to her CPR, although by now she was certain what she was doing was futile. She stopped long enough to race downstairs and unlock the back door.

Adrenaline drove her until she heard the clatter of heavy footsteps on the stairs and felt the presence of people in the room.

"It's okay, miss, we'll take over." A broad hand touched her arm. Gratefully she relinquished her position. A slight dark woman took her shoulder and led her away. "Hey, it's okay. You did fine."

The room swarmed with people, lights, equipment, shouted commands. She could hear the bump of machinery being dragged up the stairs, and shrank back out of the way, suddenly feeling irrelevant.

She wanted Ben. Through her confusion, her worry, her fear, that thought ran like a beacon. Ben would fix everything. She asked a passing EMT, "May I use the phone?"

He nodded. "Sure. Got an extension in another room?"

She nodded and went out into the hall to find a couple of uniformed policemen climbing the stairs toward her. "Ma'am," one said as he passed by her into the room.

She dialed Ben's apartment, left word on his answering machine, then dialed his cell phone to find he was out of range or didn't have the thing on. She called Elizabeth and asked if she had any idea where to find Ben.

"No, sorry. What is it, Annabelle?"

"I think Grandmere's dead."

"Oh, my dear. I'll be right there."

"Please, no. There are about a dozen people working on her right now and her doctor's on his way."

"Call me if you need me. In the meantime I'll try to find Ben and send him to you."

As the phone hit the cradle, the energy drained from her body. She sat hard in the small chair beside the telephone and simply stared at the floor.

In the half hour between the time she'd spoken to her annoying, annoyed grandmother and the time she'd arrived at the house, whatever had made Grandmere human had simply gone away and left behind this tiny, empty shell. Was this the way her mother had looked? Had Annabelle recognized even then the absence of personhood? Surely not. But if she had caused it to happen, what then?

The bedroom door opened and the big man came out and motioned to one of the uniformed officers. "Okay, Bill, come call it."

Call it? "Excuse me," she said to the second policeman. "What's happening?"

"Uh, miss, they weren't able to revive her."

Her hand flew to her mouth. She'd known, but words made it seem real, final.

He touched her shoulder. "Ma'am, trust me, after this long without oxygen to her brain, you wouldn't have wanted her to live. It's better this way." Then lamely, "I'm sorry for your loss."

The first policeman came to her. "Sorry, ma'am. Afraid she was gone before we got here. Guys said you did CPR?"

"I tried."

"Did she have a doctor?"

"Yes, I've called him. He should be on his way over."

"Good, because we're going to need a death certificate. Otherwise we have to take her to the morgue for an autopsy." He glanced back over his shoulder. "With a death certificate, you can call the funeral home right off, set up the funeral."

"Thank you."

"We'll wait with you."

"Yes, thank you. Can I see her?"

The two men glanced at each other, then the first one said, "Sure. We'll come with you."

The people and equipment were already trailing

down the stairs. Each of them gave her a sad smile
and a passing "Sorry, ma'am."

She thanked them absently.

The only light in the bedroom now came from
Grandmere's bedside table lamp and the light over
her portrait. Slowly Annabelle walked to the side of
the bed and took the frail bird claw in her hand. It
already felt cold and hard. She wanted to cry, but as
usual her eyes stayed dry. She leaned over and kissed
the waxen cheek. She could taste the expensive powder her grandmother wore.

"You tried your best, old girl, I know you did,"
she said softly. "I wish we'd been happier together."

"Annabelle?"

She jumped and turned to find Dr. Renfro, red-
faced, rotund, anxious, and still wearing his bedroom
slippers.

"Oh dear," he said. "I thought she had a few
months still."

"Doctor?" said the policeman.

He brushed a hand down his face. "Oh, she was
in end-stage cardiac failure. I just thought she had
more time. One never knows, of course, not for sure.
I'll give you a certificate. Do you have a form?"

"Yes, Doctor." He produced a folded yellow form
from his shirt pocket and glanced shamefacedly at
Annabelle. "Just routine, ma'am."

She nodded.

"Heart failure. The system just shuts down all of
a sudden." Renfro turned to Annabelle. "Were you
with her when she expired?"

Annabelle shook her head. "I talked to her earlier.
She seemed fine. I was late because I had a flat tire,

and by the time I got here—I can't have been more than thirty minutes—I found her like this.''

"Just went to sleep. An easy death, really." He patted Annabelle. "She would have hated dying in a hospital. All those tubes and things," he said in a good imitation of Mrs. Langley's voice. Then he shook his head. "Now, Miss Annabelle, you come on out of here. We'll go downstairs so I can make you a drink."

"We'll be going, if that's okay," the policeman said. "Sorry again, ma'am." He started down the stairs.

"Annabelle?" Ben's voice came up the stairs toward her. The feeling of relief that swept over her surprised and dismayed her.

"Ben!" She met him at the head of the stairs. When he wrapped his arms around her, she buried her head against his shoulder.

"Mom found me at the Hunt Club," he whispered into her hair. "I came as soon as I could. I am so sorry."

"Blessing, really," said Dr. Renfro over his shoulder. "I'm taking this young lady to the kitchen to see if I can find her some brandy."

"I'll be down in a minute," Ben said, giving her one final squeeze. "I owe Mrs. Langley a valediction."

He watched Annabelle drift down the stairs as though she wasn't quite certain where her feet were, then he went into Mrs. Langley's room. The light was still on over her portrait. The contrast between the vibrant young woman in the picture and the tiny husk that lay on the bed was about as chilling a memento mori as he'd ever come across.

He stood beside the bed with his head bowed. She looked different, somehow, and not merely because life had left her. It took him a moment to realize that she had no lipstick on. Probably come off during CPR.

A single hot-pink smear ran from the corner of her mouth up her cheek.

He felt a frisson of disquiet. He'd never seen anyone that died so neatly, so perfectly arranged. He picked up one of her frail hands. The nail on her index finger was split, the polish ragged around the edges. She must have struggled when she felt herself having some kind of attack. He looked on the bed for tiny fragments of pink, but found none. Strange.

Dr. Renfro was satisfied, the police were satisfied. He should simply walk away. That would certainly be the best course for Annabelle. But the lawyer— the criminal prosecutor—in him wouldn't allow him to walk away. Not till he knew for certain.

He moved the bedside lamp so that it reflected into Mrs. Langley's face. He bent close and gently lifted one of her eyelids.

An instant wave of nausea swept over him. He lifted the other eyelid, then closed both and stood silent beside the bed. Even in the bedside light he could see the petichiae, the tiny hemorrhages in the whites of her eyes.

He picked up one of the down pillows piled beside Mrs. Langley. Fine old linen, freshly changed and still bearing creases from the iron. Mrs. Langley had never laid her head on this pillow.

Hardly daring to breathe, he turned it over.

The smear of lipstick on the underside was definitely Mrs. Langley's color. He replaced the pillow the way he had found it.

He felt suddenly as though Mrs. Langley were watching him sardonically, accusing.

He had the authority to order an autopsy. Annabelle might never forgive him. But Mrs. Langley had retained him as her attorney. And he was damn certain someone had smothered her to death.

Would Annabelle be blamed *again?*

CHAPTER TWELVE

HE FOUND HER in the butler's pantry under a single pale light. She held a crystal snifter of brandy in both hands as though she were warming herself over a candle flame. Renfro leaned against the cold stove.

Ben wrapped his arms around her from behind. "I'm so sorry about your grandmother."

She leaned back, and he savored the warmth of her body against him. That she trusted him made what he was about to do even more difficult.

"Young man, I am glad that you are here to look after Annabelle." Renfro stood and rubbed his hands together as though he were drying them. "Mrs. Langley was a very old patient of mine." He smiled gently at Annabelle. "You know, my dear, I'd be lying if I said she was a dear friend. But it is always difficult when a life ends, no matter how expected. We always think we have a little longer to say goodbye."

Then he turned to Ben. "I'll give the funeral home a call from my car." He glanced at Annabelle. "Someone needs to stay here with Annabelle until Mrs. L. is picked up. She shouldn't be alone."

"She won't be. I'll walk you to the door." Ben took Dr. Renfro's arm. "I'll be right back, Annabelle."

Annabelle nodded. She kept her eyes on the swirling brandy as if she might be able to read something in its depths. He ached for her. Lord knew how much additional pain he was about to cause her.

Once they were out of earshot, Ben asked Renfro casually, "So you're satisfied with heart failure as a cause of death?"

"What else?"

"You examined the body?"

Renfro drew himself up. "I've been Mrs. Langley's doctor for almost forty years. I know my patients inside and out. Literally."

"So you're not surprised?"

"God simply decided to take her tonight instead of six months from now. A blessing all around. Doctors are not soothsayers. We can only give a rough estimate as to how long a patient will last."

Ben nodded. "I realize this is an imposition, but I'd like to show you something, if you have the time." He glanced in the open kitchen door. Annabelle hadn't moved. She wouldn't even notice he was gone.

There was still time to back out. Renfro might look at this evidence and discount it. What then? Let it go?

Moments later they stood at the old lady's bedside.

"Would you mind checking her eyes, Doctor?"

Ben watched him lean over and shine the light on Mrs. Langley's face as he pried up her lids. Ben heard the sharp intake of breath.

"Now, Doctor, would you take a look at this?" Ben reached for the pillow, turned it over and presented it to the doctor as though it were a silver tray.

Dr. Renfro looked at it a moment in puzzlement,

then his eyes widened. "Hell," he whispered. "Must have rolled over in her sleep and couldn't roll back."

"Annabelle said she found her lying on her back with her hands folded. No struggle."

"Nothing else it could be. An old lady who was dying anyway. A locked house. Unless…" His eyes cut toward the open door.

"No way."

"As much as I like Annabelle, there is history, you know. She's done it before."

"No, dammit, she hasn't. That's gossip, and vicious gossip at that."

"We know very little about genetic predisposition, my boy."

"I knew I should have left it alone."

"We still can, you know. Mrs. Langley was terminal. Maybe Annabelle couldn't bear to see her in pain."

"If somebody smothered Mrs. Langley, Annabelle had no part in it."

"Then perhaps Jonas or Mrs. Mayhew."

"According to Annabelle, Beulah left the house before Mrs. Langley called her."

"Perhaps the EMTs got lipstick on the pillow. I'd much rather not order an autopsy, but in the circumstances it would be best." Dr. Renfro looked down at his patient sadly. "There were times I'd cheerfully have throttled her myself."

"But you didn't."

"No."

"Neither did Annabelle."

"If you say so." Dr. Renfro sighed. "I'll call the medical examiner's office and tell them we have one to transport. I'll go downstairs and tell Annabelle and then come back upstairs to wait until they show up. Unless you'd rather break the news to Annabelle.''

''I'll tell her. You go ahead and make the call to the M.E.'' He started for the bedroom door.

Behind him, he heard Dr. Renfro pick up the receiver and ask for the M.E.'s number. Then he called after Ben, ''I hope we're both wrong. For everyone's sakes.''

AFTER TEN MINUTES of carefully explaining what he and Renfro had discovered, Ben still wasn't certain Annabelle completely understood. She sat at the kitchen table, both her hands in his. Hers felt icy despite the brandy.

She kept shaking her head. ''Grandmere didn't struggle. She just went to sleep.'' She looked up at Ben. ''Nobody even knew she was alone but me. She was fine when I spoke to her, and I wasn't more than thirty minutes getting here. That's when I found her.''

''You're certain she was dead?''

''Yes, although I did CPR on her until the EMTs got here.''

''She was lying like that, quietly on her back?''
Annabelle nodded.

''Was the house locked when you came in?''

''The back door was locked. I never checked the front. Nobody uses it, anyway.''

''Stay here.'' He was already on his way to the front door. The big, seldom-used door was not only locked but chained. Damn.

Once he notified the police about the suspicious

death, they'd send someone back to secure Mrs. Langley's bedroom. But Ben had a little leeway before he had to make that call.

He went from room to room downstairs, turning on the dim lights as he went. Nothing seemed to have been disturbed. No obvious signs of burglary. Dust kittens sat in the corners and cobwebs festooned the ornate ceiling molding.

The solarium on this floor was the twin of Mrs. Langley's solarium above, surrounded on three sides by floor-to-ceiling windows that could be cranked open on pleasant days.

Dust lay thick on the sills of every window except the last one in the corner by the wall. That sill looked as though it had been freshly cleaned. Using his handkerchief, he shoved the window. It moved silently outward without his touching the crank and opened more than wide enough for someone to slip in.

He shone his penlight outside, hoping for a footprint in a flower bed. Instead he found a flagstone path swept clean of leaves. Mr. Jonas was much too neat. He bent close to the latch and saw faint scratches, as though someone might possibly have used a screwdriver or even a nail file to open it. Easy. A child could do it.

So someone could have come in from outside. A burglary that just happened to take place while Mrs. Langley was alone? That was stretching coincidence too far. But why would somebody kill the old lady now? She'd be gone in another few months.

Only one possible reason. Ben had been stirring up Chantal's murder case. Maybe someone was afraid that since she knew she was dying, Mrs. Langley might reveal secrets she'd never told in all these years. So that person had taken matters into his or her own hands?

Ben shut the door to the room behind him so that no one would disturb what he'd found.

If the autopsy proved Mrs. Langley had been smothered by person or persons unknown, Annabelle might need the evidence of a possible intruder to show that she was innocent. He felt the flesh on the nape of his neck creep. He was already thinking as though this was a murder case in which the woman he loved would be a suspect. Again.

And guess who'd done it to her? Again. The Jackson family seemed fated to act as nemesis to the Langley family. Somehow he had to make Annabelle understand fully why he couldn't simply let Mrs. Langley's death fall through the cracks. He did not have the right to make that choice. No one did.

As he pushed through the swinging door to the pantry, he heard voices.

Annabelle sobbed against the broad chest of a man with shaggy gray hair and a full beard. The man turned to stare at Ben through hazel eyes filled with something akin to hate.

"This your doing?" the man asked.

Annabelle sniffled, ran her fingertips across her cheeks under her eyes and shook her head. "It's not his fault, Jonas. He had to do what he thought was right."

So this was Jonas. One of the few people with keys to the house. Much better, however, to leave hints that a stranger had entered through a window.

Jonas made no offer to shake hands, but kept his arm around Annabelle's shoulders, holding her against him as though to shield her from Ben.

He was Ben's height, six foot two, and held himself as erect as a four-star general. His hands were large and heavily callused—a real workman's hands attached to heavy-muscled arms. He must be in his fifties, although he had the broad sloping shoulders of a weight lifter and the narrow waist and trim hips of a runner.

His face was lined and sun-bronzed. His nose had been broken and badly reset. A white scar bisected his left eyebrow and ran down over his cheek to disappear into the beard.

Ben glanced at the man's hands and wrists. No scratches. But he had no reason to believe that Mrs. Langley's broken fingernail meant she'd tried to fight off an attacker. Besides, Jonas's alibi would probably check out, more's the pity.

"What happens now?" Jonas asked.

"I call the cops, and Renfro waits upstairs until they secure the bedroom. If the M.E. finds suspicious circumstances, then tomorrow the homicide detectives will want to interview everyone about their whereabouts tonight."

Jonas smiled down at Annabelle. When he looked at her, his whole face lit. "It's going to be okay, honey. We don't even know there's anything to worry about yet. Get on over to my place and wait for me. I want to speak to Mr. Jackson here for a moment."

He loves her, Ben thought. *And he dislikes me intensely.*

"Annabelle?" Ben's voice sounded anguished even to his own ears.

"I'll be fine. I...I need to be alone a few minutes anyway." She left without a backward glance. Her back was stiff and straight, her head high.

"You know what they'll put her through?" Jonas snarled the moment the back door shut. "Wait'll the press gets ahold of this."

"I'm sorry, but I'm an officer of the law."

"Screw the law. People matter, not law."

"Yes, people matter. They have the right not to be murdered in their beds. There's such a thing as justice."

"Oh, that's rare, that is. Justice. You come from a long line of men who care about justice, don't you?"

Ben took a deep breath. Much more of this and he would deck the man. Who could probably beat the crap out of him. "Where were you this evening, Jonas?"

"Oh-ho, the butler did it." Jonas laughed. "Forget it. First off, I'm only an occasional butler. Plus, I got a roomful of professional landscape designers will swear I came in to the meeting at six forty-five and didn't leave until twenty minutes ago."

"We'll check as a formality. Glad you're excluded." He wasn't. The more suspects the better. "Do you know how to get in touch with Mrs. Mayhew? She shouldn't have to walk in on this."

"Ought to be back in half an hour or so. Count her out, too. She was running out to her car in the back when I left for my meeting."

"We'll check."

"Those goons from Homicide will check, you mean," Jonas said. "You don't know for sure somebody killed her."

"No, but there are enough signs to make an autopsy appropriate."

"If someone had a hand in her death, it's somebody she drove to it in her lifetime. Her death leaves Annabelle free to go back to New York where she belongs and make a life for herself far away from this place."

"You've just provided Annabelle a great motive."

"Annabelle was quite prepared to stay for six months or more," Jonas retorted. "However long her grandmother lived."

"Unless she had some special reason to want to leave now. I don't want to think I could be that reason."

"Well, you are opening up the old Langley case."

"What do you know about it?"

"What everybody has said through the years." Jonas drove his hand through his shaggy hair. "Man, you have a real talent for opening cans of worms. Don't they give you enough to do?"

"You're not the only one who feels that way. In the long run I think I can help Annabelle. Secrets hurt."

"Crap. You want her name cleared so she'll be a political asset rather than a liability." Jonas smiled wolfishly. "She tells me a lot. Ought to be able to finance your campaign chest single-handed now that the old lady's dead. Annabelle will be rich. How about that for a motive? Where were *you* tonight, Counselor?"

"Having dinner with witnesses. Do me a favor, Jonas. Don't mention that old case to the detectives if they show up tomorrow. I'll wait here for the police and then I'll take Annabelle home."

He pulled out a card and quickly wrote a name and number on the back of it. "This is a defense attorney who hates my guts. Call him first thing tomorrow for her. If the detectives want to question Annabelle, tell her to say, 'I want a lawyer present before I answer any questions.' Got that?"

"A lawyer? Great. You tell her."

"I intend to, but she seems to listen to you."

"She won't say a word to the cops without a lawyer, even if I have to sit on her. You available to represent her?"

"Unfortunately, no."

"Might be lucky. Your father didn't do such a great job, did he?" Jonas took the card and looked down at the name. He seemed to relent slightly. "Thanks for this."

"I'll take her home after the cops come."

"You get in trouble if you do?"

"At this point, I don't give a damn."

"DON'T SAY another word about tonight to me either," Ben said to Annabelle on the ride home. "If the cops question you, don't even give them your name without a lawyer present. They'll be very sympathetic and say you don't need a lawyer if you're innocent. Don't believe that for a second."

"But—"

"What we said earlier could be called off the record, but I might be called as a witness or deposed. I certainly will not be assigned to this case. I'm too close. Anything you tell me from this point on, I'd have to divulge.''

"Divulge all you like, Ben. I killed her.''

"Annabelle!''

"If I hadn't had to change that damn flat tire, she wouldn't have been alone. I could have saved her if I'd gotten there sooner.''

"What flat tire?''

"I picked up a roofing nail somewhere. Lord knows where.'' She reached into her purse and pulled out the broad-headed aluminum nail. "Exhibit A. It's a miracle I didn't have a blowout. It went flat in your mother's backyard.''

"Did you call a garage?''

"I changed the tire myself. I'm driving around on one of those little-bitty spares.''

"Where's the tire?''

"In my trunk. Where else would I put it?''

"Yeah.''

"Poor Mrs. Mayhew. She was so upset.''

"Uh-huh,'' Ben said absently.

"She must have been terrified this afternoon when she got that call from the emergency room. She dotes on her grandbabies.''

"She says she was too upset to remember the voice.'' He pointed to her lap. "That roofing nail may not have gotten into your tire by accident. Maybe somebody wanted you out of the way. I don't know many women who can change a tire by themselves.''

"That's too crazy. I refuse to believe anybody did this to me.''

Fine. Let her think that for the moment, Ben thought.

"I certainly don't blame Mrs. Mayhew for staying over for dinner once she found her grandson wasn't in the emergency room with a broken leg after all," Annabelle continued. "I would have, in her place. She assumed I was with Grandmere." She turned her face to the window. "I should have been. I'll never forgive myself."

"You may not be the one who needs forgiveness."

"What?"

He put a hand on her knee. "Sorry. I know you're exhausted. Jonas and I agreed you shouldn't be alone tonight. I'll bed down on the couch at your place."

"Elizabeth is twenty steps away."

"Not the same thing. Don't fight me, I'm staying. I'll take you to pick up your car tomorrow morning." He pulled up in Elizabeth's backyard and switched off the engine. "Come on, time for bed."

The light over his mother's back door came on, and he groaned as Elizabeth trotted over to the car.

"I'm so sorry, Annabelle. Can I get you some hot chocolate? A brandy?"

"I'm just so tired." Annabelle sounded close to tears again.

"Of course you are. Ben, take this child upstairs, put her to bed, and don't you dare leave her."

"Yes, Mother."

"I mean, leave her in the bed, not…oh, you know what I mean." She turned on her toe and went back in the house.

"That's the first smile I've had in what seems like days," Annabelle said.

"Want me to carry you?"

She simply raised an eyebrow and climbed the stairs to her apartment.

"IT'S NOT EVEN MIDNIGHT," Annabelle said as she dumped bedclothes onto the couch in her living room. "I ought to call Vickie in New York, and the funeral home and—"

"Stop." Ben took her hands and pulled her down onto the sofa. She resisted. "I'm so sorry."

"You had to…"

"No. Sorry Mrs. Langley's dead. I know you loved her."

Resistance melted and she clung to him, sobbing as she had earlier on Jonas's chest. "I did love her. I hated her, but some part of me loved her. And she was all I had. There's nobody left."

"There's Jonas." He stroked her hair.

"He may not even want to stay. Anyway, the house may have to be sold. And the gardens."

"Don't take your fences early." Suddenly he sat bolt upright. The letter! Mrs. Langley's letter of instructions. And the box! Would he be free to open it now?

"What is it?"

Heart pounding, he lay back on the couch. Part of him longed to go straight to his apartment and rip the box open. But it would keep. Tonight was all Annabelle.

She needed him now. And that was a better feeling than he could ever remember having.

A few minutes later he felt her relax. Her breathing became slow and regular. Her eyes closed. The long, dark lashes brushed her cheeks. She sighed and wriggled deeper against his chest. He brushed his lips across her damp forehead. He wished he could hold her this way forever, keep her safe in his arms away from anything and anyone who would hurt her.

He hadn't felt this protective since Judy died. The women he picked didn't need his protection. He'd chosen them because they were self-sufficient, never made demands on him, never sought emotional support. He could walk away without a moment's guilt.

Gently he slid his hands under her and managed to struggle to his feet without disturbing her too much.

This always looked so easy in the movies.

He carried her to her bedroom and knelt to lay her on the bed.

As he did, her eyes opened, and she caught her breath.

"It's okay, get some sleep," he whispered.

She caught his hand. "Don't go."

"I'll be right outside."

"No. Here. Stay here."

"I'm not sure that's a good idea."

She raised herself on her elbows. "I'm not offering a repeat of the other night. I'm asking you to stay here because I don't want to be alone. You on your side, me on mine. Please. At least until I can get to sleep. Then you can go home or out to the couch."

She had no idea what she was asking of him. He closed his eyes. "Sure."

"Thanks." She rolled onto her side. He covered her with the duvet, slipped off his shoes and tie, undid the top button of his shirt and unbuckled his belt.

He stretched out on the far side of the bed and crossed his arms over his stomach.

This wasn't precisely the way he'd envisioned taking Annabelle back to bed. At the moment, what she needed from him was comfort. His body, however, had the morals of a bull elk in October. Remembered passion might be sweet, but not nearly as heady as the passion of the moment. He moved onto his side so that his back was to her. Once he was certain she was asleep, he'd move to the couch.

"Ben?"

"Yes?"

"Will they arrest me for murder?"

He caught his breath, turned, wrapped his arms around her and pulled her into him so that she fit against him like a spoon. He could feel her shivering. "Not if I can help it."

"It's logical," she continued. "There's only my word that I found her…dead…. How long does it take to smother somebody?"

He pulled himself up on one elbow. "We don't know she was smothered."

She rolled onto her back and looked up into his face. "You think she was, don't you?"

"I don't know."

"Why would anybody do that?"

"I don't know that either." He closed his eyes and raised his head. "No matter what I do, it turns out wrong. I wish I hadn't stayed in her room to check things out. I should have simply let Dr. Renfro sign the certificate."

She sat up and wrapped her arms around him. "No! I know you couldn't do that. Besides, if somebody did…kill her…they ought to pay for it, shouldn't they?''

He lay down again with her still against him. ''Not if it hurts you.''

She sighed deeply. ''You won't let that happen.'' The end of the sentence slurred a little as she slid into exhausted sleep.

Could he prevent the hurt? She trusted him, needed him. He wasn't certain he was up to the job.

CHAPTER THIRTEEN

ANNABELLE WAS CERTAIN that the fiery dream would come tonight, but if it did, she was too deep in sleep to remember it when she awakened.

She woke because she was burning up. She fought her way to the surface, and realized with a start that she lay hard up against Ben's back with her arm thrown across his hip. No wonder she was hot— Ben's body was like a furnace.

Ben's body. For a moment she wished that he were truly unconscious because she wanted to touch him, to run her hands along the hard muscles of his shoulders, over his chest, down his belly. She wanted to explore how he felt when he was relaxed. Wanted to know every inch of him.

She felt her breathing quicken and her nipples swell. From just the thought of him? Did most women react that way? Did they feel that pleasurable ache between the legs that made her long to have him touch her, invade her once again?

Obviously Momma had, at least from the stories Grandmere told of her liaisons.

In the ordinary course of her life, Annabelle did not touch men except to adjust a collar or a shoulder seam on one of the gorgeous male models she occasionally worked with. Definitely not a sexual experience for either of them.

This was different. Instant arousal. Match to the flame—all the clichés Vickie had fed her on their long evenings together when Vickie had tried to convince her that she should get out more, date more, become a woman of the world.

A woman of the world was the last thing she wanted to be. It would have been nice to be a wife, assuming she could have kept her career going at the same time, but if her genes were any criterion, she was likely to be as round-heeled as Momma. She was certainly no lady, not the way she felt about touching Ben.

He deserved better.

Ben stirred sleepily, captured her hand and pulled it across his chest. Great. Now what was she supposed to do? Lie here all night and literally stew in her own juices?

She began gently and almost without breathing to work her hand out of his grasp.

She was nearly free when he woke so quickly and so completely that she yipped in surprise.

He turned over and slipped his arms around her. "What time is it?"

"Almost morning, I think."

"Lovely way to wake up." He nuzzled her throat.

"Ben…"

He stopped her with a kiss.

She wasn't even certain he knew where he was or who *she* was, but the moment she felt his hips move against her she realized that if she'd had any idea of exploring him in a state of relaxation, she could forget about it. Ben was long past that.

And so was she. All her good intentions to be a lady went out the window in a fever of longing.

Her only conscious thought was that if her wantonness bothered Ben, he gave no sign of it.

And then she abandoned herself to sensation.

This time there was no pain, only pleasure in such waves that at one point she seemed to merge into Ben and he into her. She wanted the waves to break indefinitely.

At last she got her chance to explore his body to her heart's content until her explorations with tongue and fingertips aroused him again. This time he pulled her on top of him.

Afterward he held her naked and sweating in his arms. "Ben, I'm so sorry, I didn't mean—"

"Sorry?" He kissed her hair. He ran a hand over his forehead to get his own hair out of his eyes. "You, my sweet, are a very fast learner."

What did that mean? She stiffened and slipped off the bed. "I've got to get started, Ben. I have a million things to do today."

"It's only five-thirty in the morning. Come back to bed."

"You'd better go home."

"My mother knows I was spending the night here."

"Don't you have court today?"

He sat up. "Hell, yes!" He swung out of bed.

He *was* beautiful. And she was vulnerable. That explained last night. It would not happen again. From here on in, she'd keep him at arm's length.

Those arms wrapped around her. "Don't worry about your grandmother. It'll be all right."

She pulled away from him. Her longing for Ben had been simple need for human touch, human warmth, an affirmation of life in the midst of death. Nothing more.

"I've got to get ready for the day, Ben. Goodbye. Thanks for staying." Talk about a stupid remark! She bolted into the bathroom and slammed the door.

On the other side of it, Ben said, "We could share the shower."

"Go away, Ben." She leaned her forehead against the mirror.

"I'll call you later."

"Thanks." She turned on the shower. Did her face in the mirror show the stigmata of her wild night of sex? No big red A on her chest, but her eyes were glowing even after her bout of tears last night.

She caught her breath. She had cried, actually cried real tears. She didn't remember ever shedding a single tear. Yet for Grandmere, she'd cried.

Or had she cried out of fear that she'd be in trouble. Would the police say she'd killed Grandmere?

And how on earth could she have forgotten about her grandmother? Did sex actually override every other emotion, every conscious thought?

Apparently for Annabelle Langley it did. Maybe she was more like her mother than she wanted to believe.

"DON'T WE HAVE ENOUGH to do already?" Phil Mainwaring sounded annoyed. "You pull an autopsy because of a broken fingernail?"

"More than that."

"The M.E. faxed the results of Victoria Langley's autopsy just after lunch. Read 'em and weep, Counselor." Phil flipped two sheets of paper across his desk. Ben leaned forward to pick them up. He didn't really want to see what he'd started, but he had no choice.

"Inconclusive? What the hell does that mean?"

"It means inconclusive," Mainwaring said as though he were explaining the word to a six-year-old. "The old lady may have been smothered—there are signs that might indicate she was—but whether that killed her or whether she died of the heart attack that happened concurrently, it is impossible to tell." Mainwaring leaned back in his chair and templed his fingers. "Moreover, did somebody else have a hand in smothering her, or was it an accident because she was in the throes of a heart attack?"

"The M.E. can't nail it down any better than that?"

"Apparently not. So, Counselor, what do you suggest we do? Send Homicide on a wild-goose chase? Waste the taxpayers' dollars?"

Ben leaned forward with his elbows on his knees, the two sheets of faxed paper dangling from his fingers. "If somebody smothered her, it's murder, even though she was old and had a heart problem."

"I agree. You going to ask for a bench warrant to pick up your girlfriend or you want me to do it?"

"What?"

"She's the obvious suspect. Hell, she's the only suspect."

"There was evidence somebody got in from out-side."

"An unlocked window? A dusted windowsill? Easy enough to fake that from inside."

"Annabelle found her dead."

"So she says."

"She's not a killer."

"So she says."

"Damnation, Phil..." Ben surged to his feet.

Mainwaring put his hands up and patted the air. "Relax, Ben. I don't think she did it. As a matter of fact, I don't think anybody did it."

"But—"

"And if someone did, what do you think are the chances we'll ever find out who? Or if by some miracle we do, what are our chances of building a case that we can take to trial?"

Ben subsided. "Somewhere between no-how and no-way, I'd say."

Mainwaring nodded. "You got it, grasshopper."

"What do you want to do about it?"

Mainwaring shrugged. "Toss it into the cold-case files. Who knows, maybe five years from now some notorious felon will add Victoria Langley to his confession."

"Nothing else?"

"Let the family know they can have the body picked up and schedule the funeral." He smiled at Ben. "Don't look so depressed. We work the cases that we can reasonably expect to win. Is that not Mainwaring's First Rule of Prosecution?"

"Yeah. You're right."

Mainwaring stood up and came around the desk to

clap his hand on Ben's shoulder. "We live in the real world. It is not perfect. We do the best we can."

Ben nodded.

"Take comfort in the fact that you nailed that little bastard MacCauley's hide to the wall this morning. He's not going to be out of jail until the third millennium, if I know the judge who's going to sentence him. See what happens when you fight cases you can win?"

"JONAS, I've asked Beulah Mayhew to stay on and help get this house ready for Grandmere's funeral," Annabelle said.

"Good idea, but you're going to need more than Mrs. Mayhew, tough as she is. I can do some of the heavy work, but I'm no house cleaner."

"I wouldn't ask you to. I'm getting in a cleaning team first thing tomorrow morning. While I'm running around making arrangements for the funeral, Mrs. Mayhew can supervise. The cleaners are bonded, but I'll feel better if she's here."

"When are you having the funeral?"

"As quickly as possible, don't you think? I thought maybe tomorrow afternoon. I'll order the food."

"People will send food."

"There aren't many people her age left to send food. It won't be enough."

"Enough for what?"

"For afterward, of course. Jonas, you know the way these things work. People will expect to come by the house afterward. With the publicity and

Grandmere's social standing, we could have a crowd. We have to have coffee and a buffet for everyone.''

''Here?''

''Where else? You don't mind serving, do you?''

He drew himself up. ''As a matter of fact, I do.''

Her face fell. ''Please, Jonas. I know it's an imposition, but there just isn't anybody else I can count on.''

''What about the caterer's people?''

''All they do is put the stuff out and leave. You really don't have to do anything except make certain there are clean glasses on the bar, cups on the buffet, and the coffeepot is full. Please, Jonas, don't you desert me too. I don't think I can handle much more.''

His face softened. ''I'm sorry. You took me by surprise.''

She relaxed and hugged his waist. ''Thank you. And of course you'll be a pallbearer.''

''I will not.''

''Jonas, you were about her only friend, and closer than family. You have to be a pallbearer. I'm pulling teeth trying to get six men to carry her out to the hearse after the service and then up to the gravesite.''

''I am a gardener. I never was a friend.''

''Yes, you were. The two of you had a great relationship when you weren't screaming at one another.''

Once again he capitulated. ''Very well, Miss Langley.''

''Don't, Jonas, please.''

''What about that interfering nincompoop you've fallen for? Is he going to be a pallbearer?''

"He's not a nincompoop. He was just trying to do his job. And he is going to be a pallbearer, though I haven't told him yet."

"Nincompoop, I say." He patted her head. "And I'll call him worse than that if this autopsy business blows up in our faces."

"It won't."

"Her obituary comes out tomorrow morning. Then we'll see."

The telephone rang. Annabelle jumped.

Jonas frowned at her and got his hand on the receiver before she could touch it. "Langley residence. May I tell her who's calling?" He handed the telephone to Annabelle and whispered, "Says he's her lawyer."

Annabelle nodded and took the telephone. "Yes? Of course. I'll be here." She glanced at Jonas in panic. "Fifteen minutes? Sure. Better to get these things over with as quickly as possible."

She hung up the telephone. "Grab a dust rag and throw me one. That lawyer's on his way over. I will not have him think we let this place fall down around our ears." She rolled off a dozen sheets from the paper towels that hung above the sink. "If you'll knock the spiderwebs off the chandelier in the front hall, I'll dust the tables in the living room. He doesn't have to see any more than that."

Five minutes later, Jonas stuck the handle of the feather duster into his back pocket. "Does the chandelier meet with your approval, madam?"

She rubbed her nose and left a streak of dust on its tip. "Have to do. If we keep the lights low, maybe he won't notice."

"Come here." Jonas pulled her over to him, took a sheet of paper towel from his hip pocket and scrubbed her nose. "You always were a snotty little kid."

"Thanks." She smiled at him. "Do you have any idea why we've got this junior partner coming over? Whatever happened to Foster Gray, Esquire?"

Jonas shrugged. "Died, I suppose. He must have been a hundred."

The doorbell rang. "Oh, Lord. Don't you dare leave me alone with this guy for one minute, you got that?"

He inclined his head gravely. "As madam commands."

She hit him on the shoulder on his way to answer the door.

Ten minutes later Foster Gray the Third squared the creases in his perfectly cut navy suit for the umpty-umpth time and cleared his throat again. His perfectly cut auburn hair, which Annabelle would swear was touched up, was bent over the legal document in his lap.

"Can't we just skip all the whereases?" Annabelle asked.

Young Mr. Foster flashed her a brilliant smile that had probably cost his father a pretty penny in orthodonture. "We're nearly there."

Annabelle raised her eyebrows at Jonas, who stood in the archway like a member of the praetorian guard.

"All right, you understand that you are to serve as executrix without bond, which means you agree to carry out the terms of this will?"

"Yes, yes."

"Fine. Now to the bequests. First, you, Annabelle Chantal Langley, are to receive one million dollars in trust to be administered by...there's a series of trust stuff here you probably don't give a damn about."

So he was human after all.

"You don't get the principal until you marry or turn forty, whichever comes first."

Annabelle smiled. "Well, Grandmere obviously wanted me to have a long wait. Did she have that kind of money?"

"You bet."

"What about Jonas?"

"She leaves him ten thousand dollars outright, and tenancy of his apartment rent free, and a free hand in the gardens for as long as he chooses to stay and the gardens remain intact."

"That's all?" She jumped up. "Don't you worry, Jonas. There's got to be enough income in the trust to get you started in your landscaping business. We'll work it out."

He nodded and pushed her gently back toward her chair. "We'll talk later."

"But—"

"Annabelle." His tone was a warning.

"Oh, all right."

When she was seated again, Young Foster cleared his throat and continued, "As for the rest of the estate... Everything, the house, the grounds, all her personal possessions, go outright to Raymond Horatio Langley, her son." He grimaced. "If we can find him."

"My father?"

"I'm afraid so."

"Jonas, for God's sake, tell him. *Somebody* tell him."

Jonas didn't move from his position, but he cleared his throat. "Mr. Raymond Langley may well be dead."

"That does present problems."

"I'd say that," Annabelle cooed.

"But not to worry. She made provisions." The lawyer read silently for a moment. "Ah, basically, the will states that if Raymond Horatio Langley has not been found within seven years, or if it is proved he predeceased his mother, then the portion of the estate that should have gone to him will be sold, and the proceeds divided equally free and clear between her granddaughter—that's you—and her loyal gardener, Jonas Arkwright."

"Seven years?" Annabelle shouted.

"Quiet, Miss Annabelle."

She turned to him. "That's wicked, Jonas. Vicious! I don't give a damn about me, but you…"

He shook his head. "Not now." He scowled at Young Foster, who was watching the interplay avidly.

"Don't worry," Foster continued. "She says that while the search for her son is going on, things are to continue precisely as they have been—Jonas is to receive his usual salary plus an annual raise of ten percent so long as he stays in the apartment and looks after the grounds as he has done in the past." He beamed at Jonas. "She did not intend to throw you out on the street, Mr. Arkwright."

Annabelle started to speak, but Jonas glared at her.

Foster cleared his throat. "Ah, and there is a single codicil, added just last week," he said. "Rather peculiar. I must admit I didn't understand it at the time. We have always acted for the Langleys in such matters."

"Just tell us what the codicil says, Mr. Gray." Annabelle asked.

"She has added a coexecutor to serve without bond with you, Miss Annabelle." He looked up, bewildered. "Nothing wrong with that. I mean he's a great guy, but I don't know why she picked him."

Annabelle felt her heart flip. "Just...tell...me...his...name."

"Old college buddy of mine. Ben Jackson. He's an A.D.A."

"I'LL CONTEST the will. What's the point of waiting seven years *not* to find my father," Annabelle said. Jonas sat in one of the wing chairs with his feet on the coffee table in front of him. Annabelle paced the room.

"No, you won't." He took a swig from the bottle of beer in his hand. "It says if you contest and lose, you lose all rights to your inheritance."

"I don't care about my inheritance! I make good money in New York and I'll make better. She cannot do this to *you!*"

"That's my call, not yours. And I forbid you to contest."

"Jonas, how can you sit there so calmly? She's turned you into an indentured servant for seven years while we hunt for my father."

"Maybe we'll discover he really is dead."

"Oh, great. Then you get enough money to start your own landscaping business but you lose your gardens. You've spent your whole life making these gardens live."

"Not my whole life. Things grow, they mature, and eventually they die. No big deal."

"Okay. Here's another plan. First thing tomorrow we check how much income that trust will give me annually. Then we use it to get a business loan—make me a partner, if you want to. You can start your landscaping business."

"We'll see."

She kicked at his foot. "How can you be so calm?"

"I've learned to be patient."

"Well, I haven't. I can't believe Ben Jackson's my coexecutor!" She yanked her hair back from her temples. "He does not need another excuse to bug me."

"We'll buy a fax machine. Then you can fax one another."

She narrowed her eyes at him.

"Well, if you really don't want to see him in person…" He lifted his glass in silent salute.

She began to chortle. He shrugged and grinned back. In a moment they were both laughing. Annabelle could hear an edge of hysteria in her voice.

"What's so funny?"

Ben Jackson stood in the doorway. "The door was open. I hope you don't mind."

Annabelle pointed at Ben, looked at Jonas, and burst into laughter again.

"My fly unzipped?"

That made it worse.

"Uh—what am I missing here?" Ben sounded uncomfortable.

Annabelle pointed at him, tried to cut off her laughter, then started all over again.

Finally, as she was gulping her way quiet, Jonas said solemnly, "Mrs. Langley has unwittingly bestowed upon us the gift of laughter, sir. At your expense, I fear. You seem to be the icing on Miss Annabelle's proverbial cake."

That did it. By the time the pair of them settled down, Ben had gotten himself a beer and come back to join them.

"I'm sure wherever she is, that makes her very happy," Ben said solemnly.

Annabelle snickered, but clapped her hands over her mouth.

"Now, if you two are through with your celestial send-off, I've got news."

That sobered them. Jonas's feet came off the coffee table with a thump. Annabelle sat up and reached for his hand. He took it and held it hard.

"Hey, it's all right."

"She wasn't smothered?" Jonas asked.

"We're not sure. And since we're not sure, we're not going to pursue it. It'll go down in the cold cases as a possible suspicious death."

"And the newspapers?" Jonas asked.

"Nobody has to know anything except that she died in her sleep."

"Thank God."

Annabelle started to cry. "What's wrong with me? I've never been able to cry."

"Don't knock it," Ben said, and moved to the sofa

to put his arm around her. "Be grateful that you have feelings to let out."

"Indeed, sir," Jonas said, and released her hand. "I'll leave you alone if I may. I want to check on my azaleas before dinner."

CHAPTER FOURTEEN

BEN PICKED UP the memo from the Parole Board.

The only reason Mrs. Langley could possibly have had for adding Ben's name as coexecutor of her estate was because she thought he could find the long lost Raymond Langley. He hoped he wouldn't fail her.

He knew from past experience that people on parole disappeared every day. They simply vanished until they committed another crime, fingerprints were checked with the FBI's data base, and bingo, the old name and status as a paroled felon popped up.

Ray Langley had disappeared the moment he got out of jail—at least according to Mrs. Langley.

But his parole records were right in front of Ben. Raymond Langley had religiously reported to his Shelby County Parole Officer every week until he was discharged at the end of his sentence. He had, so far as anyone could tell, never committed another crime.

Then, the day he got off parole, he vanished. As he had every right to do.

If he were living quietly in another state with another identity, another driver's license, he could be impossible to trace, even if he were alive. If he were dead... Ben didn't even like to think about the problems.

He put down the memo and read the instructions in Mrs. Langley's letter for the twentieth time.

"No one is to know about the box until after my funeral." Okay. That he could handle. It was the rest of the stipulations that made him crazy. He stared up at the box. Why not just open the damn thing? Nobody'd ever know. If Beulah Mayhew ever asked him, he'd lie. She probably wouldn't ask, however. She might not even come to the funeral this afternoon.

So far he was batting a thousand on helping Annabelle. Whatever he did made things worse. He ought to burn the damn box or toss it into the Dumpster on his way out.

He knew he wouldn't. He'd at least make an attempt, however vain, however limited, to carry out Mrs. Langley's wishes.

He'd already partially failed her. He knew in his heart that someone had killed Mrs. Langley. It smelt like murder. His buddies in Homicide always said he had a nose for it. That had always given him kind of a sense of pride in the past. Now he wished he'd developed a nose for perfume instead.

He shoved the blankets back in front of that blasted box, stuck Mrs. Langley's letter of instruction in his breast pocket and ran a comb through his hair one last time. He hated serving as a pallbearer. He only hoped he didn't let the old lady slip down the steps of the church.

THE CHURCH WAS FULLER than Ben would have imagined possible, although a good many of the attendees were on walkers and in wheelchairs. The church blazed with flowers. He sat behind Annabelle and a tall, painfully thin young woman in sunglasses who wore a black silk sheath that raised his mother's eyebrows in approval.

He didn't need to be introduced to know this must be Vickie, the New York roommate.

Dr. Renfro and the other pallbearers sat on Ben's row. Jonas slipped in at the far end after the service had started, and kept his head down throughout. Maybe he really did miss the old girl. A couple of times when Ben looked at him, he seemed to be genuinely moved.

Ben tried to speak to Annabelle at the graveside, but she was surrounded by mourners. He gave up and followed Jonas back to the limousine that had brought them from the funeral home.

"That girl staying at the house?" Ben asked.

"Miss Vickie is not staying. I believe she is catching an afternoon flight back to Manhattan."

"Ah." Ben relaxed. One afternoon wouldn't give Vickie enough time to persuade Annabelle to return to New York, would it? He had a grace period to convince Annabelle to stay in Memphis until the will was admitted to probate. By that time maybe she'd have given in and consented to at least an engagement.

At the house, Jonas went immediately to the kitchen. "Would you mind opening the door when people arrive, sir?" he asked. "I'm going to have my hands full getting the food and drink ready."

"Sure."

Again, the number of people who called at the house staggered him. The Langley name must still mean something even after Mrs. Langley's years as a recluse. As was the way with such gatherings, this one turned into a real party—old friends who liked but seldom saw one another bringing each other up to date on their lives. Mrs. Langley might be the occasion for the party, but she was definitely not the main topic of discussion.

Phil Mainwaring escorted Ben's mother, who also wore a simple black dress and pearls—almost the twin of the one Annabelle was wearing. And Vickie, for that matter. Amazing how different clothes looked on different women.

Annabelle had coerced her hair into a severe roll on the back of her head, but she managed to look as though she was going to throw off her shoes and run barefoot through the roses any minute. God, he wanted her. She was all he thought about these days.

"Ben, stop drooling," his mother whispered.

He wiped his chin. "I am not drooling."

"Metaphorically. The look on your face is unmistakable. Watch it."

The doorbell rang for the twentieth time. Ben was too far away to answer it, but Jonas was passing by with a tray of empty wineglasses. He set the tray down and opened the door. "Good afternoon, Dr. Renfro," he said, and went about his business.

Ben's mother's eyes widened.

"What is it?" he said. "Have I got clam dip on my lapel or something?"

Elizabeth turned and watched Jonas push through

the door into the butler's pantry. "Who is that, Ben? One of the caterer's people?"

"That, Mother, is the famous Jonas, gardener extraordinaire."

"Ah. He came after my time. Don't suppose I've ever met him." She turned to Mainwaring, who was speaking to Councilman Adler. "Phil, dear, do you mind getting me another glass of wine the next time you go near the bar?"

"Sure."

"Elizabeth, you are, as always, the prettiest filly in the stable," Adler said, and kissed her cheek. "And how about our boy here, huh?" He clapped Ben on the shoulder. "Going to be the finest D.A. we've ever had."

"I resent that!" Mainwaring said.

"Present company excepted. You're going to be the best judge."

"Excuse me. This filly has to repair to the stable," Elizabeth said, and left the men together.

ANNABELLE SAW ELIZABETH slip through the doors into the butler's pantry. Probably looking for the bathroom. Annabelle sauntered after her, hoping that no one would stop her. She had to get away from these people if only for a minute. Her head was beginning to throb.

"Hello, Ray."

Elizabeth's voice from the pantry floated out to Annabelle.

She froze with her hand on the outside of the pantry door.

"Madam?" Jonas's voice was even, unhurried, a little puzzled.

"Don't, Ray. That might work with everyone else, but not with me. I knew who you were the moment I heard your voice, before I so much as glanced at you. The hazel contact lenses are a nice touch. Don't they bother your eyes?"

"My name is Jonas Arkwright, madam. I'm afraid you have me confused with someone else."

"The silver tray you're holding has your finger-prints all over it. So does your apartment. So does this house, come to that. I can get Ben to check them against Ray Langley's prints, but why bother? I have enough old pictures of you from high school. Faces and bodies change, Ray. Ears don't."

Annabelle leaned against the door. She felt sick at her stomach, hot and cold at the same time.

The male voice sounded infinitely tired, but gentle. "I've tried to avoid you all day, Liz. I knew I'd screwed up the minute I opened my mouth in there."

"Why, Ray? Why the masquerade?"

Annabelle burst through the door. "Yes, why, Ray?" Her voice twisted over his name. "You can't be Ray. I've seen your pictures. I've known you for years." Her voice rose dangerously.

Elizabeth grabbed her arm. "Keep your voice down." She turned to the man Annabelle had always known as Jonas. "We'll get rid of everyone as quick as we can. Come along, Annabelle." She turned to Jonas. "Don't even dream of disappearing, Ray. Not now." She shook her finger at him. "Promise!"

He nodded. "Annabelle..." He reached out to her.

She fought her tears, turned on her heel and thrust through the baize door without a word.

Annabelle had no idea how she survived the next twenty minutes or what she said. People were kind, so she must have said appropriate things and sent them away with courtesy. She wanted to stand in the middle of her grandmother's living room and scream at them all to get the hell out.

"There." Elizabeth shut the door on Dr. and Mrs. Renfro. "The last of them. Go home, Phil. Ben will bring me later."

"What's happening?" Phil asked.

Elizabeth shook her head. "Later, darling. Estate business. Trust me." She kissed his cheek and shoved him toward the front door. He protested, but she kept shoving. Finally, he gave in.

"Call me later?"

"Of course, Phil."

"What is it, Mother?" Ben said the moment the front door closed on Phil Mainwaring's back. "What's happened now?"

"Sit down over there on the couch and keep your mouth shut. Hold on to Annabelle."

"I can't sit down," Annabelle said. "And I don't need anybody holding me."

"Okay."

"Mother, what are you up to?"

"Wait." Elizabeth shoved open the pantry door. "Get in here."

Jonas shambled into the living room. He'd aged a dozen years in twenty minutes. Underneath his tan, his face was gray, his eyes bleak.

"Benjamin Jackson, may I introduce to you Raymond Horatio Langley."

"What?" Ben was on his feet in an instant. "No way can this be Ray Langley."

"Prison changes a man," Langley said sadly.

"I'll say." He stared at Jonas. "I think you'd better start at the beginning."

Jonas turned to Annabelle, his hands raised in supplication. "I couldn't tell you, don't you see? I had to stay to protect you. To keep a barrier between the pair of you."

"A barrier? Protect me? From Grandmere?" She turned away in disgust.

Elizabeth stepped in almost casually. "The scar changes your face considerably. How on earth did you get it? You're lucky to have kept your eye."

He seemed grateful to be able to talk about the specifics of his appearance. "Another prisoner went after me with a homemade knife."

"And your beautiful nose? I always loved your nose. Very patrician. Now you look like a fighter who's lost too many bouts."

Jonas laughed shortly. "Broken three times. Once by a guard. Twice by prisoners who resented my friendship with the warden. Prison doctors don't pay too much attention to non-life-threatening problems like broken noses."

"The man I saw in the mug shots had narrow shoulders," Ben said. "He was skinny and hunched."

"I hope you never find out, young man, but one of the few privileges granted to prisoners is the use of weight-training equipment. I used it. Often. I had years to build my body. I needed to be strong in order to survive.'' He smiled sadly. ''I came out tan and fit in body, if not in spirit. They never broke me, but they came close until the warden took an interest in me. That's where I took landscaping courses. Redid the grounds for the entire prison. Makes a man tough.'' He looked down at his hands. ''These aren't banker's hands any longer.''

''How did you manage not to be recognized for all these years?'' Ben asked. ''You grew up in this town. With these people.''

''By staying away from the few people, like Elizabeth, who might recognize me even with the way I look now. Not so hard. Nobody looks at gardeners. I grew the beard, wore hats and sunglasses and kept my mouth shut. Until today. I tried to get out of being a pallbearer and serving at this reception, but I couldn't see any way to avoid it without hurting Annabelle.''

''Hurting Annabelle? You didn't want to hurt Annabelle? Why?'' Annabelle asked. ''Why did you have to lie in the first place?''

He reached out to her. She shrank back.

''I made a bargain with my mother. I needed to be here to watch over you, but the last thing I wanted was to expose you as the murderer's child whose father was home on parole from prison.''

''And she accepted that sort of devil's bargain?'' Ben asked. ''Her own son? Living as a servant? A gardener?''

Jonas walked to the fireplace and stared down into the bouquet of flowers on the hearth. ''I gave her no choice. At first she demanded I go back to the bank, but I refused. Before I went to prison she knew I wanted to quit banking, start my own landscaping business. That's what Chantal…'' He glanced at Annabelle, then squared his shoulders. ''That's what your mother and I argued most about. She didn't want to be married to a common laborer.''

''But you didn't start a business,'' Elizabeth said sadly.

''How could I, Liz? I had to stay away from people who had known me. They were the very people who could afford landscape designers. So my mother gave me the Langley gardens to do with what I liked, and swore to keep my identity secret.''

He raised his eyebrow and shrugged. ''I doubt she had difficulty keeping her mouth shut. She didn't want anyone to know I was her gardener either.''

''Why didn't you just take me away?'' Annabelle pulled him around to face her. ''You could have told me, and we could have gone somewhere together, somewhere nobody knew us. We could have started over. I would have had a real father, for God's sake.''

''The first seven years I was here, I was still on parole. I couldn't leave the area legally even if I'd wanted to. I couldn't simply disappear without becoming a wanted man again. If I was caught—and I would have been—I'd have been sent back to prison. What would have happened to you then? Besides, I had no money, no prospects, no fake identification. I'd have been lucky to get a job flipping burgers.''

''You think I would have cared about money?''

''I cared about the money *for you*.'' He tilted his head to look down at her. ''The best schools, a decent place to live…''

"Decent?" Annabelle's voice rose.

"She knew I was watching her."

"You took me to art classes. You bought me my first bike and my first roller skates and my first sewing machine. You taught me to drive. I *loved* you!"

He winced at her use of the past tense. "I love you now, then and forever, whatever you may think of what I did. I tried to be here for you always, when the kids were nasty to you at school, when she got on your case…"

"But you weren't there every minute. Not the time I was alone with Grandmere listening to her pour all that vitriol into my ears. I came to you, but I came to you as my friend, not as my father! Damn you, do you know how many times I fell asleep longing for my father? Just needing to know he was alive and not hurt or dead somewhere?"

"I couldn't tell you. I had to protect you."

"Protect me, or watch me? Make sure I wasn't turning into what Grandmere always feared?"

"Never."

"She told me. A week before she died, when Ben was here, she finally told me that you actually saw me kill my mother."

"What?" Jonas grabbed her shoulders and bent his knees so that he could look in her eyes. "I never said that, Annabelle."

"Why would she say it then?"

He wiped a hand across his forehead. "Maybe she'd come to believe it herself."

"What *did* you see?" Ben asked quietly.

Both Jonas and Annabelle jumped at the intrusion of a third person's voice.

Jonas glanced at Ben once, then walked over to stare out the front window at the gardens beyond. "I came home about midnight and found Chantal dead in front of the fireplace in a pool of blood. And Annabelle curled on the hassock sound asleep." He closed his eyes. "Cradling the gun against her chest." He felt behind him and sank onto one of the wing chairs. "I'm sorry."

Annabelle's face drained of color. "So it really is true. I did do it."

"No, it's not." Ben went to her. "I told you, you couldn't have shot her. You weren't tall enough."

She closed her eyes. "Unless I was standing on top of the hassock when I shot her."

"All in the past," Elizabeth said. The other three had forgotten she was in the room. "You did what you thought was right about Annabelle, Ray. Whether that was a good thing or not, I have no idea. But it's done. Annabelle, you love this man and he adores you. The fact that he is your father does not change that fact."

"Doesn't it?"

"No, it doesn't. He went to prison to protect you, and he has given up the possibility of a career to stay here and garden for his mother so he could watch over you."

"It's all been a lie."

"Not the love. Nor the caring." Elizabeth went to Ray, slipped her hand under his elbow and smiled up at him. "I never believed you killed her. I've never stopped wondering where you'd got to either. I, for one, am damn glad I've finally found you again." She added, without taking her eyes from Ray's face,

"He's a good man, whatever you may think now, Annabelle."

"With an excellent motive to kill his mother," Ben said.

"I have an alibi, remember?"

"You could have hired someone."

"Why now?"

"You told me yourself you wanted to free Annabelle to go back to New York, get her away from me and the reopening of the Langley case."

"Not guilty. Nor is Annabelle. And this time I won't roll over the way I did before. I'm not going back to prison for something I didn't do."

"She did it," Elizabeth said.

"What?" They all turned to her.

"Mrs. Langley. I've always believed she killed Chantal. She hated her enough. Look what happened. Suddenly Chantal is out of the picture, Ray is in prison, the case is closed, and little Annabelle is safely in the arms of her Grandmere to be molded into the perfect new Langley debutante."

"Only I didn't cooperate."

"No you didn't, thank God," Ben said. "Could that be why you blanked it out, Annabelle? You saw your grandmother shoot your mother?"

"I don't know."

"I may know how to find out. Sit down, people," Ben said. "I have a story to tell you."

They sat silent while he told them about Mrs. Langley's box. When he was finished, no one spoke for a moment, then Ray Langley said, "Burn it without opening it."

"What?" Annabelle gaped at him.

"I mean it. Burn the damn box. It's time she stopped manipulating our lives even from beyond the grave. If she wants it opened, then it means more trouble and pain for somebody. Burn it."

"Don't listen to him, Ben," Annabelle said. "Open the box. We need to know what's in it."

"There's one small problem," Ben said. "Mrs. Langley stipulates that the box be opened only in the presence of several people. You, Annabelle, my mother, Ray Langley...I thought he was going to be the tough one to locate...and one other person. My father."

"Oh, dear," Elizabeth said. "Hal would never fly all the way down here for that."

"Are you bound and determined to do this?" Ray asked.

"I just told you. My father..."

"Was standing in the back of the church during Mother's funeral," Ray said. "He came in late and left before the end of the service, but he was there. I'm not likely to forget his face, even with twenty years of wear on it."

CHAPTER FIFTEEN

"ARE YOU SURE you saw Hal?" Elizabeth asked Jonas.

"Positive. He looked like hell, frankly. Suit hung on him."

Elizabeth reached for the telephone on the side table, pulled off her pearl earring and dialed. "He may have called me at home and left a message." She waited, then punched her code and listened. After a moment she caught her breath and hung up the phone. "He's staying at the Hampton Inn on Poplar and wants me to call him there."

"Damn!" Ben said. "How long's he been there?"

"Darling, I am not psychic. Why not ask him?" She dialed the phone again and asked for Hal Jackson's room. "Hal?" Her voice sounded cool. She glanced at her son. "Of course. I'll pick you up in twenty minutes. I'm sure Ben will be happy you're in town as well."

Ben made a sound as his mother hung up.

"Well, aren't you? Happy, I mean? You don't have to drag him off that boat of his and pour him onto an airplane."

"Bring him to my apartment."

"After dinner."

"Mother..."

"I was married to the man. He holds no terrors for me." She stood and smoothed her dress. "Besides, if he really does look like hell, I may just gloat a little."

"If you're sure."

"I'm sure." She turned to Jonas. "Nine o'clock? Ben's apartment? And keep your temper?"

He nodded. "If I can."

She swept out.

"Do you want me to leave too?" Ben asked Annabelle.

"I don't want to be alone with him." She nodded at Jonas.

"Annabelle, you've known this man all your life."

"I have not. I have known *Jonas*. This man is a stranger." She turned to Jonas, who sat looking up at her as though he was afraid she'd strike him. "I'm sorry—I don't even know what to call you!"

"Call me Jonas."

"Fine. Would you care to join Ben and me for dinner?"

He smiled ruefully at her formal tone. "No thank you. Ben, I'll see you at nine."

"You won't run?"

"I haven't so far. Why should I now?"

"WHY DON'T WE PICK UP something and go to my place?" Ben asked. "You need to kick back. We both do."

"Ben, I want you to know how grateful I am for what you've done so far."

"Interfering, you mean?"

"It's all been with the best intentions."

"God, talk about a condemnation."

"I want you to know I'll always consider you a friend."

He slammed on his brakes and turned to her. "I don't want to be your friend. I want to be your lover, and eventually, I want to be your husband."

"Not going to happen. You knew that from the start."

"Things have changed."

"Not for me."

"You know you're not a killer."

"I don't know that, and even if I did, that's not the whole problem."

"Screw my career, if that's what you're worried about."

"You'll never understand."

"The only thing I could understand is that you don't want me. And you'll have a tough time convincing me of that."

"I can't talk about this tonight."

"So I'll feed you, then we'll talk. What do you fancy?"

"I want a very large steak in a very public restaurant, and then I want the biggest piece of chocolate cake you can find."

"Really? Can I take you to the club?"

"Not in this or any other lifetime. We've been through enough of that sort of thing at the Peabody."

He didn't press. Maybe he was learning after all. Annabelle ate her steak as though she hadn't been fed for days. She kept her eyes on her plate and said next to nothing to Ben, who watched her with awe as she downed the steak and trimmings, then finished chocolate cake, ice cream and the fresh kiwi fruit comfit. As he handed over his credit card to the waiter, she said, "Let me. I'm a rich woman, remember?"

"No way. I invited you." His cell phone rang. "Damn. Phil? Mother had a minor crisis. She should have called you… No, it's nothing for you to worry about. I'll tell her you're anxious about her…. I beg your pardon?" His eyes widened, his smile broadened. "Yes! Congratulations, Your Honor!"

"Good news?"

"Phil had a call when he got back from the funeral. Barring confirmation problems, he is now a real bona fide judge."

"That means you're going to be a real bona fide district attorney, doesn't it?"

"I guess it does."

She took his hand. "I'm glad for you, Ben. You'll do a wonderful job."

"Not without you."

"Uh-uh. Better sign that check. We're going to be late for your party."

JONAS WAS WAITING for them outside the door to Ben's apartment. Once they were inside, he said nothing, but sat in one of the chrome chairs in the shadows beside the window wall.

"Would you like a drink?" Ben asked.

Jonas shook his head.

When Annabelle came back from the bathroom, she set her handbag on the side table and took the other chrome chair. "Jonas?" she said gently. "Daddy?"

"You don't have to call me that."

"I did a lot of thinking during dinner and in the car over here. I don't know how I feel about what's happened. All I know is that I don't want to lose you."

He took her hand. "And I couldn't bear to lose you."

"So let's take it one step at a time, all right? We'll work it out."

He nodded, his eyes brimming with tears.

Ben had been watching silently from the kitchen. He froze when the doorbell rang. "I'm not sure I can do this."

Annabelle went to him. "Sure you can. We'll all be here for you."

He stared down at her. Suddenly he was the needy one, and Annabelle hadn't turned away from his weakness. He nodded and went to open the door.

"Ben, I've brought your father," Elizabeth said. She stepped in, kissed Ben on the cheek and walked over to Jonas.

Ben stared at the man on his doorstep. Rode hard and put away wet. Ben remembered a big florid man. This one had shrunk inside his skin so that it hung in bloodhound dewlaps under his chin. His cheeks and nose were tan, but with an underlying tinge of the red of rosacea. His eyes were still piercing, but the whites were veined with red.

"Hello, son," Hal boomed, and held out his hand with that kick-ass grin back in place on his face.

Ben ignored the hand. "Please come in and take a seat so we can get started. You know why we're here?"

"Your mother told me the whole thing. Ray? How you been? And this can't be little Annabelle? She's the spitting image of her mother."

Annabelle flinched. Elizabeth intervened. "Sit down, Hal. I'm worn-out, and I'm sure these people are in worse shape than I am."

"Mom," Ben asked, "have you spoken to Phil?"

Elizabeth shook her head. "Went completely out of my head. He'll be worried."

"Actually, he's elated. The judgeship came through."

"Oh, Ben, that's marvelous! Let me use your phone. Just give me a moment."

With Elizabeth in the bedroom talking to Phil, the rest of them stared at one another.

"Sorry about your mother, Ray," Hal said finally. "Always liked the old piranha."

"Is that why you came to her funeral?" Annabelle asked.

"Seemed the right thing to do. And see my family at the same time."

"What family would that be?" Ben asked his father.

"Come on, Ben, can't we let the past lie dead and buried?"

Ben surged to his feet. "Hardly seems fair when you're still alive."

"Ben!" Elizabeth snapped from the bedroom door. "You have a job to do. Leave the recriminations for later."

Ben took a deep breath. "Right as usual. I'll be right back."

He half stumbled to the bedroom and toward his

closet. The rage he felt stunned and frightened him. So much for becoming a robot, for having no feelings. He leaned his forehead against the doorjamb. A moment later he felt arms around him.

"It's okay," Annabelle whispered. "Don't let him get to you."

He buried his face in her hair and clung to her. "Why can't I let it go? Mother has."

"No, she hasn't. She just conceals it better."

"If she can, I can," Ben said. "Here, toss these blankets on the bed while I get this dad-blasted box."

When he laid it on the coffee table, he realized his father had a glass in his hand. He waved it at his son. "It's only diet soda. Found it in your cabinet. I was thirsty." He poked the box with an index finger. "So this is the Great Box. No explosion. That's something. Open the damn thing."

"Not yet." Ben pulled Mrs. Langley's letter from his pocket. "This was included with her instructions. It's a letter to all of us. I'm supposed to read it aloud to you all before we open the box."

"Oh, for Christ's sake, Ben!" His father threw up his hands. "I need a real drink."

"No, you don't," Elizabeth snapped. "Shut up and listen."

He subsided, grumbling.

Ben began to read.

"'*If Mr. Jackson, Junior, is as honorable as he purports to be, then you are all assembled like the vultures you are, but I am dead, so I cannot enjoy your discomfort.*'"

"Old bitch," Hal whispered. Ben shot him a glance.

"'After you have read this letter aloud, Mr. Jackson, you may unwrap my presents and do with them as your conscience dictates. I underline the word conscience, *because I suspect that you are the only person there assembled who has one.*

"'First, I must tell you why you are together.

"'Elizabeth Jackson. You are here because this debacle is your fault.'"

"What?" Elizabeth gasped.

"'If you had married Raymond, he would never have become prey to that creature from the black lagoon.'"

Elizabeth laughed.

"'Harold Jackson. You were a drunkard, a ladies' man, a completely dishonorable barrister, but I thought you were a superb defense attorney and the only man capable of saving the Langleys. Instead, you allowed us to be dragged through the mud and lost me my son.'"

"I had help." Hal flipped his index finger off his forehead toward Ray.

"'Raymond, my son, you betrayed me most deeply. You ignored your primary obligation to me, the family and the bank. If you were balked by Elizabeth, you should have married some equally suitable young lady, taken your rightful place in the bank, and in time moved into the mansion with your sons to assume my place in society. Instead, you married a rutting whore who could not by any stretch of the imagination be considered either suitable or a lady.'"

"Got that right," said Hal. Elizabeth slapped his arm.

"'Moreover, when you returned from prison you

forced this outrageous bargain upon me and became a common laborer, a servant in the house where you should have been master. I can only hope that watching your daughter grow up without knowledge of your relationship has provided you a taste of the hell you put me through.''

"Daddy," Annabelle said. "I'm so sorry."

"True hell would have been separation from you."

'''Finally, my granddaughter, spawn of the whore, who has always been a wild child, who carries the heritage of the trash from which her mother sprang, who, despite everything I have done for her, persists in disobedience, and who has abandoned me in my final days to die alone…'''

"I did not!" Annabelle said.

'''…alone,''' Ben repeated.

'''She will carry the stigma of her birth to her grave, and will, I hope and pray, neither marry nor procreate…'''

"Damn her!" Ben snarled, then continued reading.

'''…and so bring the glorious Langley line to its dishonorable end. May the contents of this box assist her in her decision.'''

Ben looked up. "It's signed Annabelle Victoria Mason Langley."

"I never knew I was named for her," Annabelle said.

"You wouldn't have been if I'd had my way," Ray said, squeezing her hand. "Chantal thought it might make her more generous toward us." He smiled at her. "But now I think it suits you. Redeem the name, my dear."

Ben dropped the letter onto the coffee table. "My

father was right. We should have burned the damn thing.''

"Open the blasted box!'' Hal said, and slammed his glass onto the side table at his elbow.

"It's already open. Annabelle, you want to do the honors?''

She shivered. "If we have to do this, then you unwrap that stuff.''

He plucked the layers of tissue off the top and dropped them on the floor. "What the…'' He caught his breath, reached in and began to pull out a piece of cotton flannel in some sort of bunny print.

"No!'' Ray grabbed at it, but Ben moved too quickly for him. "Dear God,'' Ray said, and sank onto the couch. "How did she find it?''

"It's a child's sleeper,'' Elizabeth said. "What's that stuff on the front?''

"Blood,'' Ray said.

Annabelle began to keen softly.

"Handprints,'' she said in a faraway voice. "I wiped my hands down the front of my jammies. They were all wet and sticky.''

Ben folded the pajamas carefully. "Annabelle, you want me to stop?''

"No, please.''

He tugged at the edge of a piece of white fabric that stuck for a moment under some of the other items. Then he unfurled a length of white lace hand over hand like a conjurer pulling a scarf from a top hat.

Annabelle whimpered. Ray wrapped his arms around her. "Don't look, sweetheart.''

"I have to." She pushed him away and went slowly to Ben.

"He's right," Ben said, attempting to shield her face against his jacket.

"I have to, don't you see?" She touched the lace. "It's bloody too, isn't it?" She turned to Elizabeth. "Last week I got a drop of blood on a piece of white lace, and when I looked, it seemed as though the entire piece was dripping with it." She ran her fingers down the lace. "This is what I was seeing, isn't it, Daddy?"

Ray dropped his head into his hands. "The gun was wrapped in it. You had it in your arms."

"I don't think I'd better go on with this."

"You damn well better," Hal stormed, "or I will."

"Shut up, Jackson," Ray snapped. His powerful hands clenched into fists. "You're here under sufferance. Don't push your luck."

"Yes, shut up." Elizabeth added. "Go on, Ben, if there's worse to come we'd better know."

"Not much more. Big velvet box of some sort."

"Chantal's jewel case," Ray whispered.

Ben slid the lid back. Inside lay a jumble of jewelry. Ben held it out to Annabelle.

"Let Elizabeth. I don't want to touch it."

"Here, Ben, if there's one thing I know, it's jewelry." Elizabeth took the box from Ben, set it on the coffee table and began to finger the pieces. "Most of it is flashy costume stuff, but quite expensive." She held up a pair of diamond ear clips. "These are real."

"I never saw her wear them," Ray said. "They

can't be real. I couldn't have afforded to give her diamonds that size.''

"Somebody did," Annabelle whispered.

"Oooh, this is a really lovely bracelet. Coral and turquoise set in silver and gold. Not outrageous, but not cheap either.'' Elizabeth shoved aside some other pieces and held up a string of large black baroque pearls. She ran one of the pearls along her front teeth. "Real. Very expensive."

Ray had gone to stand at the window with his hands in his pockets. Elizabeth glanced up at him. "I take it you didn't give her these either.''

Ray shook his head without turning around.

"Ah, what have we here? A lovely antique lava-liere watch. The diamonds are old, but they're very nice, and so is the watch. Is this from you, Ray?''

Again he shook his head. "I wonder if it still works." Elizabeth began to tease the winding stem gently. The watch began to tick. "How about that?" She laid it back in the box. "What's this? A casing from a bullet?''

Ray reached for it, but Ben forestalled him. "Leave it on the table.''

"And finally," Elizabeth said, "the brass ring. Or in this case, the emerald ring. My, my. Must have cost a fortune.''

Ben heard his father's quick intake of breath. His red face had gone ashen, and his breath was shallow. Ben hoped his mother wouldn't look up, because he'd be willing to bet she'd guess, as he did, that the ring had been a present from Hal. For favors received.

The watch gave a single chime. Everyone jumped,

then laughed nervously. Elizabeth picked it up. "Pooh, it's stopped already." She started to turn the stem again. "It's stuck. I don't want to break it. Probably dirty. Here, Ben, you do it."

He took the watch and clicked it open. A tiny sliver of paper floated to the floor. "Something holding it." He picked up the paper and read, "'Someday a time for us.' Nice sentiment."

"But not from the same period as the watch," his mother said, reaching out for it. "The inscription comes from a song in a Broadway musical in the fifties, I think."

Ben slid the paper back into the watch and clicked the case closed. "We'll leave it as it is for the moment. Is that everything?"

"Yes," Elizabeth answered. "Anything else in the box?"

"No."

"What I don't understand is how Mother found those things," Ray said. He came back and sank into the same chair. "I thought I hid them so well nobody would find them."

"*You* hid them?" Annabelle asked.

He nodded. "After I got you cleaned up that night, I had to do something with the scarf and pj's. I didn't think the police would have any reason to search the house, but I couldn't take a chance, so I wrapped them in newspaper and stuffed them behind one of the rafters in the back of the attic."

"Nobody searched because you didn't give them a reason to," Hal said. "You copped a plea before I had a chance to open my mouth. Why the hell didn't you tell me about the scarf and pajamas, Ray? It would have been evidence to support your story. A jury might have believed me if I'd had them. Nothing would have happened to Annabelle, man, she was a child. It was an accident, pure and simple.''

"No," Ray said.

"Did you kill Chantal?" Ben asked. "Did your mother?"

"No."

"Then why was the gun downstairs in the first place, and loaded?" Ben was getting into his prosecutorial stride. Apparently he was carrying the others along with him because nobody questioned his authority.

"Because, dammit, Chantal was going to blow my head off with it when I came home!"

CHAPTER SIXTEEN

"YOU WANT TO KNOW the whole story?" Ray asked. "You want Annabelle to hear it?"

"Annabelle wants to hear it," Annabelle said. "No more secrets."

"I need a drink," Ray said. "My mouth's so dry I can't form the words."

"We all do," Elizabeth said. "Sit there. I'll get us some sodas. None of us needs any alcohol, agreed?"

When she came back with the soda, Ray drank his greedily, then took a deep breath. "We'd been fighting for months," he said, "mostly over my leaving the bank and starting the landscaping business, but the last few weeks Chantal had seemed almost happy. I thought we might finally make a go of that travesty of a marriage for Annabelle's sake, if for no other reason." He took Annabelle's hand.

"That evening I came home late from the bank. She was furious. Said mother had been nasty to her again, and that she wasn't about to take it another day. She told me she was going to take Annabelle back to Lafayette with her, and I'd never see her again."

"She wouldn't have gotten away with that," Hal said.

"Mothers got custody in those days, unless they were unfit."

"Which she was."

"The only way I could prove that was by dragging us all through the mud. She knew I was licked. We had the worst fight we'd ever had. I could hear Annabelle on the staircase, and I tried to stop it, but Chantal was like a crazy woman—like she was egging me on."

"She may have been," Ben said, and took Annabelle's other hand. "Do you remember any of that?" he asked her.

She shook her head. "Nothing."

"Finally, she went too far," Ray continued. "I've never hit a woman before that night or since, but I slapped her. Hard. She laughed at me. I knew if I stayed in that room another minute I'd do something I'd regret worse, so I stormed out. I picked up a bottle at the liquor store on the corner, drove down to Riverside Park and sat in the car and drank. I drank a lot in those days."

"So did I," Hal said. "Plays hell with the liver."

"I don't really like the taste of the stuff, but I wanted to get drunk. Then I started worrying that she'd gotten me out of the house on purpose so she'd have time to pack and run away with Annabelle."

"How long were you by the river?" Ben asked.

Ray waved a hand. "I don't know. Several hours. I wasn't really drunk, and on the way home I started thinking about what she'd said when I left. She'd said, 'If you come back to this house I'll kill you.'"

"We've all said things like that," Elizabeth observed. "I certainly have." She glanced at Hal, who slumped in his chair with his eyes half-shut in concentration.

"That was about the time that woman up north shot her husband. She said she thought he was a burglar," Hal said.

"Chantal joked about that a lot," Ray answered. "How easy it would be if you were a good actress and could convince the police you'd done it by accident. I think she took the gun downstairs to shoot me when I came in the door."

"That's the sort of crazy thing Chantal would think she could get away with," Hal said.

"When I found her and Annabelle, all I could think of was working the same story in reverse—I'd woken up, hadn't realized Chantal had gone out, had come downstairs and shot her accidentally."

"I told you at the time that story wouldn't hold water, Ray," Hal said. "You should have kept your mouth shut until I got there instead of spouting off to the police the way you did."

"I know that now. At any rate, I used the scarf to wipe Annabelle's prints off the gun..."

"Stupid thing to do, I always said so," Hal said.

"I cleaned Annabelle up, re-dressed her, took her to my mother's, hid the scarf and pajamas and scrubbed up the mess I'd made in the bathroom, and prayed Annabelle wouldn't remember in the morning what had happened the night before. She'd barely opened her eyes when I cleaned her up. I've always wondered whether Chantal gave her something to keep her quiet."

Annabelle sat up. "Could that account for why I can't remember?"

"Absolutely," Elizabeth said. "Probably paregoric. Can't get the stuff so easily now, but every mother had it in her medicine cabinet then—child gets cranky, fill him full of paregoric and he sleeps like an angel for hours."

"So maybe I'm not crazy for not remembering?"

"You never were," Ben said.

"Maybe I really didn't know what I was doing?"

"You didn't do anything. Believe me," Ben insisted.

"Go on, dammit," Hal said to Ray. "Most of this I've heard, but the others haven't. My esteemed son may be a little more charitable toward the old man once he hears what idiot clients I had to deal with."

"Hal!" Elizabeth said.

"He's right, Liz," Ray continued. "I knew Chantal didn't commit suicide, so there was no way she could have powder burns on her hands, and I'd scrubbed Annabelle's until they were almost raw. But if I went with the burglar story, then I had to have powder burns on my hands. I'd already wiped the gun, so there wasn't any residue left, so..."

"You fired a second shot," Ben whispered.

Ray nodded. "Through the carpet under the hassock. I doubt the police moved the hassock. In any case, nobody saw the second bullet hole. And I had my powder residue."

"I should have known," Ben said. He hit himself in the head with the flat of his hand. "When I checked the reports, I noticed that Chantal's fingerprints were on four of the shells, including the empty one that supposedly killed her. Ray's fingerprints were on one shell that hadn't been fired."

"That's the one I replaced after the second shot." He pointed to the tissue-wrapped casing lying on the coffee table. "I didn't dare leave the second empty cartridge where the police could find it, so I stuffed it upstairs with the other things. Mother must have gone over that house with a fine-tooth comb when she was thinking of renting it out. Now, Hal, do you see why I couldn't go to trial? I had to short-circuit all the evidence gathering. I pleaded down to second, so nobody checked."

"There was another man," Elizabeth said quietly.

"There were always other men," Hal snapped.

"Including you." Elizabeth picked up the emerald ring and tossed it across the table. He caught it in midair. "Never give your mistress the same jewelry you give your wife, dear."

Hal glanced at Ray. "Elizabeth, I swear—"

"Don't bother. I'm not married to you anymore, thank God."

"Wait a minute." Ben held up a hand. "Before the two of you get into it. What do you mean there was another man, Mother?"

"Simple. I remember the dress that scarf went with. If was a very elegant and expensive cocktail dress. You don't put a dress like that on to run away to Bayou Teche. You put it on because you're expecting company. That's why she had to get Ray out of the house."

"Mother, you're a genius." Ben glared at his father.

"Wait a minute. We may have had a thing, but it was over long before that night."

"Where were you? You weren't home. Mother's already told me that."

"Who remembers after all this time?"

"While we're on the subject, when did you get to town this time?"

"I told you, I came for Mrs. Langley's funeral."

"Before or after she died?"

"What the hell are you talking about?"

"It's a simple question."

"I've been here for a couple of days. Looking up old friends. Setting up some business deals."

So his father could have gotten into the Langley house and killed Mrs. Langley. He definitely knew the layout of the house and which windows were simplest to get through. Ben would go into that when there weren't all these people around. He'd get the truth out of Hal. The truth about Mrs. Langley and the truth about his walking out all those years ago. The whole story.

THE NEXT MORNING Ben stuck his head inside Phil Mainwaring's door. "Good morning, Your Honor."

"Get in here, Ben." Mainwaring didn't sound elated. He sounded angry.

"Sure. Congratulations."

"Sit. What is this crazy story Elizabeth tells me about Ray Langley being Victoria Langley's gardener and your father being in town two days before she died?"

"That's about it."

"God in heaven. I told you to leave this thing alone, Ben. If the newspapers get hold of it, you can kiss your appointment goodbye."

"There is no story. Not so far as the newspapers will see."

"Send Annabelle back to New York at least until your appointment is secure." Mainwaring sounded plaintive. "Councilman Adler has already been on the horn to me this morning. He's setting up a meeting to discuss your future, and he'd better get the answers he's looking for."

"It's no business of Adler's."

"Ben, Ben, Ben." Mainwaring sighed. "He came to the funeral yesterday because the Langley interests still pull a lot of financial weight in this part of the country, but he does not want to be reminded of his youthful peccadilloes every time he looks at your date."

"Adler? He must be, what, seventy?"

"And with enough great-grandchildren to swing a close election. He wasn't always close to seventy, you know."

"What do you expect me to do?"

Mainwaring slammed his palms down on his desk. "Do you want this appointment or don't you?"

"You know I want it. I can make a contribution."

"And I want it for you. You're far and away the best man for the job. So send Annabelle Langley back to New York, pack your father off to wherever he came from and go back to doing the job you're paid for, dammit."

"I'm not sure I can do that."

"Jesus H. Christ! Why not?"

"Don't you ever have to *know*, Phil? Just know the truth for its own sake?"

"No, dammit, not unless knowing helps me win a

case. And listen to me closely, my friend, *there is no case.*"

"If somebody else killed Chantal Langley, and Raymond went to jail for it, there's been a gross miscarriage of justice."

Mainwaring sighed again, deeply, and said more in sorrow than in anger, "He copped to it, Ben. Nobody railroaded the man. If he chose to go to jail to protect his daughter or his mother, the choice was his."

"And if there was somebody else?"

"Who?"

"Someone Chantal expected."

"Bull hockey."

"Phil..."

"I'm asking you—no, *telling* you for the last time. Drop it. Go back to work. I'm going to be peddling like mad to get that appointment for you as it is. Don't make it harder on both of us."

"BRITTANY'S COMING this morning to pick up her dress," Marian said over her spectacles as she put down the telephone in the workroom.

Annabelle frowned over the tops of hers at Marian's face.

Marian shrugged. "Thought you might want to avoid her. Is she still going to the Steamboat Ball with Ben?"

Annabelle clipped the threads at the end of the seam she was sewing with brutal efficiency. "How would I know?"

"He hasn't asked you?"

"I wouldn't go if he did. I'll be going back to New York soon anyway."

"Uh-huh. Why, since you're obviously crazy about him?"

"Am not!"

"You are too."

"All the more reason to leave town. He needs a Brittany clone."

"He needs you to keep him humble."

"Humble? Ben?"

"Lately I'd say he's pretty humble. He's in love with you."

Annabelle flushed.

"Would it be so bad to marry Ben? You could keep working for Elizabeth. It's not the Champs Elysées or even Fifth Avenue, but it has other advantages."

"I'm from a line of woman men take to bed. They don't marry us."

"Your father married your mother."

"My point exactly. He shouldn't have. Everybody tells me how much like her I am. Who's to say I wouldn't betray Ben the way she betrayed my father?"

"You may look like her, but you are not like her. Not a bit."

"Did you know her too?"

Marian nodded. "She took Hal away from me."

"What?" Annabelle wasn't certain she'd heard right above the noise of the sewing machines.

"Elizabeth knows. It was short-lived. We were all a lot younger. Elizabeth forgave me for the affair, but

I never forgave myself. Hal was simply irresistible to women. To me, certainly.''

''Hard to believe looking at him now.''

''I'd rather not.'' Marian picked up her embroidery hoop and began carefully laying down a padding stitch to mend a satin-stitched flower on a christening gown.

''Do you know why he walked out on his family?''

''Yes.''

''And why he lives on a boat and looks like a derelict?''

''Possibly.''

''Does Ben know?''

''Part of it, not all. Elizabeth told me.''

''If it's a secret...''

''Not from you.'' Marian laid down her hoop. ''Hal hit his midlife crisis about the same time he got a very rich widow off on a shoplifting charge. He had some psychologist testify that she had an obsessive-compulsive disorder, when she simply wanted a diamond tennis bracelet and didn't want to pay for it. I suppose it was inevitable that they had an affair.

''Only this time it was serious. He saw himself driving a Ferrari and being a member of the jet set— being as famous as F. Lee Bailey. He thought Elizabeth would roll over and play dead—take any settlement he offered. She didn't. She wound up with everything but his shorts.

''By that time the bimbo had moved on to greener pastures, but when Hal wanted to come back, Elizabeth said no. She'd finally had enough. He started drinking even more than usual, and was apparently playing the commodities markets on margin. He borrowed some of the firm's money.

"When they found out, they hushed everything up, replaced the money, bought Hal out on the stipulation that he wouldn't practice law in this state again. That's when he disappeared. I didn't know where he was until Ben said something."

"Are you still in love with him?"

Marian laughed. "Hal? You can't be serious. I'd sooner love a Gila monster. He was the most self-absorbed man I've ever known, even if he was a brilliant lawyer. Ben comes by his talent honestly. But until you walked into his life, Ben was in danger of developing that same self-absorption. If you walk out on him..."

"I have to do what's best for both of us."

"Yes, you do. Just be certain you know what it is."

The telephone rang again. "It's the intercom. Brittany must be downstairs for her fitting. You want to come or not?"

"Not."

Marian patted her on the shoulder in passing. "I'll find out whether she's still going to the Steamboat Ball with Ben."

"YOU HAVE TO STAY here until the will is admitted to probate," Ben said desperately.

"No, I don't," Annabelle said. "You can handle it."

"Your father needs you. My mother needs you. I need you."

"Planes fly both ways." Annabelle held up the

evening paper. "It's not on the front page, or even the first page of the Metro section, but it's here, all right, in the story about Phil's appointment."

"Doesn't mean anything."

"Ben, it does. Just a couple of questions about our possible new D.A.'s involvement with the scandalous Langley clan. If I stay, it'll get worse."

"I don't give a damn."

"You should. I've told you over and over that I am not the right political connection for you." She had no intention of telling Ben that wasn't her greatest worry. Even sitting across the table from him in an out-of-the-way restaurant, she wanted to jump his bones. Her mother's daughter.

He grabbed her hands. "Make me a bargain. Come to the Steamboat Ball with me on Saturday."

"I thought you had a date."

"Brittany is going with her new man, Trent what's-his-name. In one of my mother's dresses that she got at a ridiculously low price and in about half the normal time. I ought to charge her a commission."

Annabelle laughed. "I don't have anything to wear."

"Yes, you do. I talked to Marian this afternoon. Mother has half a dozen dresses from the 1880s that could be altered for you. You'd be the most authentically costumed woman there."

"We're taking those dresses apart to use the fabric. They're not costumes."

"They are until you dismember them. Come on. For once in your life, take a chance, face them down.

It'll be just like Mother's party—everybody'll be crazy about you."

"Look what happened at your mother's party."

"You won't have another flashback. Now you know most of what happened. You didn't simply wipe everything out—you were drugged."

"I don't know."

"Please. If you're not having a good time, if you don't feel comfortable, we'll leave." He took a deep breath. "And I'll drive you to the plane for New York myself."

"Really?"

"Cross my heart." He didn't tell her that he'd probably be on the next one following her. He'd get a job on Wall Street. He hated corporate law with a passion. Or he could join the prosecutor's office. He heard they always needed recruits. He could pass the New York bar.

One step at a time. First the party.

"All right."

"Great." He took her hands again. "Now, I'll follow you home. Dumb to bring both cars."

"Smart. I'm going home alone, Ben. If you set one foot in my living room, things will get out of hand."

"That's what I'm hoping."

"Forget it. You've conned me into the blasted ball. Don't press your luck."

ELIZABETH SPAT the final pin out of her mouth and sat back on her haunches. "That dress might have been made for you."

"I can't breathe," Annabelle wheezed.

"You're not supposed to breathe. You're supposed to loll around with smelling salts."

"I'm supposed to dance." She grimaced and worked her hands around her waist. "I'm serious."

"Oh, all right. Marian?"

Marian sat at her table with her stocking feet on the sewing chair in front of her. "I can add a gusset under the arm. It won't show."

"The russet silk is perfect for you," Elizabeth said. She pulled her bare feet around so that she sat tailor fashion at Annabelle's feet. "And I have the perfect jewelry—a velvet ribbon with my great-grandmother's amber slide. Thank God you have enough hair so that we don't need to put a rat on your head."

"I beg your pardon."

Elizabeth flipped her hand. "One of those fake hair-bolster things the ladies wore."

"I really don't want to do this."

"I'll be there. You can cling to me. It'll be fun showing you off to all Ben's cronies."

"His cronies?"

"Oh, yes. The back-room boys will no doubt be interested in meeting you before they abandon the ladies for cigars and rum and back-slapping."

"This thing is political?"

"Everything is political, my dear." Elizabeth stood up easily. "Don't you worry. You and Ben will be the best-looking couple there."

CHAPTER SEVENTEEN

"YOUR FATHER WANTS to move home, to this house," Elizabeth said. She sat on her bed across from Ben, who lay stretched on her silk chaise longue.

"I'll bet he does."

"I said no."

"Good."

"I said that if he wanted to sell his boat and move back to Memphis, I'd be happy to help him find an apartment, but that was as far as I would go."

"Mom." Ben shook his head sadly. "Before you know it, you'll be giving him half the furniture from this house and painting kitchen cabinets for him."

"If I do, that's my choice." She leaned back. "He's tired and I don't think he's very well. Ben, he's like a stranger to me. I feel absolutely nothing toward him except pity. He says he can practice law, never let his Tennessee license lapse."

"You mean, I might be facing my father in court?" Ben sat up so quickly he banged his head against the light over the chaise.

"Possibly, although he says he doesn't do criminal law any longer."

"God, how I would like to kick his butt in front of a jury."

"The old bull versus the young bull? I don't think it would be an even contest these days."

"Once, just once, I'd like to send one of his damn guilty clients so far up the river he'd never come back again to hurt anyone else."

"That wouldn't bring Judy back."

"No, but she might finally rest in peace."

"You're the one who needs the peace. Can Annabelle bring it to you?"

"In a heartbeat, if she'd just get over worrying about what people think. I want to marry her, Mom."

"Phil says—"

"Screw what Phil says. You told me I ought to get a life. Now, when I've finally got the chance for one, you give me what Phil says."

"I didn't say I agreed with him." Elizabeth climbed off the bed and sat on the end of the chaise. "You follow your heart, now that you've finally discovered you have one. I'll back you all the way."

"I'M SO SORRY to chicken out on you this way," Elizabeth said to Annabelle, who was standing on a dressmaker's platform in Elizabeth's living room, while Marian was busy fastening the tiny hooks and eyes that ran from below her tailbone all the way to the low-cut back of the russet silk ball gown. "I feel just awful. I think you and Ben must have infected me."

"Go straight to bed," Marian said. "I'll come upstairs to check on you as soon as I get Cinderella off to the ball. There. Go look in the mirror in the front hall. Mind that train. Slip the string over your middle finger to keep it off the ground."

Annabelle looked into the pier mirror. She saw a real throwback, way beyond Chantal—to Chantal's great-grandmother, maybe, if she'd had the money to buy a russet silk ball gown inset with Brussels lace. She jabbed one of the long hairpins deeper into the nest of curls that started at the crown of her head and tumbled down almost to her shoulders. "Ow. I think you pinned these things directly to my scalp."

"Don't grumble," Marian said. "You will be the most beautiful woman there. Trust me."

"I agree." Elizabeth leaned back on her hands. "I knew I bought that dress for a better reason than cannibalizing it for somebody's prom dress. God, I think my eyes are crossing." She pulled herself up. "Phil will murder me, but what can I do?" She half stumbled from the living room with a feeble wave over her shoulder.

"She didn't want to go anyway," Marian said. "I suspect she's not nearly as sick as she'd like us to believe."

"Why not? She'd look gorgeous in that rose matelasse."

"Phil is going to have to move to Nashville, and apparently he's been putting the screws to Elizabeth to marry him after all these years. I think she's ducking the issue."

"She doesn't want to marry him?"

"Or anybody else."

"Is she still in love with Hal?"

Marian laughed and stretched out on the turquoise love seat. "Not a chance. I don't think in her heart of hearts she's ever truly loved but one man."

Annabelle opened her mouth to ask, when the

doorbell rang. Marian sprang up and went to open it. "Colonel Jackson, suh," she said, and curtsied. "You do look handsome in your frock coat. Please come in, suh."

"Maid Marian, I presume."

Annabelle clutched her hands across her stomach at the sound of his voice. What would he think? She glanced down at her bosom, which definitely spilled over the top of this dad-dratted mass of silk and whalebone she was hooked into.

"How's Mom?" he said.

"She'll be fine. Miss Annabelle, your gentleman caller has arrived."

He smiled at Annabelle, looked her up and down, and gaped.

"Shut your mouth, Ben Jackson."

"I feel as though I've stepped through a time warp. You should be strolling the deck of a riverboat instead of attending a ball at the Hunt Club."

"And you, sir, should be downstairs cheating at cards."

"Shall we go? Can you fit into an ordinary car?"

"We can try." She flipped her train up with a practiced toe and caught it on her finger. Marian nodded in approval as she swept by.

Oh, Lord, what had she gotten herself into this time?

"THERE, SEE, it's not so bad." Ben swung Annabelle around in the arc of a waltz.

"I can't breathe, and everybody's staring."

"Because you're beautiful."

"Because my bosom is popping out of this dress."

Ben raised his eyebrows and grinned down at her. "That would definitely enhance the party."

Annabelle blushed.

"Look, there's Phil. Doesn't look pleased." Ben swept Annabelle by the punch table and said as they waltzed by, "Mother really is sick as a dog."

"I know," Phil called. "Inconvenient."

Ben stopped dancing, took Annabelle's hand and strolled over to Phil. "You look as though you just stepped in from the plantation garden. Where did you get the swallowtail coat?"

"It's my grandfather's," Phil said. "Your mother made the brocade vest for me." He bent over Annabelle's hand in her lace mitt. "You look even lovelier than your mother."

Oops. Annabelle tried to give him a gracious smile, but it came out a grimace.

"May I borrow Ben for a couple of minutes?"

"Phil…"

"Couple of people in the conference room want to speak with him. He'll be back in time for the next waltz, or if he's not, I will be," Phil said with a smile. He guided Ben off expertly. Ben gave a despairing shrug of his shoulders, and Annabelle tossed him what she hoped was a 'hey, it's okay' smile.

She took a cup of punch and retreated behind the nearest potted palm. She'd barely had time to slake her thirst when Phil appeared at her elbow. "Ben's on his own in there. So, may I have this dance?"

"We don't have to."

"But I want to. I promised Ben you wouldn't sit even one out."

"It's not necessary."

But he had already put his gloved hand around her waist. He lifted the other and she slid hers into it. "Okay," he said. "Here we go."

Annabelle wondered how soon the band would feel comfortable swinging into modern dance music. These waltzes and polkas were exhausting. When the music finally stopped, Phil pulled a handkerchief from the pocket of his swallowtail coat. "Whew! I'm too old for this."

"Never too old, Your Honor," said a young man walking by. He clapped Phil on the shoulder, smiled curiously at Annabelle and kept walking. Annabelle felt her face flush.

"Don't worry. He has no idea who you are, and wouldn't care if he did."

"How long is Ben going to be?"

"No idea." Phil pulled out a heavy gold full hunter watch on a long chain and clicked it open. "He's only been gone twenty minutes. It's ten-fifteen exactly." The watch chimed a single note. He smiled and slid it back into his pocket. "Now, how about some more of that punch."

Annabelle fought to keep the muscles of her face relaxed, her smile in place. She'd heard that bell before. Heard it night after night in her dreams. It sounded like a doorbell, but sweeter, silvery. Phil took her hand and apparently felt no tension, because he led her to the punch cart and handed her a crystal cup of punch before he poured himself one.

"Beautiful watch," she said casually.

"One of my finest. I collect antique watches, but I don't wear this one often. It was my great-grandfather's." Phil chatted on easily. "I don't sup-

pose I've worn it more than once or twice since..."
He took a breath. "Since he left it to me."

Annabelle's throat was suddenly dry. She swigged
punch greedily.

"Hey, honey," said a passerby. "That stuff can
be lethal if you're not used to it."

She stared down at the cup. "It tastes like fruit
juice."

"Artillery punch often does," Phil said cheerfully.
"Should I get you some coffee?"

"That would be lovely. Thank you. I'll just go sit
on the terrace."

"I wouldn't. It's about to storm. Come with me."

"I'll see if Ben's through with his meeting."

"No! Don't interrupt. Ben's clinching his appointment in there."

"Okay. Then I'll wait here."

She *had* to tell someone. She watched Phil amble
off, then practically ran to the ladies' room and called
Elizabeth. "Answer, dammit."

"Hello."

"Elizabeth, it's Phil. It was his watch I heard the
night my mother—"

"You have reached the establishment of Elizabeth
Lace. Our business hours are..."

She hit the phone and hung up. She didn't dare
face Phil again. She'd give herself away. He'd realize
she knew. She slipped out of the ladies' room and
ran toward the front hall, her train looped over her
arm.

"Annabelle," Phil called. "I've got your coffee."

She pasted a smile on her face. "Sorry, Phil. I'm

afraid the punch disagreed with me. I'm just going to catch a cab home.''

"Don't be ridiculous. I'll take you.''

"Please, no!'' She backed away from him. "Ben needs you. Tell him I'll be waiting for him at home, will you?''

Before he could say another word, she took to her heels and ran out the front door and down the steps. She said to the young man at the foot of the stairs, "I need a cab.''

"Can't flag cabs in Memphis, ma'am,'' he said. "Have to call one. In this rain it'll probably take thirty minutes at least.''

She glanced over her shoulder. Through the pier mirror she could see Phil standing in the hall watching her.

"Leaving so soon?'' Brittany came through the door behind her. She did look marvelous in the dark red lace gown that Annabelle and Marian had crafted from Elizabeth's designs. "You and Ben have a spat?''

"I don't feel very well.''

A black Mercedes drew up at the foot of the steps and Trent Wellfleet leaned over. "Come on, Brittany. I've had enough of this Old South crap.''

Annabelle grabbed Brittany's arm. "Please, would you drop me by my house?''

"Why, I—''

"Please, it's really urgent.'' She could see Phil walking toward her.

"Thanks. That's sweet of you.'' She scrambled into the back seat of the Mercedes and slammed the door.

Brittany slid into the front. "Honey, I guess we'll have to make a stop on the way to the club. Okay?"

Trent stared at Annabelle. "Lord, honey, you act as though somebody's after you. Okay, let's go." He drove off as Phil opened the front door and started down the steps.

"Too much artillery punch," Annabelle replied. "I promise I won't throw up until I get upstairs to my own place."

"Good," said Trent.

"BEN, DO YOU WANT this appointment or not?" Councilman Adler asked from his place at the head of the table.

"I want it very much, Councilman," Ben said. He'd been trying to keep his temper for the last twenty minutes of interrogation. He'd expected congratulations and claps on the shoulder. What he'd gotten was a star chamber in which fifteen men and women flung questions at him about where he stood on everything from the death penalty to privately run prisons.

So far he'd done damn well, although he resented the inquisition. Now, however, with what Ben suspected was a setup by Adler, State Senator Cissie Margate, chairperson of the board of the local shelter for abused women, had brought up the Langley autopsy.

"Hardly necessary, was it?" she'd asked. "The medical examiner has his hands full without your exerting undue influence based on your hunches."

"I still believe Mrs. Langley was smothered," Ben

said, "but I agreed with Phil Mainwaring that we'd never be able to make a case."

"I hate to say this, Ben, but if the media get ahold of this mess it could blow up in all our faces."

"Are you saying that I shouldn't have asked for an autopsy?"

"Now, don't get huffy, son," Adler said, brandishing his cigar. "Everybody knows those Langleys have been jinxed for twenty-five years. You ought to be concentrating on putting gang members behind bars, getting the drugs and the prostitutes off the streets, making downtown safer for the tourists. Don't waste your time on cases that have been closed for more than twenty years. Bad for business, my boy."

"I intend to do all of those things, Councilman, and I'm grateful for your input—for the input of everyone here. Cissie, you asked me a question earlier, whether I really want this job. All of a sudden I'm not so sure. I don't intend to pick my battles based on what's good for business in this town, but what makes the average-Joe home owner feel safe in his house and his kid safe at school. If I think there's been a miscarriage of justice, then even after twenty years, or fifty, if I last that long, I'm going to dig. If you want a man to run the district attorney's office on that principle, then I'm your man. If you want someone to run my department based on what does or does not please you and the chamber of commerce, then get yourself another boy."

He nodded pleasantly, turned on his heel and walked out.

He'd done it now. Given up the one thing he'd

always thought he wanted. He ought to feel miserable, but he felt elated. He had to find Annabelle.

He searched for her, asked about her, and couldn't find either her or Phil. They couldn't have left, surely. He'd only been gone thirty minutes or so. Had she had another of her flashbacks? God, he hoped not, for her sake. She'd feel she'd let him down for the last time.

He went out on the front porch. The young man handling the cars huddled under a gold umbrella. Cold rain was driven nearly sideways by the fierce April winds. He shivered in his frock coat.

"Hi. Seen a woman in a kind of red-brown dress with a train?"

"Yeah. Left about five minutes ago with a big blonde and her boyfriend in a Mercedes. She looked real unhappy. Then a couple of minutes later some gray-headed guy came out and wanted his car. Thought he was gonna belt me when it took a couple of minutes to get it out from behind a couple of others. Went off to get it himself. Man, was he P.O.'d."

"Phil?" She must have had another flashback and Phil went after her to see she got home all right.

While Ben was standing there, Phil drove up behind a red Miata parked at the foot of the stairs. A thin woman whose name he should remember brushed past him. "I hate these stupid masquerades," she said. And ran down the stairs to the car.

Meanwhile, Phil was honking his horn imperiously. Ben turned up the collar of his coat and plunged down the stairs. "Phil," he said, and beat on the side of the car. "Open the window."

"Got to go, Ben, emergency."

"What? Can I help? Where's Annabelle?"

"Went home. Touch of migraine. Said to tell you to please stay for the rest of the party and call her in the morning."

"Hell, no."

"She insisted." A bell began to chime. Phil cursed, yanked his watch out of his breast pocket and slammed it on the seat. "Good night, Ben," he said, and nearly drove over Ben's feet as he slewed around the Miata.

What had his tail in a crack? The one thing Phil never, ever did was treat any of his precious antiques lightly. Have to be something major to make him slam his great-grandfather's watch down that way. Ben turned around to ask for his car. "Sure, mister. Take a minute, though. This rain's turning the lawn into soup."

He'd call Annabelle from his car to see if she was all right. Come by, maybe spend the night.

The front door opened behind him. "Ben, get your tail back in here," Cissie said. "And stop being so easily offended."

"Cissie, I told you…"

"Ben Jackson, I am old enough to be your mother and I've known you all your life. Get in here this minute." She held the door for him.

Reluctantly, he went.

The same cast of characters sat around the same table, but somehow the atmosphere had changed. "Okay, Ben, you win," Adler said. "It's your department. You have two years to prove you can handle it before the voters get to vote you up or down.

We'll give you all our support. Best of luck, Mr. District Attorney.''

Ben felt the elation start at his toes and spread upward until he was grinning like a madman. "Thank you. I won't let you down."

"And date anybody you like," Cissie added with a raised eyebrow at Adler. "Your private business is your business. I sure don't want anybody checking up on who *I* date, do you, Mr. Adler?"

Everybody began to laugh. Now came the back-slapping. All he could think of was fighting his way out through the congratulations to get to Annabelle. He glanced at the grandfather clock in the corner of the room. Eleven o'clock. Phil and his crazy chime-every-fifteen-minutes watch—Ben had thought it was later. As the clock began to chime, he froze.

The night of his mother's party, it wasn't only the wine on the lace that had set Annabelle off, it was also that single chime from his mother's birthday present. An antique clock from Phil, the collector of antique watches and clocks.

Ben recalled Chantal's antique lavaliere—a present with a romantic inscription. Could Phil have given her that gift? Ben had never even dreamed Phil might have been one of Chantal's lovers. Phil, his mentor, his father figure, his boss. Not a killer. Ridiculous.

"Oh, damn," Ben whispered.

"I beg your pardon."

"Sorry. Got an emergency."

"Ben?" Cissie called after him.

He kept running. He'd forgotten he'd asked for his car. It sat to the side in front of the stairs. He jumped down the front stairs, flung himself behind the wheel and spun out.

He was the one having hallucinations. Phil Mainwaring was the most honest man he'd ever known. He'd loved his wife. Never would have cheated on her. Couldn't kill anybody.

But Annabelle would have heard the watch chime when she was dancing with him. Had it triggered a final flashback? Had she remembered at last who had been in the room with her mother when she was shot?

The moment his hands were free he called Annabelle's number. Answering machine. His mother's. Same thing. Phil's. Same thing. Ray Langley. No answer, no answering machine. He couldn't remember where his father was staying, so he couldn't call him. Marian's roommate said she was at Elizabeth's looking after her.

Should he send a squad car to check on Annabelle? If he was wrong, she'd never forgive him. If he was wrong, neither would Phil.

But what if he was right? He felt the car start to hydroplane in the high water overflowing the gutters. A minute later he slammed broadside into a curb in a wall of water. The car died instantly.

"THANKS, Brittany." Annabelle crawled out of the back seat and raced for the door to her apartment. She glanced over her shoulder. Elizabeth's house was totally dark. No matter. She was overreacting. Once inside with the door locked, she could take off this ridiculous dress, put on some jeans and wait for Ben. Sooner or later his meeting would be over.

She needed his assurance that she was crazy even to suspect Phil Mainwaring.

She flung the chain on the front door behind her and pelted up the stairs. She was amazed she only tripped twice. She turned on every light, and began to claw at the hooks and eyes of the russet silk.

She hoped she hadn't ruined it in the rain. Silk spotted so badly, and the dress was almost a hundred years old. Elizabeth would fire her.

She wouldn't have to. If nothing else, tonight had forced her to see that she'd been right all along. She couldn't stay in Memphis. If she could go weird at the sound of a watch and suspect someone like Phil Mainwaring, she'd better get back to New York. Ben promised this date would be his last demand. If she hated it, he'd let her go.

Would he?

The trick was not to give him the chance. She needed to be on a plane out of town before he had a clue she'd left.

"Ah!" The last hook came loose. She pulled the dress off her shoulders and eased it low enough to step out of it. She laid it carefully on her worktable to dry. She stepped out of petticoats and the waist nipper, took them with her into the bedroom, pulled on a pair of jeans and a T-shirt. She'd deal with her hair later.

She walked back into the room and reached for the telephone.

"I wouldn't do that," said Phil Mainwaring's pleasant voice. He stood at the top of the stairs with his arms folded across his chest.

CHAPTER EIGHTEEN

"HOW DID YOU get in here?" Annabelle asked. She was suddenly acutely aware of her thin T-shirt and her bare feet.

Phil shrugged. "When you've been around a house as long as I have this one, you know where the spare keys are kept. Your chain didn't catch, by the way. You ought to be more careful."

"You really didn't need to follow me home." She tried to sound as natural as possible. "Now that you're in, I'd really like you to leave."

"Oh, why?"

"Because I'm expecting Ben any minute."

"No, you're not. I suspect he'll be quite late, what with the celebration and the champagne and all."

"He got the appointment?"

"Yes, he did. And he'll be very good at his job. I taught him." He sauntered into the room. They might have been a pair of casual acquaintances about to share a drink, except for Phil's wary eyes, and his clenched fists. "You're terrible at concealing your feelings, you know."

She laughed nervously. "So I do care about Ben. I admit it."

"That wasn't what I meant. I saw the look on your face when you heard my watch chime while we were dancing.'' He shook his head. ''I used to wear that watch everywhere. Then I stopped wearing it at all, after… The last five years, I've worn it to the Steamboat Ball, but I should never have worn it tonight. I wouldn't have if I'd had any idea you'd seen me all those years ago and heard my watch chime. Or that you'd remember after all this time.'' He sighed deeply. ''Careless of me. Where were you hiding that night?''

''I'm sorry, Phil, I don't have the faintest idea what you're talking about.''

''Don't bother to lie. Be honest. I promise I'll be honest back.''

''Very well. I was on the stairs in the dark.''

''I see. I thought you didn't remember.''

''I didn't. Not all of it. I remembered the lace and the blood, but I blanked out the rest until tonight when I heard that chime. Suddenly I was back there seeing it all clearly.''

''Pity.'' He leaned on the sink as though he was suddenly bone-weary. ''Why couldn't Ben let the whole thing be? All he had to do was walk away, forget the Langley case, send you packing to New York where I didn't have to look at you. But men and their hormones. It's a real shame.''

''Why did you hate looking at me? Am I so much like my mother?''

''You're more beautiful on the outside than she was. But you lack her inner fire. She was wild, on the edge, like a feral cat, ready to scratch and bite.''

''You loved her.''

''She would have destroyed me.''

''How could she?''

"Meredith, my wife, had the money, the social connections. We were on our way to the governor's mansion, maybe the senate. I had the *right* wife. I knew enough not to be unfaithful to her."

"But you were, weren't you?" Annabelle said. "With my mother."

"I couldn't stay away from her. So I thought, fine, I'll have her once, and then I'll be free of her, but it wasn't like that. Every time I touched her I wanted more, more passion, more of...her. I couldn't think about anything all day except Chantal in my arms, on a motel bed, in the back of my car, anywhere and everywhere she'd let me."

"No one knew?"

"Meredith had already had one heart attack. She couldn't...wouldn't be a wife to me. Sex frightened her, she couldn't catch her breath."

"That's your excuse? You needed a woman?"

"I needed Chantal! If it had been some casual liaison with a prostitute, Meredith might even have approved. But not Chantal—and not a love affair."

"Chantal told you she wanted to take me and go back home, so you killed her."

He began to laugh. The amusement sounded genuine. That made it even more dangerous. "I could have fought that. Chantal loved me too. She wanted to marry me."

"People get divorced every day."

"Oh, no, divorce was not appropriate for our Chantal. She didn't believe in it, whatever she told your father. She had some insane plan to shoot Ray and say it was an accident. I was supposed to handle the case and make everything go away safely."

"So Dad was right. She planned to kill him."

"That still left Meredith between us." His eyes glowed with tears. "I loved Meredith. She was fragile, but we both thought she'd live a normal lifespan. I never dreamed she'd die five years later."

Annabelle gulped. "She wanted you to kill your wife?"

"She said how easy it would be—a little extra digitalis and a death certificate reading natural causes."

"Just like Grandmere."

"Yes, dammit, the way it would have worked with your grandmother if Ben hadn't stuck his nose in where it didn't belong. Thank God the medical examiner said the autopsy was inconclusive."

"I'm sorry, Phil, I can't feel much sympathy for you because you didn't want to kill your wife. You were perfectly willing to kill my mother and my grandmother."

And me, she thought. She had to keep him talking. Surely when Ben discovered she was gone he'd come looking for her—furious, probably, but that didn't matter as long as he got here in time.

"I wanted Chantal in my bed, not on my arm at political functions. That night, I looked at her standing by the fire in her white lace dress—too tight, too short, her breasts almost bursting over the top. Her long brown legs in those high-heeled sandals with no stockings and painted toenails. I saw her for the first time as my colleagues would see her. As she'd be in ten years. Coarse. A beautiful, wild slut. Men bed sluts, they do not marry them. That's what I've tried to tell Ben, but he refuses to listen. You will destroy his career as completely as she would have destroyed mine if I'd let her.''

Stung, she stared at him. That's what she'd been telling herself, telling Ben. She was like her mother.

But it wasn't true. She wouldn't destroy Ben's career, because in truth she was *not* like her mother. She would never consider hurting another human being, and she felt passion for one man and one man only—Ben. She started to protest, but his words stopped her. He seemed to be speaking to himself, almost unaware that she was in the room.

''I didn't plan to kill her, you know, just talk some sense into her. But she wouldn't listen. When I wouldn't agree to her plan, she shrieked at me, threatened to shoot me, to say I'd tried to rape her. She'd have ruined me. She was out of control. We struggled, and the gun went off. It was an accident.''

''One bullet, a perfect shot. And no powder burns on her dress?''

''I took the gun away from her and shot her, but it was still self-defense. She would have shot me.''

''Right.''

He held out his hands in a gesture of supplication. ''I'm not a murderer. I'm an honorable man. I've spent my life making up for what I did.''

''Really? What about letting my father take the blame? What about me and the gossip? And Grandmere?'' She felt tears start. ''Why did you have to kill my grandmother? She'd never done anything to you.''

''Ben told me Mrs. Langley told him she knew something about that night that she'd never told anyone. I couldn't take the chance she knew about my relationship with Chantal. I was never on anyone's list of suspects, couldn't afford to let Ben start thinking about me now. She was dying anyway. I simply put her out of her suffering. Euthanasia isn't murder.''

"Framing me for her death isn't honorable either. You're the one who called Beulah and got her out of the house. Did you shove that nail in my tire so I'd be late?''

Phil grimaced. He seemed to be in real pain. ''Not to frame you. I just needed a few minutes with no interference. I was sure I could get one of those old solarium windows open without breaking a windowpane, and I did.''

"How nice for you.''

"She managed to scratch my wrist once, but she didn't struggle. Probably glad to have it over with.'' He seemed to be talking to himself. ''Ben was never supposed to see the body, much less suspect she'd been killed by an outsider. Why can't he leave things alone?'' Phil rubbed his hand over his forehead. He seemed desperately tired.

"Am I to be a mercy killing too?'' She knew the moment the words left her mouth she'd said the wrong thing. Phil seemed to come to his senses. His jaw hardened, his eyes narrowed.

"Yes. Very, very sad. You'd made up your mind to give up your lover for his career, and you were grieving for your grandmother. You came home and took an entire bottle of sleeping pills.''

"I don't keep sleeping pills.''

He brushed that aside. ''I stole some from Elizabeth's medicine cabinet several days ago in case I should ever need them myself. When I leave here, only your fingerprints will be on the bottle.''

''I'm supposed to take my medicine like a good little girl? Forget it. Besides, Ben will never believe it.''

''The evidence will speak for itself. He'll grieve a decent interval, and then he'll marry some cool blonde who'll kiss babies with him. You'll actually be doing him a favor.''

''No, I won't.'' Annabelle flung up her head. ''Ben loves me. And I love him. If that means I have to kiss other people's babies, I damn well will. What I won't do is let you kill me.''

Not now, not when she finally understood that the love she had for Ben was right. Not now that she knew she was nothing like her mother. Not now when she'd found her father and knew that he was not a killer. She was not a killer, either. Life was suddenly full of possibilities.

''You have no choice.''

''Sure I do. You know, Phil, you're really kind of a dolt.''

''What?''

''Yeah.'' Annabelle might lose against Phil's superior strength, but she'd go down fighting. ''I don't think Grandmere knew a thing about my mother's murder. She was simply making up tales so she could be the center of attention and make everybody else miserable.''

''Then she was the dolt.''

''And me? I didn't have any idea you were the man in the living room that night. I never saw your face. I only heard the shot and came downstairs in time to hear that silly watch you were wearing chime the quarter hour. If you hadn't worn that watch to-night, if I hadn't recognized the sound from all those years ago, I would never have suspected you. Never.''

She leaned back casually against the edge of the worktable. Her shears lay beneath the russet silk dress. She felt their outline. She put her hand behind her casually. "If you want to get rid of me, you'll have to do it face-to-face. Ben will know it's murder for sure, and he'll never rest until you're on death row. That I promise you.''

"Bitch!'' He lunged at her.

She grabbed the scissors and backed away from him, but not fast enough. He grabbed her arm and pulled her toward him.

"Ben's on his way! He'll find me!'' she shouted.

She jabbed the point of the scissors into his hand. He screamed. Blood ran from the gash.

She raced toward the stairs, only to find herself yanked back by her hair. He wrapped his good arm across her throat. She couldn't breathe. With the other he grasped her wrist.

"Drop them!''

She held on doggedly. He twisted her wrist until she screamed.

"You'll be comatose or dead when Ben finds you.'' He forced her arm against the edge of the ta-ble. "Drop them!''

He cracked her wrist against the edge of the table. Her fingers went numb. The shears clattered to the floor.

"Once you lose consciousness, you'll take every damn sleeping pill I shove down your throat."

She couldn't breathe. She saw rainbows behind her eyelids.

This could not happen.

One moment she strained against him, the next she slumped boneless in his arms.

He didn't expect it so soon or so completely. For an instant his grip relaxed. She twisted away, but her foot caught on the edge of the silk that had slipped to the floor when she grabbed the scissors. Gasping, she went down on hands and knees. Her knee hit hard. She screamed with pain.

A second and he'd be on her again. She grabbed for the scissors and scrambled under the table.

"Bitch!" he snarled. "Come back here."

"Fat chance!" She drove the points of the scissors up as hard as she could into his thigh.

His blood spattered her face. Salt stung her eyes, drenched her shirt. Real blood.

"Damn you!" he screamed. He twisted away from her. She could see his hand clapped to the spurting wound. "You've hit the artery. Help me!"

She backed up toward the far side of the table as he fell full length on the other side.

"I'll die, damn you!"

She dragged herself to her feet. Did he mean it? She hesitated only a moment, then dialed 911.

As soon as she'd given the address, she grabbed a piece of white lace and tied a tourniquet around his upper thigh. His head was thrown back, his teeth bared, eyes closed. He rolled in pain and grasped his leg in both hands.

"Lie still," she said. "You'll make it worse." She began to twist the tourniquet. She had to look at what she was doing to set it correctly.

That was a mistake. Phil grabbed her hair and yanked her back.

"I killed you once, I'll do it again."

This time he lacked the strength to hold her. She twisted away from him, feeling hanks of hair rip loose, and scrambled out of reach on hands and knees.

When she looked back at him, he was crying, one hand on the tourniquet, the other raised in supplication. "Chantal, I love you."

"Annabelle!" Ben's voice, Ben's footsteps, racing up the stairs. And behind him other heavier feet.

He saw her on the floor, and as she reached her arms to him, his eyes widened. "He's hurt you, you're bleeding."

"His blood," she managed to say. She sounded hoarse. Her throat hurt.

The room was suddenly filled with police and EMTs. Sirens screamed outside.

Ben crushed her in his arms.

"She tried to kill me," Mainwaring said. His eyes were starting to glaze, but his voice was strong.

"I wish she had, you bastard," Ben snarled.

"Ben? Ben?" Elizabeth called from the foot of the stairs. A moment later she began to cough. "What on earth's going on up there?"

"Stay out, Mother."

"Nonsense. Is Annabelle all right?"

The instant she saw Annabelle covered in blood

her hands flew to her mouth. Then she saw Phil writhing on the floor.

"My God, Phil, what did you do?"

"Tell them, Elizabeth, tell them she's a killer."

Elizabeth merely stared at him openmouthed.

"He's the killer," Annabelle said from the circle of Ben's arms. "Check his coat pocket. You'll find your sleeping pills, Elizabeth. He was about to set up my suicide."

"But why?"

"Because he killed Chantal," Ben said grimly.

Annabelle stared up at him.

"Took me long enough to catch on. I was afraid he'd kill you."

"But how..."

"I refused to believe you'd run out on me, and then I heard that stupid watch. Phil and his damn antique clocks. I remembered the watch in Chantal's jewelry box, and suddenly I thought, why not Phil? By that time he had gone after you."

The men hefted Phil onto a stretcher and carried him past Elizabeth.

"Elizabeth, tell them. I'm a judge!"

"Not yet you're not," Ben said grimly, then to the policemen, "Call Homicide, take him to the prison ward at the Med. And put him on suicide watch."

One of the cops shrugged. "Sure, if we manage to get him there before he bleeds out." He jerked his head at Annabelle. "Take her too?"

"I'll bring her later."

"Whatever you say."

"Ben, can you do that?" Annabelle asked. "I did stab him. Twice."

"You were afraid for your life. That makes what you did self-defense. Besides, you're going to be my prize witness at his trial." He glanced at the stairs. "If he lives that long."

"I always knew there was something about Phil," Elizabeth said. She sneezed three times and blew her nose. "God, I really do feel awful."

"Come on, Mother, you did not know there was something any more than I did. He's been like a second father to me most of my life. I never once guessed he was anything but the world's finest mentor."

"I did too know." Elizabeth sniffed. "Why do you think I never married him? Never went to bed with him, for that matter. We were fond of each other, but there was certainly no passion." She sniffed again and coughed. "Used it all up on Chantal, apparently. I'm going to bed. Annabelle, the guest-room sheets are clean." Annabelle looked up. "Well, darling, you can't stay here."

"I don't imagine I'll get much sleep once Ben takes me down to the police station."

"Tomorrow is soon enough for that."

"Oh, Elizabeth, I think I ruined the russet dress."

"Don't worry about it. You're alive, that's all that counts." She hugged Annabelle hard.

"Don't cry, Elizabeth, please."

"When I think about—" She turned and flew down the stairs.

"Ben, go after her."

Ben shook his head. "In a little while, when I'm sure you're safe. I don't think she wants to see me right now. Poor Mom. I pray she can convince herself that she always did think there was something odd about him.''

Suddenly Annabelle wrapped her arms around Ben. "Oh, Ben, darling. I'm so sorry. He was your friend too.''

"He was an A.D.A. back when Chantal died. He could have skewed the case from the sidelines without anybody the wiser. I should have at least checked him out. I never guessed...''

"Don't beat yourself up. It's all right.'' She looked up at him with shining eyes. "You'll make it right.''

Ben buried his head against her shoulder.

"I wasn't trying to kill him,'' she whispered. "But I didn't want to die before I...'' Her voice trailed off.

"What?''

"Before I got a chance to tell you I love you.''

"Now you believe you could never kill anyone?''

She said in a small voice, "I may have killed Phil.''

"Self-defense.''

"I wasn't worried so much about being a killer. Not after we made love the first time.''

He held her away from him. "What do you mean?''

She dropped her eyes. "I'm not a virgin any longer, and after the way I reacted I'm as wild as she was. Phil said it tonight. Men bed sluts. They don't marry them.''

Ben began to laugh. "That, my darling, is the way a woman is supposed to act with the man she loves.''

"Then it's all right?''

He nodded solemnly. "It is not only all right, but I highly recommend it. And wait until I get you on

our honeymoon and really start some intensive instruction.''

''Ben, New York...''

''If you want to live in a cold-water flat on the
Lower East Side while I struggle along as a lowly
A.D.A., that's what we'll do. I can prosecute any-
where.''

''No! If Elizabeth will have me, I'll be happy to
work for her, and planes fly both ways, and there's
the Internet. I promise I'll learn to kiss babies.''

''Our own, maybe. Nobody else's.''

''I don't want to waste the rest of my life without
you. That's what I discovered tonight. We're worth
fighting for.''

He bent his head and kissed her, deeply and yet
gently.

His hand had slipped under her T-shirt when they
heard footsteps on the stairs again. ''Blasted police
state.''

''What the hell happened here?'' Hal's voice.

''Annabelle!'' Ray Langley rushed to his daughter.
''Are you all right?''

''How did you hear?''

''Breaking news on TV,'' Ray said. ''Phil Mainwaring? I can't believe it.''

''That bastard! He was the A.D.A. sitting second
chair on Chantal's death,'' Hal said. ''I always said
he was crafty.''

''Is he going to live?'' Annabelle asked anxiously.

''Who knows?''

''He going to hire you for his defense, Dad?'' Ben
asked coldly.

''I hope he tries.''

"What are you and my father doing together anyway?" Annabelle asked.

"Talking about old times, making peace," Ray said shamefacedly. "We're both too old to hold grudges."

"And about my homecoming, young Ben, and my future," Hal said softly. "I'd like to do some pro bono work for Phil's prosecution. You're going to need somebody who was around at the time. I intend to kick Phil Mainwaring's butt all the way to prison and back."

"I COULD PROBABLY have gotten him off, you know," Hal said to his son. He blew gently on the cup of coffee in his hand and leaned back in the chair across from Ben's desk.

"I know," Ben said. "At least he had the gumption to give us a deathbed confession."

"How's Annabelle handling it?"

"Better than I would have thought. She didn't mean to hit an artery, and anyway, that's not what killed him. The doctor said his idiopathic system shutdown. I think he wanted to die. He couldn't have lived with the disgrace of a trial, and he wouldn't have survived a week in prison."

"All those cronies that made him a judge have some pretty fair egg on their faces. Ought to keep them off your case for a while."

"Yeah." Ben put down his cup. "Dad, why are you here?"

"I've put in papers to work in the public defender's office." He grinned at his son. "Too old to change my spots."

"I see." Ben sounded grim.

"But too old to let my ego get involved either. Our adversarial justice system may not be the best in the world, Ben, but damned if I've ever found a better one."

"It's not a game."

"No. And I won't play it that way. I'll work to help people I truly believe are innocent."

"Like Elmer Bazemore?"

Hal sighed deeply. "I chose not to see the evidence that Bazemore was guilty. I was as horrified as you were when he killed Judy. I'm asking your forgiveness for that, for the way I treated your mother and you and your brother. I've long since made restitution to my old law firm—you don't need to know the details—but if we're going to see one another around the courthouse, I'd like to have lunch with you occasionally."

"And my mother?"

Ben shook his head. "Funny, old Mrs. Langley may finally get the daughter-in-law she wanted all along, the way Ray and Elizabeth have been looking at one another."

"I'm glad. Ray's a nice guy when you get to know him."

"I always thought so. You know, Ben, everybody was trying to do the right thing here. Even Phil. And it all came out wrong."

"What's that mean?"

"Elizabeth and I thought we were right to marry. Ray thought he was right to keep his marriage to Chantal together at any cost. Then he thought he was right to take the blame for his daughter. Mrs. Langley thought she was right to berate Annabelle about her background and her criminal tendencies. I thought I was right to let Ray cop a plea. You thought you were right to try to change Annabelle, whether she wanted to be changed or not. Now, thanks to your pigheadedness, we may all get a second chance. I'm proud of you, son.''

CHAPTER NINETEEN

"THIS WHOLE BIG-WEDDING thing was your idea," Vickie said. She towered over Annabelle in a slim black silk dress with a wide antique Battenberg lace collar. "You can't funk wearing the first dress you've designed for Elizabeth Lace now."

"I should never have designed this damn train. I feel as though I'm towing a barge."

"It's gorgeous. I'm so jealous. Here you are a full-fledged designer for a well-known specialty house, and I'm still doing knock-offs for Seventh Avenue showrooms."

"Not for long. You'll make it, and then other houses will be stealing from you."

"All right, Annabelle. Are you calm enough to get this show on the road?"

"I can't go out there," Annabelle said. "All those people staring at me." She shuddered.

"People are supposed to stare at the bride, you ninny. The church is packed. Ben's brother, Steve, is already up front doing his best-man routine...I swear, the man is a hunk! And tall enough even for me."

"Leave Steve alone, Vickie. His mother says he has issues."

"Big deal, so do I. I'll put my issues up against his issues any day." Vickie twitched her eyebrows.

"The point is, I am terrified to be the center of attention. What if I trip going down the aisle? Or fall up the steps?"

"You won't. Just calm down. The priest is at the altar, the ushers are getting ready to walk Ben's mother down to the first pew, Marian's hovering outside waiting to arrange your train and veil, and your father's in the vestibule acting as though he's on the verge of a heart attack and yanking on his morning coat as though he were strangling. Will you come on?"

"I thought I could do it, but I can't. Not even for Ben."

"Fine. Then sit here and stew." Vickie slammed the door to the bride's room behind her. Annabelle grabbed the latch and shoved it into place. She couldn't sit down. There was too much antique lace in the dress, the veil, and entirely too much in the train.

Why had she agreed to this full-dress travesty? She'd be bound to step on her veil, tear the lace and yank it off the back of her head. Something horrible would happen. It always did when she was the center of attention.

"Annabelle?" Ben spoke from outside the door.

"Oh, Ben, I'm so sorry. I can't go through with this."

"You can't marry me?"

"Can't I marry you in a pair of jeans in front of a justice of the peace somewhere where nobody knows us?"

Dead silence. For much too long. Then Ben's voice again. "Sure."

"What?"

"What matters is that you marry me and that it's the happiest day of our lives. If that means jeans and a justice of the peace, I'm up for it."

"You mean that?" She leaned on the inside of the door.

"We can't sneak through the vestibule—too many people will see us and wonder where we're going. How about if I slip around to the window, you climb out, we run for my car, stop at Wal-Mart to buy you some jeans and stuff, and head off to Tunica? We can get a Mississippi marriage license in twenty minutes, and I'm sure we can dig out a justice of the peace who knows me. We can be married in a couple of hours."

"What would all those people think? We can't just leave them sitting there."

"Your father can make the announcement that we've eloped. We can be back in time to meet everybody at the reception."

"You're serious."

"Yes."

She leaned her forehead against the door. It felt cool. She could hear Ben breathing on the other side.

"You think you can get that dress through the window, or you going to strip to your underwear first?" he asked. He sounded incredibly matter-of-fact.

He really did mean it. He would walk out on his own wedding, a churchful of people, if that's what she wanted. Scandal and all.

She took a deep breath. "No, I'm not going to strip down to my underwear. Ben, darling, I do love you."

"Glad to hear it. Makes the whole day kind of

pointless otherwise. I love you back, by the way, in antique lace or jeans. Even better in nothing at all.''

"Oh, Ben!" She took a deep breath. "Nope. This was my idea, my coming out, and I refuse to funk it. Find Vickie and my dad, will you, darling? And go down front and wait for me. Let's get this show on the road."

"Yes!" came Vickie's voice. "I knew you wouldn't chicken out."

"Come on, honey, unlock the door," said Ray. "I'll hold you up."

"And don't you dare mess up the veil," added Marian. "I worked on that dress for four months. Now I want to see you married in it."

"For Pete's sake, Ben, is the whole congregation out there?"

"Not everyone," Ben said. "Mom's down front. I love you. I'll see you in two minutes. I promise, you won't fall up the stairs."

Annabelle crossed her fingers. "From your mouth to God's ears. Grandmere, wherever you are, you finally got your wish. I'm finally going to act like a Langley."

She waited until she heard Ben's footsteps move away before she opened the door. Vickie and Marian stood outside smiling at her. "That's the prettiest dress we've ever made," Marian said. "No way was I going to let you sneak out without showing it off. Now, come on."

She took her father's arm and stood at the head of the aisle while Vickie, her only attendant, walked to the front of the chapel.

Her father beamed down at her. "Daughter. I never thought I'd be able to call you that."

"I never thought I'd have a dad to give me away, either." She smiled a little mistily. "But then, I never thought anybody'd want me as a gracious gift."

"Here we go," he said as Marian gave Annabelle a small shove.

"Don't you dare trip over that gown," Marian whispered.

The church was festooned with so many flowers that it looked like an indoor garden. As Ben watched Annabelle glide down the aisle toward him in her beautiful gown, he thought of the way he'd pictured her in a field of lilies of the valley. She was more lovely than he'd dreamed.

But it wouldn't have mattered to him if she'd actually slipped out that window, just so long as she became Mrs. Benjamin Jackson before the afternoon was out.

As he moved beside her and took her hand, he smiled into her eyes—her wonderful eyes. Doe's eyes, but no longer wounded. Open, trusting, loving.

As his mother had predicted, love had jumped up and bitten him. More important, it had given him the gift of Annabelle.

He squeezed her hand and began to repeat his vows.

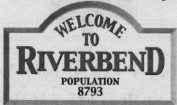

HARLEQUIN®
SUPERROMANCE

#924 BIRTHRIGHT • Judith Arnold
Riverbend

Aaron Mazerik is back. He isn't the town's bad boy anymore, but some people still don't think he's good enough—especially not for Riverbend's golden girl, Lily Holden. Which is fine with Aaron, since he's convinced there's even *more* reason he and Lily shouldn't be together.

Riverbend, Indiana: Home of the River Rats—small-town sons and daughters who've been friends since high school. These are their stories.

#925 FULL RECOVERY • Bobby Hutchinson
Emergency!

Spence Mathews, former RCMP officer and now handling security at St. Joe's Hospital, helps Dr. Joanne Duncan deliver a baby in the E.R. After the infant mysteriously disappears a few hours later, Spence and Joanne work closely together to solve the abduction and in the process recover the baby girl—and much more!

#926 MOM'S THE WORD • Roz Denny Fox
9 Months Later

Hayley Ryan is pregnant and alone. Her no-good ex—the baby's father—abandoned her for another woman; her beloved grandfather is dead, leaving her nothing but a mining claim in southern Arizona. Hayley is cast upon her own resources, trying to work the claim, worrying about herself and her baby.... And then rancher Zack Cooper shows up.

#927 THE REAL FATHER • Kathleen O'Brien
Twins

Ten years ago, Molly Lorring left Demery, South Carolina, with a secret. She was pregnant with Beau Forrest's baby, but Beau died in a car crash before he could marry her. For all that time, Beau's identical twin, Jackson, has carried his own secret. Beau *isn't* the father of Molly's baby....

#928 CONSEQUENCES • Margot Dalton
Crystal Creek

Principal Lucia Osborne knows the consequences of hiring cowboy Jim Whitely to teach the difficult seventh graders. Especially when Jim deliberately flouts the rules in order to help the kids. Certain members of the board may vote to fire Lucia and close the school. But Lucia has even graver consequences to worry about. She's falling in love with Jim…and she's expecting another man's child.

#929 THE BABY BARGAIN • Peggy Nicholson
Marriage of Inconvenience

Rafe Montana's sixteen-year-old daughter, Zoe, and Dana Kershaw's teenage son, Sean, have made a baby. *Now what?* Rafe's solution—or rather, proposal—has Zoe ecstatic, but it leaves Dana aghast and Sean confused. Even Rafe wonders whether he's out of his mind.

CNM0600